A Lie For A Lie

Julie Corbin

HODDER

First published in Great Britain in 2020 by Hodder & Stoughton
An Hachette UK company

This paperback edition published in 2020

1

Copyright © Julie Corbin 2020

The right of Julie Corbin to be identified as the Author of the Work has
been asserted by her in accordance with the Copyright, Designs and
Patents Act 1988.

Images pp.44, 86, 126, 129, 295 © Shutterstock

A CIP catalogue record for this title is available from the British Library

Paperback ISBN 978 1 473 66324 4
eBook ISBN 978 1 473 66323 7

Typeset in Plantin Light by Palimpsest Book Production Limited,
Falkirk, Stirlingshire

Printed and bound in Great Britain by Clays Ltd, Elcograf S.p.A.

Hodder & Stoughton policy is to use papers that are natural, renewable
and recyclable products and made from wood grown in sustainable forests.
The logging and manufacturing processes are expected to conform to the
environmental regulations of the country of origin.

Hodder & Stoughton Ltd
Carmelite House
50 Victoria Embankment
London EC4Y 0DZ

www.hodder.co.uk

For Ali and Jo, great friends and fellow warriors

Prologue

I tell a lie – it's the wrong lie.

I choose it without thinking about the consequences.

And I get much more than I bargained for.

Serves me right?

You be the judge.

Chapter One

It begins with a phone call from the headmaster's secretary. 'Mr Wiseman would like a word.'

'Did he mention a time?' Anna asks, phone in one hand, bloody gauze swab in the other.

'Immediately,' she tells her. 'That's what he said. Ask Sister Pierce to come and see me at once.'

'Okay.' Anna glances at the boy on the examination bed: Angus Rutherford, sent up from the pitches after colliding with a classmate. 'I'll finish up here and come straight across.' She returns the phone to its cradle and takes a closer look at the cut on Angus's head. She feels around the wound and pulls the skin together before holding the edges in place with wound closures that are almost immediately soaked in blood. 'This needs to be stitched.'

'Will I have to go to hospital?' Angus asks. He is a gentle boy who becomes a tiger when he plays sport; it's not the first time Anna has had to patch him up.

'I'm afraid so.' She wraps a dressing bandage around his head from the base of his skull to just above his eyes. 'Tell me if it's too tight.'

'Will I be able to play on Saturday?'

'No contact for at least three weeks, possibly more.'

His whole body slumps. 'Sir will go nuts.'

Anna soaks a cloth in hot water and wipes away the blood drying in patches on his cheek. 'It's just one of those things, Angus,' she says. 'Happens to all the best players.' She removes her gloves and drops them into the bin. 'I know it's upsetting but at least you don't have a serious concussion or you could be out for the whole season.' She helps him off the surgery bed. 'Have a seat in the waiting room and I'll ask Nurse Whitlock to organise your trip to hospital.'

He hobbles towards the door, his hand resting protectively on the head bandage. He's almost over the threshold when he looks back and says, 'Thank you, Sister Pierce.'

'You're welcome.' She smiles, feels it fix on her face as she breathes in. She holds the air in her lungs for a few seconds and allows herself to think about why the head wants to see her. She's known Owen Wiseman for almost two decades. They sing in the same choir and have children of similar ages, but she rarely speaks to him about work. Owen normally stays out of the day-to-day running of the school. He's more concerned with pupil numbers and budgets, governors meetings and child safeguarding.

It must be something serious otherwise he would catch her when their paths crossed in the corridor or at choir practice.

She goes to find Geraldine Whitlock, who is standing in front of the whiteboard in the office planning the HPV vaccination schedule. Her list of names is written in small, neat handwriting with arrows and asterisks in contrasting colours; woe betide anyone who messes with her system.

Anna tells her about Angus, and then, 'Owen's asked to see me. Hopefully I won't be long.'

Geraldine gives an audible sigh. She's close to retirement and by her own admission has had enough of increasingly demanding parents and antisocial shift work.

'I'll be back as soon as I can,' Anna says.

Geraldine nods acceptance and Anna leaves her to it, knowing full well that if any children do appear they won't linger if they see Nurse Whitlock's on duty. Short shrift is her prescription for most things.

Anna shields her eyes as she comes out into the late September sunshine. The sky is a wispy blend of blue and white, and a welcome breeze blows up from the coast. The medical centre sits at the western edge of the school campus, close to the playing fields and the boarding houses, and more than one hundred metres from the clutch of buildings that make up the main school. She walks up the hill, passes the pre-prep and nursery on her left, and the chapel on her right, the latter a grand building, more cathedral than chapel.

The head's study is on the far side of the lower quad, in the main building, which was originally a twelfth-century monastery. She takes a short cut through a concealed door off the quad into the oak-panelled hall then up the stairs to the waiting area outside his office. His secretary glances up at her but doesn't smile. Anna doesn't take it personally; she rarely smiles. 'He's on a call with one of the governors,' she says. 'Have a seat. He shouldn't be long.'

Anna sits on the plush sofa opposite the window. 'Do you know why he wants to see me?' she asks.

'He requested the minutes from the pastoral care meeting,' his secretary tells her. 'Might be something to do with that.'

'Right.'

Thursdays always begin with the pastoral care meeting, three of them gathered in the deputy head's study: Anna, Lynn Sykes, head of pastoral care, and Peter Williams, the deputy headmaster. That morning they discussed the children they were concerned about – a bereaved child in Year Five, a child who was suspended after he was caught smoking, another child, and another, until 'Victoria Carmichael,' Peter said, looking at Lynn. 'You wanted to flag her up?'

'She's made a poor start to this term. We're only a few weeks in and she's already been in trouble half a dozen times or more. Last week she was in Saturday detention but almost immediately afterwards was caught stealing another girl's make-up.'

Lynn and Peter discussed her lack of focus and questioned whether her home life had worsened but Anna didn't comment. She should have, she realises as she sits outside the head's office, because she has a feeling that this is the reason she's been called in. She's also worried about Victoria – Tori as she's mostly called – but she didn't add to her colleagues' comments because she felt enough was said and, anyway, her concern has been minuted on many previous occasions.

Now she's wondering whether she has made an error of judgement.

The door opens and Owen glances out. 'Anna.' He waves her inside his study and towards a seat. 'Thank you for coming across.'

'No problem.' She sits down in front of his desk and watches as he removes his jacket before taking his seat opposite her. She thinks he might mention the piece they're singing for choir this term – Bach's Mass in B minor, an ambitious piece that's challenging all their voices – or the fact that both their sons are in their first year at the University of Glasgow studying engineering.

He doesn't. 'I'll get straight to the point.' He rests his elbows on the desk. 'It's about Victoria Carmichael.'

He pauses and Anna senses him trying to read her expression. Anxious about what's to follow, she says, 'I did wonder if she was the reason you'd asked to see me. I know I didn't raise any concerns at the meeting this morning. I should have,' she acknowledges. 'But I felt Lynn and Peter were thorough in what they said.'

'What should you have raised?' he asks, his tone interested.

'Well … I'm also concerned about Tori. She's been difficult with me lately, didn't show up for our mentor's meeting last week, was ten minutes late for my SRE lesson.' She rocks forward in her seat. 'And she's been visiting the medical centre more than she normally would. She was upset yesterday afternoon when I wouldn't put her off swimming.' She feels a tremor begin in her thighs and she crosses her legs to smother it. 'She is okay, isn't she? She hasn't hurt herself or anything? Please tell me she hasn't?'

Owen understands where her thoughts are headed. 'No, no.' He shakes his head. 'She's not hurt herself. That's not why you're here.'

Anna lets out a sigh of relief. 'Thank God! I was beginning to really worry.' She's spent her whole career caring for children and it would be her worst nightmare if anything were to happen to one of them. 'Thank God,' she repeats, shaking her head against the horror of it.

'So she visited the medical centre when you were on duty yesterday?'

'Yes.'

'Did you write an account of her visit?'

'I did. As I do with every child who steps through the door.'

He pushes his laptop across the desk towards her. 'Could you show me the entry, please?'

She logs herself onto the system and quickly accesses the medical files, an area closed to all staff members apart from the four registered nurses. She clicks on Victoria's file and then on the last entry: 24-09-19, 14.35. She turns the screen round so that Owen is able to see it. 'There's nothing confidential in this entry,' she says.

He reads aloud: 'Victoria wanted to be excused from swimming. I asked her why and she said, "Because I can't be arsed." I explained that this wasn't a valid reason, that she was timetabled for swimming club and that with a positive attitude she might even enjoy it. She then told me it irritated her eczema. (She has never been diagnosed with eczema.) I asked her if she wanted to show me her skin but she told me it was none of my business. I suggested she speak with Mr Groom re swimming, as she had in fact signed up for the club. She told me she didn't like him. I asked her if she wanted me to speak to him and she said no. I then asked her if there was anything else I could help her with and she said, "There's no point. You're as much use as a chocolate fireguard." She left the surgery. I will catch up with her at supper to make sure she's in a better frame of mind. Anna Pierce.' He glances up from the screen. 'Did you catch up with her at supper?'

'I saw her but didn't speak to her. She was sitting with Pippa, Hester and Isobel.'

Tori barely ate anything at supper. The email from her dad was burning a hole in her pocket. She glanced around the room, her eyes searching for Sister Pierce, but she couldn't see her. And there was no one else for her to talk to. The girls were making it obvious they didn't want her around. 'You need to stop stealing,' Isobel told her. 'How many chances do we have to give you?'

'I didn't steal your make-up, Hester,' she said.

The three girls looked at one another, eyes rolling, faces hardening.

'And she didn't visit you again later that evening?'

'Not exactly.' Anna explained she was busy after supper because the mother of one of the junior girls had come to her for advice. Her daughter was off sick but she had bundled her into the car when she came to pick up her son. A day child, so strictly speaking not Anna's responsibility, but she had a raging fever and the beginnings of a rash. Anna took one look at her and immediately called an ambulance. 'While I was on the phone, Tori was in the waiting room but she could see I was busy. We didn't speak.'

Owen sits back in his seat and gives an audible sigh. 'Anna, there's no easy way to say this.' He clears his throat, clearly reluctant to voice the words. 'Victoria has accused you of assault.'

Chapter Two

Anna's mouth falls open; the blood drains from her cheeks.

'She told me that she came to see you yesterday evening, sometime after supper,' Owen continues. 'And that's when you hit her.'

Anna shivers. 'I – I didn't!' Her eyes are filling now. She blinks away the tears, embarrassed and confused. 'I don't ...' White noise echoes inside her skull; her whole body is quaking, shaking. She stares down at her feet, tapping on the wooden floor as if being directed by a crazed puppeteer. 'I ...' She crosses and re-crosses her legs, uses her hands to press down hard on her thighs. 'I – I didn't.'

'I'm sorry, Anna.' His expression is sympathetic. 'I can see this has come as a shock to you.'

Anna suppresses the urge to shout out – A shock? *A shock?* You think? She gets quickly to her feet and walks across to the window, clutches the sill with both hands. S2 boys push and shove their way out of the door directly below her and run across the gravel to reach the newly mown grass, the crunch of their boots sending gravel sparks up from their heels. Her eyes follow them as they race towards the regiment of beech trees that underline the school's perimeter. And then they begin to throw rugby balls backward and forward between pairs.

Although her eyes are watching, she doesn't see them.

Her attention is taken up with the battle inside her. She is trembling, her teeth chatter, her limbs pulse. An electrical live-wire courses through her from the crown of her head to the soles of her feet. She wants to run, out of the room, through the woods, back to her house, seek the warmth of the familiar, the comfort of home, because an accusation like this is serious. Colleagues have lost their jobs for less.

Breathe.

Just breathe.

She turns back to Owen. 'What did she say exactly?'

He holds her eyes. 'She said that you were angry with her and that you raised your hand—'

'I was angry?' She's frowning. She blinks several times. 'About *what*? When am I *ever* angry?'

'I asked her what had made you angry but she wouldn't tell me.'

'That's because it's a bare-faced lie!'

'I understand your frustration, Anna.' He sighs. 'But as you know, we have to take all allegations of assault seriously.'

Owen is not only the head teacher but also the safeguarding lead and while he is legally required to remain impartial, his eyes are kind and it allows Anna to relax. Just a little. 'Have you informed ...' She falters.

'I have informed social services,' he confirms.

'What will ...?'

'The allegation will most likely be handed over to the police.'

'Will I be charged?' she asks, her voice barely audible.

'I don't know.'

'And in the meantime?' A rising panic empties into her throat. Panic tinged with hysteria because God knows she's done everything she can for this girl. *Everything*.

And to say that she hit her? 'I've never hit a child,' she tells Owen. 'I've never slapped a child. Or pushed a child. I've barely even shouted at a child, and that includes my own. Even Noah, who was very naughty at times and would climb on everything, raid the fridge, went through a phase of hiding his grandad's glasses. He thought it was funny. And sometimes—' She stops, stares up at the ceiling: at the chandelier that was gifted by parents after their four children achieved better grades than they thought they would, spent their years at Bishopglen happy and loved. Yes, loved. Because it would be impossible in a job like hers not to grow fond of children, not to go the extra mile, not to support them through the ups and downs of their child and teenage years and be proud when they left the school confident in themselves and their abilities. 'More than twenty years,' Anna says. 'And to my knowledge not one complaint has been raised against me.' Owen affirms this with a nod of his head. 'And Tori?' She frowns, disbelieving. 'How? *Why?*'

'I really don't know, Anna.'

They both leave unsaid the fact that Victoria Carmichael has been in trouble on and off since she arrived at the school. She is on a full scholarship, and while she is academically gifted, she has struggled socially, despite all the supportive measures that have been put in place.

'Fuck.' Anna swears under her breath. 'I should have seen something like this coming. And I should have spoken up at the meeting this morning.'

'It wouldn't have changed anything.'

'I know but …' She shakes her head against her own stupidity. 'I've been barking up the wrong tree. She's been really down this term and I was worried that she might begin self-harming. I spoke to Sadie about it last week.' Sadie Taymere is the senior girls' housemistress and six evenings a week she chivvies them into bed. 'I thought Tori was more likely to harm herself than lash out at anyone else.' Anna swallows the lump in her throat. 'Lash out against me.'

'Did you write an account of your conversation with Sadie?'

'Yes.' Anna knows the importance of a paper trail: *If it's not written down then it didn't happen.* She has this notice pinned up inside the surgery cupboard, an unequivocal reminder to all the nursing staff. 'Sadie felt that Tori was quieter than normal, more likely to take refuge in her room than spend time in the common room. But there was nothing she could put her finger on.'

'Could we make a guess as to what might be worrying her?'

'Her parents' divorce is one of the most acrimonious I've come across and Tori is stuck in the middle. She hasn't seen her dad for a while now.' Anna pauses to remember a recent mentor's meeting with Tori.

'My dad's related to the royal family,' Tori said to Anna. 'You wouldn't think it. Although the royal family are really messed up so maybe you would think it. That's why I'm called Victoria. I mean, we're several cousins removed and not rich or anything.' She stopped to take a breath. 'I just wish he would come and see me when he says he will.' She stared up at the ceiling, blinking back tears. 'He's living with another woman now.' She bit her lip. 'And she has a daughter.'

Anna leaned forward to hold Tori's hands. 'Your dad loves you, Tori. I'm sure of that.' Tori's eyes met hers, wanting to believe. 'How about you send him a letter or an email explaining how you feel?'

'Maybe,' she said, unconvinced.

'We can work on it together if you like,' Anna said.

Anna knows how this marriage breakdown story goes: it begins with arguments, recriminations and disappointments. Then the father leaves the mother and daughter to set up home elsewhere. The weekend visits lapse because it takes willingness and effort to keep them going. The dad meets a woman. He moves in with the woman. The woman has a daughter the same age. The man's own daughter, his flesh and blood, is replaced.

Tori's vulnerabilities had once been Anna's and she hasn't had to work hard to imagine Tori's home life. She guesses that's why Tori chose her as a mentor. Although Anna had never told Tori about her own upbringing, in Anna's experience, recognising someone who 'gets' you is an instinctive pull.

Owen is talking and Anna tries to focus on what he's saying. She hears him tell her that he has sent Tori home and that Anna will also need to stay at home until the police have reported back to him. He wants her to know that she has his support, that there is no presumption of guilt, but that the system, for obvious reasons, must believe the child. He will speak to the other nurses and ensure that in her absence the medical centre is run to the same high standards. 'Rest assured that this matter is confidential. I won't be referring to it in staff briefings. You will be taking a leave of absence for reasons that need not be disclosed.'

But Tori, Anna thinks. Will she tell the other girls? If so, it will be round the senior girls, the whole school, in no time. Isobel will be one of the first to hear about it.

How will she cope with her mum off work because she is under investigation for child abuse?

'I suggest you collect your things,' Owen says quietly.

'I can't finish my shift?' she asks. 'One of the boys hurt himself earlier today and is on his way to hospital. I'd like to follow through on his care.'

'Geraldine is also on duty, isn't she?' Owen says.

Anna nods. 'Yes, but—'

'I'll speak to her,' Owen says. 'Please don't worry about the medical centre. I will make it my business to keep a close eye.'

'It's my department, Owen,' she says. '*Mine*. It doesn't run itself. Geraldine is counting down the days to her retirement; Ali and Sheila have young families. It's not fair to load responsibility onto their shoulders.'

'If necessary I'll contact a nursing agency.' He stands up. 'But let's not get ahead of ourselves. This could all be wrapped up in double-quick time. When Victoria has a moment to reflect …?' He raises both hands, palms upwards. 'Who knows?' He walks Anna to the door. 'You know how much I respect you, Anna,' he says, his eyes catching hers. She sees focus and strength and something else – a look that speaks of their friendship. Twenty years of knowing each other, thousands of days and a wealth of experience to draw upon. 'Hang on in there.'

Chapter Three

Her legs don't belong to her. Her feet move automatically but awkwardly as if there is resistance from the stair carpet, the wooden floorboards in the main hall, the tarmacked road outside. Her feet keep moving and her body stays upright as she retraces her steps back to the medical centre. She smiles distractedly at the wriggly, giggly line of pre-preppers who are leaving for the day. One of the mothers stops Anna with a hand to her elbow. 'Sister Pierce! Phoebe was telling me that you did a teeth-cleaning session with them yesterday. She was very quick to correct me last night when we didn't clean them well enough.'

'That's great.' Anna stares down at Phoebe, who is jumping from one foot to the other, a lolly wedged in the corner of her mouth.

'It's sugar-free,' her mother blurts out quickly, sensing Anna's thoughts.

Sensing them wrongly, as it happens, because Anna isn't thinking anything of the sort. Her mind is frozen in a loop of disbelief. What the hell has just taken place? Could she really have been suspended for suspected child abuse? Really? *Really?*

She continues walking, keeping her head down as she listens to her mind race: *What has Tori said? What flight of twisted imagination has taken possession of her? Will she be believed? Could Anna lose her job over this?*

Thankfully there are no children in the waiting area.

She almost pushes open the door to the office but at the last second she hears Geraldine on the phone. 'Yes, Mr Wiseman.' A pause. A sigh. Another sigh. And then a reluctant admission. 'I think I'll be able to cover that shift.'

Anna moves away from the office and into the surgery. She needs time out, to close her eyes for a minute, and hope that when she opens them again this will all have been a dream. She goes to collapse onto the examination couch but sees it's already taken – Lynn has her feet up, backrest raised, and is reading a magazine.

'There you are!' She smiles. 'I'm hanging around because I'm taking Lois for a dental appointment but she's not ready yet and I'm damned if I'm going to wait outside the classroom for Madame Courtois to tell me that she's not working hard enough at her French.' She tosses the magazine to one side. 'My other option was to wait in the car but Julia Raeburn was heading my way and she had that look on her face. I expect she's canvassing for a teacher to be fired or caviar for the children's supper.' Her eyes narrow as she focuses on Anna. 'Are you okay?' Her expression softens. 'You're very pale.'

Anna is unable to reply. She stands, mute and vulnerable, her chin dropping towards her chest.

Lynn jumps up and leads Anna by the shoulders. 'Easy does it,' she says. 'Lie back on the couch.'

John always describes Lynn as a law unto herself but as Anna closes her eyes she knows that there is no one else she'd rather have bumped into. Like Anna, she has dual roles in the school, both as a parent and an employee, part-time in her case. She's fearless, funny and entirely focused when she needs to be. She's Anna's closest colleague and best friend.

'Take this.' She passes Anna a glass of water. 'Sip it slowly. It might make you feel better.'

Anna drinks tentatively, feels the dizzy sickness in her head begin to clear and is close to confiding in Lynn when there's a knock on the door.

Geraldine's head appears. 'Mr Wiseman's just been on the phone.' She sighs. 'Now *I* have to go and see him.' She glances at Anna and then away again as if she doesn't like what she sees. 'He tells me you're going home.' She sniffs. 'I'll take the walkie-talkie with me in case you leave before I get back.' She pulls her head away. 'I hope it's nothing serious,' she adds, her concern a reluctant afterthought.

'How that woman is a nurse,' Lynn grinds out, 'is a mystery to all of us. I have more compassion in my little finger than she has in her whole body.'

'She's been whittled away by the years,' Anna says, before adding slowly, 'And … she doesn't know what's going on with me.'

'Has something happened?' Lynn asks. Her tone is gentle and Anna's eyes fill for the second time. 'Is it Noah? Isobel? John?'

'No.' Anna reaches for a box of tissues, grabs a handful and holds them against her eyes, pressing hard enough to break up the darkness with starry lights and flashes of colour.

'Are you ill, sweetheart?' Lynn strokes her hair. 'Are you able to talk about it?'

Anna removes the tissues from in front of her face and stares at her friend. 'I've been accused of hitting a child,' she says flatly. 'I've been suspended pending an investigation.'

The look on Lynn's face is one that Anna recognises from her own reaction – disbelief, confusion and anger all rolled into one. 'What the fuck?'

'I didn't do it.'

'Of course you didn't do it! That goes without saying! Literally, Anna. Li-ter-ally,' she enunciates, then blinks rapidly before adding, 'What child?'

'Tori Carmichael.'

Lynn's jaw drops open. 'The little bitch! Is there anyone in this school who doesn't know how much she lies? How can they be taking anything she says seriously?'

'Because they have to.' Anna sighs.

'Who spoke to you?'

'Owen.'

'Well, he's not living up to his name, is he?' She folds her arms. 'There's nothing wise about suspending you.'

Anna gives a weak smile. 'Child safeguarding comes first, Lynn, you know that.' She swings her legs off the bed. 'I have to leave the premises.'

'You live here!'

'I'm allowed on the grounds, just as long as I stay away from the school buildings and the boarding areas.'

'This is ludicrous! You're the last person who should be accused of something like this.'

Anna laughs. It's short and mirthless.

'Anna? Really!' Lynn shakes her shoulders. 'Don't let this get to you. You've done nothing wrong.'

'I know.' She nods. 'I know that but … Her accusation has been reported to social services, and if the police aren't already involved, they will be soon. And then …' She bites her lip. 'For people who don't know her, she's very convincing.'

'Okay,' Lynn acknowledges. 'I get that. But the police aren't idiots. They'll question girls like her all the time. What's the story she's telling? Can you easily dispute it?'

'I'm not sure. I saw her at about half past two yesterday. She wanted to get off swimming, without good reason. I said no and she was rude to me. She flounced off in a bit of a mood but that's nothing new. She told Owen that she came to see me again after supper and that was when I hit her.'

'And did she come again?'

'She did. But I was busy calling an ambulance and she left before I was free,' Anna says. 'And I regret not mentioning her at the pastoral care meeting this morning but ...'

'I said enough for both of us.'

Anna shrugs. 'I should have said something ... We all know what she's like – up and down, sometimes moody, sometimes biddable. I spoke to Sadie last week and she said she was quieter than normal but ...' She sighs. Anna knows it's childish but she feels hurt by Tori's accusation. Anna's guidance teacher at school was her go-to person in the same way Anna has been for Tori. Anna would never have done anything to hurt her. 'I don't know why she would do this to me,' Anna says.

'Teenage girls are all fear and spite,' Lynn replies. 'They can't help but be bitchy madams, and I know it must feel personal—'

'That's because it *is* personal.'

'She wants to hurt someone and she's chosen you in the same way that most teenagers hurt their own parents,' Lynn suggests. She throws out her arms. 'I expect it's because she's jealous.'

'Why would she be jealous?'

'Because you have it all! Noah and Isobel are great kids. You and John are great parents. Your home life could make someone like Tori very envious.'

Tori had been at Bishopglen less than two months when she joined the newsletter committee and Isobel invited her home. They sat upstairs in her bedroom going through drawings

from the Junior School Design-a-Christmas-Card competi-
tion. Tori chose three and put them forward, explaining why
she thought they were the best.

'No offence, Tori,' Pippa said. 'But you're still fairly new
to the school.' She whipped one of the drawings out of her
hand. 'We can't choose Lois's drawing. She's my sister. It'll
look like nepotism.'

'And that boy won a competition last year,' Isobel said,
taking another drawing out of her hand. 'We try not to pick
the same children all the time.'

'Not this one either,' Hester Wiseman said. She smiled as
she took the final drawing from her hand. 'Sorry.'

'Why not?' Tori asked.

'Because ... well. This bit here.' She pointed to the middle
of the drawing where one of the donkey's ears was pointing
upwards. 'It looks like a cock.'

Hilarious.

Not.

Tori left them to their laughter and went to the loo. Then
she went downstairs. The washing machine was hammering
away in the utility room so they didn't hear her come into
the kitchen. Mr Pierce was sitting at the table marking
papers. Sister Pierce was on the floor surrounded by photos.
Tori sat on the chair in the recess beside the Aga and watched
them. She knew she was behaving in a creepy way but she
couldn't help herself. The scene held her attention, grabbing
her focus like a powerful magnet. Peace and harmony, home-
liness and comfort – Tori couldn't remember ever witnessing
this level of accord between her own parents. It made her
chest ache.

A couple of minutes went by before Sister Pierce spotted
her. 'Tori!' She jumped. 'I didn't see you there!'

Mr Pierce looked up and smiled. 'Fed up with the girls'
chat?'

'Sorry. I didn't want to interrupt you.'

'I don't know why I'm bothering with this.' Sister Pierce stood up, stretched out her knees. *'I make albums for Noah and Isobel but everything's online now, isn't it?'* She opened the cupboard, brought flour and sugar out on the work surface. *'Fancy helping me make some scones?'*

Tori smiled. *'I'd love to,'* she said.

I should be her daughter, not Isobel, she thought.

How would Anna describe her family life? Definitely not perfect. They have their arguments and they're perennially hard up. But then Lynn has a point: to someone like Tori, their lives are blessed.

'Shall I see whether I can get anything out of Lois?' Lynn says. 'She loves spying on Pippa so she usually knows what the senior girls are up to.'

'Let's just keep it between the two of us for now,' Anna replies. 'With any luck Tori will come to her senses and the nightmare will be over before it really begins.'

'Okay.' Lynn nods. 'I won't tell a soul. Well, only Matt.' She hugs Anna tight. *'Courage, mon brave.* You'll get through this.'

Lynn leaves to take Lois to the dentist and Anna hangs back to make sure the medical centre is left tidy. She goes through each of the rooms, checking the cupboards that should be locked are locked. She stacks the resuscitation models, still on the floor from her first-aid lesson that morning, neatly in the corner of the teaching room. Boys' and girls' sick bays lie at either end of the building and both are empty. (Give it another couple of weeks and that will change.) In the circular waiting area close to the front door, she plumps up the cushions and tidies the information section, where health promotion leaflets are spread across the table.

She leaves before Geraldine returns, making sure one of the walkie-talkies is in its cradle should a child be looking for attention. Owen didn't tell her that she should hand in her keys. So she doesn't. She slips them into her uniform pocket and heads home.

Chapter Four

It was in the 1920s that the monastery became a boarding school and every decade since, buildings have been added on: classroom blocks and staff houses, a fully equipped gym and swimming pool, a state-of-the-art science centre with a telescope and a charging point for electric cars. And, most recently, a recording studio has been grafted onto the refurbished music block.

There are almost thirty staff flats and houses spread across the extensive grounds, most of them in clusters. Not all members of staff are given accommodation; Anna is one of the lucky ones, and she lives with her family in the middle cottage of a row of three. The deputy Peter Williams and his young family are on one side. Geraldine and her husband, who is head of maintenance, are on the other.

During the cold, dark months Anna drives up the hill to work but in the fine weather she takes a short cut through the woods at the rear of the school. It's a five-minute walk along a man-made track that's narrow and twisty but well enough trodden for it to be easy to follow. As she walks she stares down at the earth to avoid tripping over knotted tree roots or fallen branches. A blessing, because focusing on her feet makes it easier not to think too much.

When she arrives home her husband John is in the kitchen making tea. She stands in the shadow of the doorway and watches him, reassured by the normality. He is listening to a quiz on Radio 4, shouting out the answers and then laughing when he gets them wrong. He's a noisy, messy cook. Steam rises from two pots, the frying pan spits and crackles. Finally she steps into the room and he catches the movement from the corner of his eye, swivels round to greet her.

'I thought you were working another double shift?' He doesn't wait for an answer but leans in for a kiss, which she returns, and then she links her hands around his waist, seeking the comfort of a long-lasting hug. 'You all right?'

'No, I'm not.' She rushes to unburden herself. 'I've had a shit day, John. The shittiest of shitty days.' Tears gather again. 'Unbelievable, in fact.'

'What happened?' John's expression is immediately concerned. 'Tell me.'

'I was called into—' She hears something drop onto the floor upstairs and jerks her head back to listen. 'Who's home? Is it Noah?'

'Isobel,' John says, pulling her close again. 'She's lost a textbook and is having one of her mini-crises.'

Anna hadn't expected this. Isobel is the head of S5, a full boarder with responsibility for the younger girls in her house. She rarely comes home during the week.

'So what happened?' John strokes her back.

'It can wait.' She forces a smile.

There's a particularly loud spit from the frying pan. John crosses the floor and tosses the contents up into the air with a cheffy confidence. 'I can delay tea.' He glances back at her. 'We could go for a walk?'

'It's okay.' She lifts a dishtowel off the back of a chair. 'It can wait.'

'You're sure?'

She nods.

'And Noah's on his way back,' John says. 'He'll be here in time for tea.'

'What? He's only been gone two weeks!'

'Probably wants you to do his washing.'

'I expect you're right.' God knows she loves her kids but she needs to get John on his own if she's to tell him about today. Anna doesn't want Noah and Isobel to know, not yet, not until she's got over the shock herself and she can tell them without crying. But now she'll have to sit through a family meal pretending all is well.

John uses a fork to stab a nugget of chicken. 'Taste this.' He holds it out to her. 'I used the spice mix Lynn recommended.'

Anna takes the fork in her hand and blows on the meat before she bites into it, tearing the chicken piece in half and passing the other half back to her husband. 'It's good,' she says.

'Better or worse than the usual recipe?'

'Better.'

There's a clattering down the stairs and Isobel flounces into the kitchen, her steps heavy with significance. 'RIP my future career.' She throws herself down on the comfy chair beside the Aga. 'I've lost my physics textbook. It'll send Mr Frank into a *rage*. He'll never give me another one and we're not allowed to share.'

'Did you write your name inside?' Anna asks.

'Of course.' She widens her eyes, her eyelashes extra long and black with mascara. 'And I wrote it on the spine too.'

'There's probably one in the school library,' her dad tells her. 'You could borrow that until your own one turns up.'

'Mum, can you look in the library for me tomorrow?' Her tone is pleading. 'At morning break we have to make a decision on the layout for the newsletter. Then straight after lunch I need to start my biology project or else I'll never get it all done.'

'Don't be encouraging your mum to do your dirty work.' John takes the dishtowel that Anna has folded into a tight, compact square and flicks it in Isobel's direction. 'You staying for tea?'

'Mum?'

'I'll help you look for it.' She's wearing more make-up than she normally does, Anna notices. Sixteen going on seventeen and with all the relationship ups and downs ahead of her. 'It might be under all the clutter in the front porch.'

'But if we don't find it?' she whines.

'You staying for tea or not?' her dad repeats.

'Is it chicken?'

'It's my improved sweet and sour chicken, green beans and sticky rice,' he says with another flourish of the towel.

'Have you put pineapple in the sauce?'

'I have.'

'*Why?*' She makes a face. 'You know I hate pineapple! God!' She throws her head back. 'Why is everything going wrong?'

Anna turns away, hiding a sigh. She's not sure she can take this level of drama. Not now. Not this evening. In school, Isobel is mature and helpful but sometimes when she's home she becomes a moany, woe-is-me teenager, and the last few months she's been even more emotional than normal.

'You can pick the pineapple chunks out of yours,' John tells her.

'I'll still be able to taste it! The juice leaks out into the sauce!'

'I'm going to have a quick shower,' Anna says, leaving the cajoling to John. 'I won't be long.'

She climbs the stairs, checking her mobile before she undresses because Tori might have already withdrawn her accusation and then there'll be no need to tell John. The first thing she sees is a message from the junior boys' houseparent telling her that Angus Rutherford has had his head stitched and has called his mum, who sends her thanks for caring for him. There are no messages from Owen. And no missed calls. And when she logs onto her school emails, she finds half a dozen routine messages from parents but nothing from Owen.

By the time she gets downstairs again Noah has arrived and is sitting at the table, beer in hand. 'I didn't expect to see you today, love.' She kisses the top of his head. 'You doing okay?'

'Fine, yeah.' Green eyes smile up at her. 'It's just a flying visit. Ed was coming home for the night so I thought I might as well cadge a lift.'

'Ed Wiseman?' Isobel asks. Noah doesn't reply. 'I'll take that as a yes.'

The cat is on her knee, turning circles before he settles himself. 'Don't let Monty's claws pull at the threads in your skirt,' Anna says to her, her hand resting on Noah's shoulder.

Isobel chooses not to hear. 'Pippa's got a thing for Wiseman.' She wrestles her mobile out of her skirt pocket, twisting her body sideways, at pains not to disturb the cat. 'I'll tell her he's back.'

Anna walks across to her daughter, lifts Monty off her knee – 'He wasn't pulling at my skirt!' – and plonks him down next to the cat flap. He sits in front of it contemplating his next move and Anna joins Noah at the table. 'So tell us all about uni,' she says, determinedly bright. 'Did you have try-outs for the rugby team?'

Noah starts talking and, although Tori's accusation is a solid weight on Anna's chest, she's able to enjoy moments of forgetting as he brings them up to date with everything that's been happening. The main event is that he's in the first team for rugby. He scored a try in his first match but, before that, he had his initiation ceremony, which involved increasingly embarrassing dares punctuated with copious amounts of alcohol, a black bin bag taped around his neck so that, 'I could have a tactical chunder into the bag.'

'You put your fingers down your throat?' Isobel asks, eyes wide.

'My stomach was so full of lager it didn't take much to make me sick.'

'Yuck!' She recoils. 'You're disgusting!'

Anna doesn't comment. She has a repertoire of what Isobel and Noah refer to as her 'voice of doom' tales and they are familiar with all of them. They include young people who have choked and died on their own vomit, been permanently paralysed from diving into water that was too shallow, and getting HIV the first time they have unprotected sex. Each of the stories is not only true but also unexaggerated.

'Not like it was in our day, Anna, eh?' John says. 'We were too skint to buy booze.'

Anna never had a 'day' at university. She met John when she was training to be a nurse and he was a second-year chemistry student. 'No credit cards. No overdrafts,' Anna affirms. 'Cornflakes for tea more often than not.'

John smiles across at her and she feels her heart skip. Still, after all these years. That's something, isn't it? Not to be scoffed at, not to be squandered. She's about to reach for his hand, just to feel the warmth of his skin, make contact with the man who is both lover and friend, husband and co-parent, when Isobel speaks.

'Changing the subject,' she says, tipping the remains of her meal into the bin – chunks of pineapple and pieces of chicken that didn't pass her scrutiny – 'I was asked to show a family round today. They seemed really nice. I think they'll sign up.' She helps herself to a yoghurt from the fridge. 'When I was taking them through the main hall, I saw you coming out of Mr Wiseman's office, Mum.'

Anna hadn't noticed her daughter but then she was too shocked to notice anything very much, and now she feels anxiety descend like a fog.

'You looked a bit upset,' Isobel says. She screws up her nose. 'Like you'd been crying.'

All three pairs of eyes are suddenly focused on Anna. 'He wanted to speak to me about one of the children,' she says, a slight tremor in her voice.

'Called to the headmaster's office?' John says. 'That's unusual, isn't it?'

His sideways glance has bite to it and Anna flinches. Has he forgotten what she'd said about having a bad day? Can't he put two and two together? Work out that whatever happened in Owen's office is the reason she's upset?

John doesn't like Owen but that's old news. Years ago he described him as an arrogant twat and he persists in saying he hasn't had any reason to change his opinion despite the fact that Owen was key in the decision-making that promoted Anna to senior nurse, gave her a significant wage rise, and offered their whole family rent-free accommodation, not to mention the reduced school fees.

'So what did he want, Mum?' Isobel says.

The chicken turns in Anna's stomach and when she swallows, the acid taste of vomit burns her throat. Suddenly her reticence feels misplaced. Far worse for Isobel to hear about it from one of her school friends, or Ed Wiseman to get hold of the news and break it to Noah when they're driving back to university.

She takes a drink of water and looks at her family. 'I won't be going into work tomorrow. I've been accused of hitting a child and will need to stay at home pending an investigation.'

Silence.

Anna doesn't breathe as she waits for one of them to react.

Isobel breaks the silence with a shrill, prolonged laugh. 'What the hell, Mum? That's not even funny! It happens to people, you know. There was that gap student in Edinburgh who was accused of punching one of the sixth-form boys.' She takes a spoonful of yoghurt and keeps talking through the gloop in her mouth. 'Turned out he hadn't done it. The boy just didn't like him. He still lost his job, though.'

John is completely still, staring at Anna. Just staring.

'Mum?' Noah says, trying to read her expression. 'You are joking, aren't you?'

'I'm not joking,' she says flatly. 'I have been accused of hitting a child.'

Isobel's mouth falls open. John slumps back in his seat. Noah is frowning as if he's trying to decipher what the words mean because they are strung together in an order that makes no sense when they are applied to his mum. Three or four seconds tick by. They are no ordinary seconds. They lengthen and expand, enough time for the air to saturate with tension. Anna digs her fingernails into the palm of her hand. The wait is excruciating. It reminds her of the time her dad told her he was leaving her mum, his words weighing as heavy as the barrel of a loaded gun.

It's Noah who speaks first. 'Who accused you?' His head is moving from side to side with tiny, disbelieving shakes. 'Why? Why would they say that? Why are they lying?'

'I don't know.' Anna takes a hurried breath and reaches for her daughter's hand. 'Isobel, don't worry about school. As far as the staff are concerned I'm on leave for an undisclosed reason.'

'What year are they in? Is it my year? Is it a girl or a boy?' She wrenches her hand away from Anna's. 'Oh my God! Does everyone *know*?' she shrieks. 'What's going to happen? Will you have to leave the school? Will *I* have to leave the school?' She runs out of breath and then she starts crying, loud, gulping tears. John reaches across to hold her and she falls against his shoulder, wailing into his shirt.

Anna stands up, pushing back her chair so roughly that it crashes to the ground behind her. There's a loud meow from Monty before he finally makes up his mind to bolt through the cat flap. Anna leaves the room and Noah follows her.

'Mum!' She's almost in her bedroom when he catches up with her. 'Mum! Wait!' He puts his arms around her. 'You must be really upset. I'm so sorry.' He's rubbing her back. 'Who is this kid? What are you supposed to have done?'

'I don't know. I have to wait to hear. Maybe from social services. Maybe from the police.' Her words are punctuated with short breaths. 'If they feel … her story is credible … they'll press charges.'

'So it's a girl? Who?' He holds her away from his shoulder, his eyes wide with sincerity. 'What's her name?'

'Victoria Carmichael. You won't know her. She came to Bishopglen after you left. She's been to the house a couple of times but it was when you were travelling.'

'I've heard the name,' he says. 'She's in the same year as Iso?'

Tori knew about Noah because Isobel used her older brother's name as a weapon. He was a key piece of her popularity arsenal. And he was best friends with Ed Wiseman. They were cool. They were going places. They were on a gap year together in South-East Asia so Tori had yet to meet either of them but she guessed that if they were anything like their sisters, she wouldn't like them much.

Anna nods. 'I've been mentoring her for the last year. I thought we got on well.' She shakes her head against her own naivety. 'She said I hit her yesterday evening, at some point after supper. She did come to the medical centre but I was phoning for an ambulance and didn't speak to her.'

'Well, that should be easy enough to prove?'

'Not really.' Her lip jumps. 'I haven't crossed any lines, Noah.' She focuses on those green eyes of his, the ones that she loves to see light up with his smile. 'I know I haven't.'

'Of course you haven't! You're brilliant at your job.'

'I'm not sure why she's doing this to me.'

'Attention-seeking?' Noah suggests. 'Is she unhappy? Did you tell her off?'

'All of the above. She hasn't been herself lately. I mean, she's often moody and difficult, and these last few weeks she's been especially so. Her parents are in the process of divorcing. She doesn't see her dad much.' Anna pauses, briefly tunes in to the low, comforting murmur of John's voice from the kitchen below. Isobel has stopped crying; John must have talked her round. He's better with Isobel than she is. Always has been. She's a daddy's girl and Noah is more her boy than John's. They didn't plan it this way. The children just naturally gravitated towards the opposite-sex parent.

'I'm sorry you've come home to this,' she says, giving Noah a sad smile. 'I would have warned you if I'd known.'

'Don't be daft, Mum.' He takes hold of her hands. 'I'm your son. I want to help.'

'And you do help.' She means that. 'Just being here is a help to me. But listen.' She releases her hands and gives his chest a small push. 'Why don't you go and catch up with your friends?'

'Well …' He looks doubtful. 'I did say I'd join some of the crew down the pub. Is that okay, though?'

'Of course. You go out.' She pushes him a little harder this time. 'And don't worry. This could all come to nothing.'

'She's probably loving the attention,' Noah says, glancing back from the doorway. 'Gives her power.'

'Knowing Tori as I do, it wouldn't surprise me,' Anna says.

'Once shit starts to get real, with the police talking to her and so on, I think she'll be honest.' His expression is hopeful. 'I'll be back before eleven. Don't worry, Mum, yeah?'

Chapter Five

She does her best not to worry. She sits down on the bed. She checks her mobile again, just in case there's a message. There isn't. Each thought that comes into her head she shuts down before it can morph and multiply, extrapolate along a line that ends up with her struck off, no longer a nurse, the whole family homeless, Isobel locked in her bedroom refusing to attend any other school, Noah home from university because he's scared his family will implode.

And John. John would insist on being upbeat but underneath she knows he would be panicking as much as she was. Money worries would dominate their family life, just like they did five years ago. And she's not sure their marriage would survive another run at that particular mountain.

She shifts her position to stare at the chest of drawers, holds her gaze for a few seconds before sliding off the bed to yank open the heavy bottom drawer. She forces her hand through a mound of old socks and forgotten underwear until her fingers feel the edge of a book. Socks jump out onto the floor as she pulls it onto her lap. She doesn't open it. She stares at the cover, finds the sight of it both cautionary and reassuring.

It could be worse.

Yes.

It could always be worse.

This is a thought that she can hold onto, expand upon, turn every which way but not discard, because it's the truth. If she barely knew this truth as a sixteen-year-old then her nurse's training hammered it home. You can't train as a nurse and not know that things can always be worse. She remembers the patients she treated who were blindsided by one illness after another or had families where bad luck showed up one day and never left, death's dark shadow cleaved to them and their loved ones like a bloodsucking leech. There was Irene with the grade IV glioma who had lost her husband in a workplace accident and her daughter to meningitis. There was Dan, the thirty-one-year-old fireman, who had saved countless lives and fought hard to save his own, clinging onto every second until organ failure shut his body down.

Anna specialised in children's nursing early on in her career because she had an affinity with children. She loved that they lived in the moment; she could make them laugh, distract them from their pain, cheer them up with hand puppets and card games. She worked in the NHS for a couple of years after she married John and then she applied to Bishopglen. John thought she was selling out – he is loyal to the public sector – but she knew that children from wealthy families could be just as vulnerable as those from poorer backgrounds because children's health and wellbeing isn't always reflected in the size of their parents' bank balance. 'There'll be children who need the support I can give them, John,' she'd said. 'Bad luck and poor parenting happen across the board.'

She was right. She made a difference to the children who were bereaved, physically or mentally ill, experiencing difficulties at home, or simply needed a kindly face during break and lunchtimes until they made friends.

And despite twenty years in the independent school sector she never forgot her time in the NHS and the courageous people she nursed.

You do your best with what's in front of you. If life throws a curved ball your way – be brave – step up.

Tori had been doing that, Anna thinks. She'd been trying to step up.

Tori finished her chemistry assignment and then stayed in the library, her fingers trailing along the spines of textbooks until she found one that interested her – a book about human interaction. She opened it at the chapter entitled: 'The Importance of Touch'. She read that if you held a hug for longer than three seconds your pituitary gland released oxytocin, a neuropeptide, commonly known as the 'cuddle' hormone.

No wonder she was miserable. Days could go by when no one touched her. Her mum had never been touchy-feely but her dad had hugged her every day when he lived with them.

She told Sister Pierce about the hormone. 'Or in my case, lack of it. Maybe that's why I've got problems.'

Sister Pierce frowned, momentarily stuck for a solution until she said, 'How about getting involved in the buddy system? I've seen you with the younger children. You're very natural with them and they like you.'

The buddy system paired senior school pupils with ones lower down the school. It was designed for the benefit of the younger children because it made senior school less scary. Tori agreed that Sister Pierce would speak to the head of lower school and within a couple of days Tori was given Lois Sykes as a buddy. She was Mrs Sykes's daughter and Pippa's sister so Tori wasn't sure it would work but within five minutes of spending time with Lois, it was clear that

she was a sweetheart. She liked skipping and always carried
ropes around with her. Tori loved the optimism of that. They
met twice a week and sometimes they played skipping games,
other times Tori would listen to Lois read. Always at the end
of it, Lois would hug her hard as if they might never meet
again. And when she saw her around school she'd shout,
'Tori! Tori! It's me!' She waved to her as if she was her very
best friend.

Even Mrs Sykes was impressed. 'You're really helping
Lois, Tori,' she told her. 'She's always struggled with friend-
ships and you're really making a difference.'

'Anna?'

She opens her eyes with a start, hears John's footsteps
on the stairs. Next thing he's sitting on the floor beside
her.

'Sorry I took so long.'

'That's okay.' She leans her head against his shoulder.
'Noah's gone to the pub.'

'I dropped Isobel back at school.' He brings Anna's
hand onto his lap. 'We found the physics textbook on
top of the piano in the common room so that helped
cheer her up.'

'So the book wasn't at home after all,' Anna says.

'No.' He sighs. 'She was still a bit clingy when I left
her. She's worried everyone will know about what's
happened.'

'Of course she is,' Anna says.

'Anna.' He strokes her hand. 'She's sixteen.'

'I know.' She sighs. 'She's upset. I understand that.'

'I'm so sorry this is happening to you.' John interlaces
their fingers and she feels warmth spread from his hand
to hers. 'What has the child said?'

'Just that …' Anna tries to swallow away the ache of

dryness in her mouth. 'You believe I didn't do it, don't you?'

'Of course. Jesus, Anna!' His expression, like Lynn's and Noah's, tells her that he has no doubt about her innocence, that the very idea of her hitting a child is absurd. 'I know you! You'd never do anything like that.'

'Thank you.' She squeezes his hand. Life is always better with John on her side. 'I wasn't going to tell the kids, but then Isobel asked the question and I thought forewarned is forearmed.' She stares down at their fingers: John's thicker and longer than hers, his hand as familiar as her own. 'Owen is hoping it won't be fuel for the gossip whores but I'll be very surprised if it isn't. God knows what will happen if the car park mafia get hold of it.'

'Aren't they busy organising the trip to France?'

'Some of them are but Julia Raeburn doesn't have a child in that year and she hasn't liked me since the head lice debacle in pre-prep.'

The 'car park mafia' was Lynn's nickname for some of the day children's mothers who, when their children have run into school, stand in a huddle in their designer Lycra plotting their next crusade. Sometimes they want changes in school policy, sometimes they pick on a particular teacher who they decide isn't up to scratch, or a child who, in their eyes, should be excluded. Other times it's all about food: too much sugar, too many white carbs. And why isn't all the food organic? Owen realised that they needed their energies channelled and persuaded them onto various parent/staff committees. This helps focus their attention but it won't hold them for long if there is a juicy story in the offing. And what could be juicier than a member of staff being accused of hitting one of the children?

'What's the name of the child?' John asks. 'Is it someone you've spoken about?'

'My accuser?' She turns to face him. 'You really want to know?'

'Yes.' He shrugs. 'A twelve-year-old boy won't lie for the same reasons as a teenage girl. And if you have history with this kid ...' He trails off.

Their eyes hold. One heartbeat, and then another until she sees she has his full, unguarded attention. 'Victoria Carmichael.' Her voice is almost a whisper. A soft, significant whisper. 'She's the one who's accused me.'

His mouth hangs open.

'Your protégée,' she adds softly, because it was John, a chemistry teacher in the local state school, who brought Tori to Bishopglen's attention, encouraged her to sit the scholarship exams, gave her a pep talk when she didn't want to take up their offer of a place, introduced her to his family, encouraged Isobel to be her friend and Anna to look out for her.

He opens his mouth to speak but is lost for words.

Anna detaches her hand and stands up. She knows she has done this deliberately, let the name drop into the air like a barrel bomb from the sky and then watch as the bomb detonates in his eyes. She's punishing him because he didn't support her at the dinner table: first there was his expression when Owen was mentioned and then he let Noah be the one to follow her from the room because Isobel's meltdown was more important than anything Anna was suffering.

Anna isn't proud of her strike back at him – it's immature. She's an adult, for God's sake! She should be above behaving like this. But just occasionally it would be nice if her feelings took priority, if he put his role as her husband before his role as Isobel's father.

'I don't understand.' John is on his feet beside her, frown lines tracking his forehead. 'What the fuck? *Why?* Why would she do this?'

'God knows. And after all I've – *we've* – done for her.' She shakes her head. 'More fool me, huh?'

'And me,' John says. 'It's insane.' He starts to pace, his expression darkening. 'She's the last person I would expect to lie.'

'John, she's always lying!'

'About small stuff, sure. But this? Threatening your career? Your integrity? This is serious.' He walks towards the door. 'I'm not fucking having it. I'll go into school and speak to her.'

'John, no!' Anna grabs for his arm, holds on tight as he pulls towards the stairs. 'John! Please. You mustn't do that.'

'Anna.' His tone is level but she can see tension in the set of his jaw. 'I'm not having Victoria Carmichael lying about you.'

'I understand you're angry. I am too.' She pulls his arm towards her, places his hand on her waist. 'Just hear me out.'

He sighs and stares up at the ceiling.

'Think about it, John,' she says. 'Tori's been sent home. If you turn up at her house, chances are she'll refuse to speak to you. Her mother will be there and you know what she's like. It doesn't take much to set her off. At the very least she'll accuse you of harassment and call the police. It could make everything worse.'

Anna had only met Saskia Carmichael once. She came to collect Tori from sick bay when she was laid low with the flu. She was dressed in a smart suit and three-inch heels, her hair blow-dried and set with hairspray. 'Is she really ill?'

Saskia asked Anna. 'Because I had a busy afternoon ahead of me and if I don't work I don't get paid.' (Tori told Anna that her mum was a pharmaceutical rep. 'She hates it but it pays well.')

'Tori has a high temperature and headache,' Anna said. She advised the need for regular painkillers and fluids, watched Saskia's eyes glaze over.

'Where is she? Is she ready?'

'She's just getting dressed. She's keen to take some work home with her so her chemistry teacher is bringing a couple of past papers over. He'll be here any second.'

'I don't know where she gets her brains from,' Saskia said. 'Not from me, and not from her dad either.' She flattened her lips. 'Definitely not from him.'

Anna watched as Tori came towards them, her face flushed. Most mums would rush over and hug their child, show sympathy, show them they're loved. But in this case, Tori was the one looking for a hug. Her arms encircled her mum's waist while Saskia held her own arms up and turned her head to one side. 'I don't want your germs, Tori! Save them for next time you see your father.'

'I get that you're angry on my behalf,' Anna tells John. 'And I love you for it.' She stands on her tiptoes and kisses beneath his ear. 'But you could be accused of putting pressure on her. And then Tori might dig her heels in even more.'

'I know but …' John's thoughts are writ large across his face. Anna watches his expression, torn between good sense and his instinct to protect her.

'Believe me, *I'm* tempted to go round to her house,' Anna says. 'Or at the very least phone her but I know I can't because anything I do could be used against me.'

'So what now?' John says. 'We let her get away with making false claims?'

'I'm hoping she'll change her mind. A night's sleep, a chance to reflect. It's possible.' She yawns, dog-tired all of a sudden, the rush and retreat of emotions sapping her energy. 'I'm shattered.'

'I'm sorry, hun.' He strokes her hair. 'Would you like a drink before bed?'

'I've got indigestion.'

'Was it the chicken?'

She smiles, soft-punches his shoulder. 'No, you diddy. The chicken was delicious.'

'Peppermint tea, then?'

'Perfect. Thank you.' She kisses his cheek, rests her head in the hollow of his shoulder. 'I haven't told anyone else except Lynn. And she won't tell anyone apart from Matt, because it might all blow over.'

'Even if she doesn't retract her statement, it will boil down to your word against hers,' John says. 'And with her past history, there's really no competition, is there?'

She hears the hope in his voice and it makes her shiver.

When John returns with a mug of tea she's already in bed. She props herself up on the pillows and sips at the tea, making a mental list of everything she needs to email Owen and Geraldine about in the morning: Angus should be added to the off games list; someone else will need to meet and greet a community police officer who is coming in to speak to the senior school about a growing drug culture in the local area; her lessons are all prepped, there are worksheets in the teaching room cupboard; HPV permission forms are due to be emailed out; a medical supplies order will be delivered; the first-aid bags need checking; she mentors three pupils and one of them is timetabled to come to see her at two.

It's Geraldine who will be on duty tomorrow, and it's difficult for any of the nurses when they are on shift alone – with four hundred and fifty pupils you never know what's going to come through the door next. Perhaps Owen has already spoken to Ali or Sheila. Whatever. She can't worry about it. Someone will have to step up until she's back at work. Fingers crossed that will be soon.

When she's finished her tea she turns off the light. The curtains are open and she watches the sky fade to navy blue. Tree outlines are darker still, their branches reaching skywards, waving at the dying of the light. Anna's mobile buzzes and the screen lights up with a message from Isobel:

Sorry I wasn't very supportive just now, Mum. No one is talking about it here! 😊 😘 😘 😘 😘

Anna replies with thanks and love, then places her mobile face down on the bedside table. In her mind's eye she sees her daughter texting from the comfort of her dorm less than five hundred metres away. Most of the senior girls have single or double rooms but Isobel and her two best friends, Pippa Sykes and Hester Wiseman, opted to share the larger room at the end of the building. The three girls have been close since they were in nursery. Occasionally one or other will have a falling out but mostly they make the trio work.

Anna wonders whether any of them have noticed that Tori isn't in the boarding house, whether they're asking each other where she's got to. And then, will Isobel put two and two together? Anna thinks not, because despite the fact that she and John encouraged them to get to know each other, Tori and Isobel are not natural friends. Tori has been an infrequent guest in their home and whenever she has visited, she's drifted away from Isobel to sit in the kitchen next to the Aga with the cat on her knee talking to Anna or John. Usually John.

Anna remembers a Sunday last year when Isobel and her friends were upstairs. Anna promised them an old-fashioned afternoon tea: home-made scones with strawberry jam and clotted cream. She knew the girls were busy with the school newsletter so she hadn't expected any help, but within half an hour Tori had come downstairs to join her and John, who was marking papers at the table. Anna didn't hear her come into the room but suddenly she was there, silent and watchful. She asked her whether she wanted to help with the scones.

'I've never made scones,' Tori told her. Her pale cheeks coloured pink as if to admit such a thing made her feel vulnerable.

Anna pointed to the hook on the back of the door. 'Grab yourself a pinny.'

'Keep calm and bake.' Tori read the front of the apron before pulling it over her head and knotting the ties behind her back. 'I'll suggest it to my mum,' she said, her tone ironic.

'We'll make extra and you can take some home to her, if you like?' Anna said.

'She doesn't eat carbs,' Tori said. She came to stand at the table beside Anna. 'Or at least, not when she's sober.'

Anna placed a hand on Tori's shoulder but before she could open her mouth to speak, Isobel walked into the kitchen. 'What are you doing?' Her expression was suspicious.

'Making scones,' Anna said, floury jazz hands held up for Isobel to see.

'I was asking Tori.' Her tone was clipped and Anna flashed

her a warning glance. 'She's supposed to be helping to pick a winner in the competition.'

'I thought we'd finished.' Tori pushed the bowl across the table towards her. 'Do you want to help?'

Tori's willingness seemed genuine but clearly Isobel was seeing something else entirely because Anna knew that her hackles were raised. Even as a small girl she struggled to control her temper and the tell-tale signs were there: tight fists held close to her sides, narrowed eyes, right foot tapping. She left the room without replying but not before eyeballing her mum. If looks could kill … Anna thought.

It wasn't until later when the girls had returned home that they spoke.

'What was all that about?' Isobel's mouth was set in an unforgiving line.

'If you're referring to the baking,' Anna said, laying her book to one side, 'Tori wanted to help.' She regarded her daughter with an open expression. 'Was I supposed to send her back upstairs again?'

'Well … no.' Her head bobbed from side to side. 'But when another girl tries to take your daughter's place—'

'Isobel!' Anna stood up. 'You hate baking!'

'I don't hate it! I wouldn't rush to do it but that doesn't mean I hate it.'

'You are my daughter.' Anna hugged her tight, felt her resistance evaporate. 'I would happily spend all day with you. You know that.'

'You think Tori's all sweetness and light,' Isobel grumbled.

'I know she's a tricky character' – Isobel snorted – 'but there's no reason for you to feel jealous.'

'Mum! I'm not jealous!' She stepped away. 'I'm amazed at you. Or not amazed – shocked, confused, surprised.' She shook her head impatiently. 'I can't find the right word, but basically, I just don't get why you're so nice to her.'

'*Because that's my job! And I feel for her. She's not had the steady family life that you and Noah have had,*' Anna said. '*And charity really does need to begin at home.*'

Isobel *wrestled with a comeback, her cheeks reddened, her lips bitten before she said quietly,* '*Honestly, Mum, you're such a sucker for a sob story.*'

Was she? Anna thinks as she lies in bed. She knows she's not always an accurate judge of character. With adults, she can be blinded by good manners and a smile. But children? Children deserve to be believed and to be given repeated chances. Don't they?

Like most teenage girls, Isobel has an aptitude for drama but Anna has to admit that she might just have a point because if she had been more sceptical of Tori's character, trusted her less, kept her firmly at arm's length, she wouldn't be in the position she is in now.

Anna relives the meeting in Owen's office and feels the rush of anxiety double her heartbeat. Anxiety, closely followed by dread. What will tomorrow bring? She closes her eyes firmly. She really is too tired to think about it. She slides down under the duvet, pulling it up and over her head until the world is shut out completely.

Chapter Six

Three o'clock in the morning and Anna is awake. She's on autopilot as she climbs out of bed and goes to the loo, barely opening her eyes. She's back under the covers again when she remembers that Noah went out to the pub. Did he get home okay? Despite the shock of Tori's accusation, she fell asleep at once and she doesn't remember hearing Noah come up the stairs. John will know if he's home but he's sound asleep next to her, his breathing a soft, rhythmic snore.

Anna sighs. She'll have to check Noah's in his bed otherwise she won't settle. Using her mobile as a torch, she pulls on her dressing gown and tiptoes along the corridor. His bedroom door is closed. She turns the handle slowly, makes a face as the mechanism gives a squeak. She doesn't shine the torch directly onto the bed but onto the floor around it. Noah's clothes are in a fallen heap on top of his trainers. She tilts the phone and the beam lifts higher. She sees his mobile on the bedside table and, beyond that, his head on the pillow. She's about to close the door again when she hesitates, remembers a conversation with Lynn.

It was a Thursday evening, Matt was on a work trip and John was staying late for a parent/teacher meeting. Anna and Lynn were lounging on one of the long, deep, ridiculously comfortable sofas in Lynn's living room. A glass of red down and another one just poured.

'Did you find out about Pippa and the mystery of the secret texts?' Anna asked.

Lynn gave Anna a guilty look. 'I did.' She swallowed a mouthful of wine. 'Promise not to tell?'

Anna raised herself up on one elbow and used her free hand to make a cross over her heart. 'Your secret's safe with me.'

Lynn glanced over her shoulder to check their girls were still in the garden: Pippa and Isobel were sitting on the swings, moving slowly back and forth while they chatted; Lois was running around with Toast, the family dog. 'I went into her bedroom when she was asleep,' Lynn whispered. 'Luckily she hadn't got her new iPhone yet so I could access her phone with her thumb.'

'What?' Anna was fully upright now. 'Lynn!'

'Don't judge me,' Lynn said. 'I'd tried every which way to get the truth out of her. Matt and I were genuinely worried that she was being bullied.'

'But—' Anna was conflicted. 'I get why you did it but she's entitled to her privacy, isn't she?'

Lynn shrugged. 'I read through every one of her texts. It allowed us to sort out the problem.' She went on to explain that Pippa was being pressured by a boy from a neighbouring school whom she'd met on the orchestra trip to Vienna. She'd sent him several nude pictures of herself. 'He was threatening to make them public unless she agreed to have sex with him.'

'Oh my God!' Anna was shocked. 'That's awful.'

'I know,' Lynn acknowledged. 'I was worried sick but Matt spoke to his lawyer and they sent someone round to meet the boy when he was walking home from school. Put the fear of the law into him. Cocky little shite, he crumbled straight away. And a week later Pippa was back to her usual self.'

*   *   *

Anna stands in the corridor outside Noah's room and stares across at her son, spread-eagled on the bed. It goes against everything she believes in to sneak behind her children's backs. But she doesn't judge Lynn's actions – she doesn't judge them at all. She knows that sometimes needs must. So far she's believed her children have told her the truth when it really mattered. But if that changed, who knows what she might do?

Anna closes Noah's door and goes back to bed.

John heads off at eight the next day. 'Chin up, love.' He climbs into the car and winds down the window. 'Keep me posted? I have free periods before and after lunch.'

'I'll call you.'

Half an hour later she's standing in the same spot saying goodbye to Noah. 'I love you, Mum. I know you'll get through this.'

She hugs him for a few seconds longer than she normally would and waves him off too.

What next? When really she should be in her surgery giving out medicines, liaising with the boarding houses, setting up for her lessons. She takes a shower, lingering under the heavy rush of water, and only stops when she begins to worry about the volume of hot water and how much it will cost.

Her uniform is the first thing she sees when she opens her wardrobe. She's not wedded to it – she knows who she is without it – but there's something about wearing a uniform that allows her to become that person: the school nurse. She's employed for her skills, her knowledge and her warmth. She's not a pushover but she is popular with the pupils: she smiles a lot, she listens, she respects confidentiality. She's spent more than twenty years, minus two stints of maternity leave, giving body and soul to her role, and this accusation from Tori is just a tiny part of the whole.

She dresses in jeans and a T-shirt and sits at the kitchen table with her laptop in front of her. She writes two emails, to Owen and to Geraldine, listing all the tasks that need to be completed over the next few days, ending her message to Owen with: 'I hope my absence is only temporary. Please let me know if you hear anything.'

Pause. Think.

Monty is weaving around her ankles, delighted to have her company. He's a ginger tom, part big boss, part pampered pooch. She picks him up and he allows himself to be cuddled, his purring a steady beat as she walks around the house. Liars are found out. That's what her life experience has taught her. The universe waits for an opportunity to show up the liar. Friendships collapse, marriages fail, countries trade blows.

Or, in this case, Victoria Carmichael retracts her statement.

But what if she doesn't?

Anna logs onto the Nursing and Midwifery Council website and reads through the fitness to practise section. She could be struck off for 'doing harm to others' – if the case is proven. But how could it be proven? Because John is right: it's Tori's word against Anna's. And Tori is a known liar while Anna has a rock-solid reputation.

Still – she should research solicitors, just in case. She's online typing questions into Google when her mobile rings.

'Just checking you're okay.' It's Lynn. 'Have you heard anything?'

'No, I haven't.' She stands up, talking and walking her way around the table. 'You at school?'

'I've just been in the staff briefing. Owen mentioned you'd be absent for a few days and that cover was arranged.' Her voice is low. 'No one made any comment. The main topic of conversation was the disruption to the timetable because of the swimming tournament.'

Anna takes a breath before saying, 'Is Tori in school?'

'I saw her earlier,' Lynn says, her voice dropping to a whisper. 'She came in to school to pick up some books.'

Her mum had dropped her off; her dad was coming to collect her. She waited for him in the car park, her arms aching under the weight of the textbooks she was carrying. She wasn't expecting to stay home for more than forty-eight hours – just enough time for Sister Pierce to pay for what she did. Her face was sore, her eye watering, and when her dad saw her, he came running towards her, cupping her face with his hands. 'My poor baby! My poor Vic! What happened?'

Is this *what it takes to get his attention? she thought.*

'Who was she with?'

'A man. Her dad, maybe?' Lynn's voice drops even lower. 'It looked as if someone must have hit her because even from a distance I could see she had a mark on the side of her face.'

'Jesus,' Anna says. 'Were there scratches as well, or …?'

'I'm not sure. I wasn't that close to her. Why? Would that change anything?'

'I don't know. Maybe.' Anna sighs. 'I'm still not exactly sure what I'm accused of. I mean, could she have done it to herself?'

'It's hard to say. But listen, how about if Matt and I come round this evening? Lois has a sleepover, so we can catch up just the four of us.'

'I don't know, Lynn.' She sighs again. 'I'm not great company.'

'It's at times like this that you need your friends.' She steamrollers on. 'I'll pick up some curry from the Indian on the way. What time is John home?'

'Usually about eight on a Friday. He stays for five-a-side football.'

'Not tonight, though, surely?'

'I told him to carry on as normal.'

'See you at eight, then?'

'I might be a bit of a sad sack.'

'I'll cheer you up. And in the meantime, stay positive. You've got this.'

'Cheers, Lynn.' Anna glances down at her laptop screen. 'Hang on! Before you go, you couldn't recommend a solicitor, could you? I might need one with me if I'm questioned by the police.'

'You heard from them?'

'Not yet. But I think I should be prepared.'

'You definitely should. Matt's business uses a firm in Glasgow. They have a range of expertise. I'll text you their details. Get onto them straight away, and mention Matt's name.'

'Cheers.'

Lynn texts her the solicitor's details and Anna gives them a ring. They make a promise to have someone present when she's questioned. She finishes the call and lifts Monty up again – he's being particularly empathetic this morning. She brings his face close to hers and closes her eyes into his furry softness. 'It's almost as if you know,' she whispers.

And then, early afternoon, a call comes into her mobile and her life moves on a step. 'Hello?'

'Am I speaking to Anna Pierce?'

'Yes.'

'My name is DC James Murray and I'm calling you from Bishopglen police station. I'm ringing in connection with an accusation made against you by Victoria Carmichael. Are you able to come to the station tomorrow for a voluntary interview?'

Anna takes a quick breath before saying, 'Should I bring a solicitor?'

'That is your decision, Mrs Pierce.'

'What time would you like me there?'

'Three thirty.'

'I'll see you then.' She ends the call and stares into the room, empty apart from Monty, who is sitting on a kitchen chair watching her.

People wormed their way into Tori's head and not in a good way – she could list those people but she was making an effort not to hold grudges. Sister Pierce, though? She was in her head in a good way.

Tori had a crush on her – she didn't fancy her, it wasn't like that – more that Sister Pierce cut through her bullshit.

'I wish I'd never come to Bishopglen,' she said. 'All it's doing is showing me a world I'll never be part of.'

'Is it, though?' Sister Pierce asked her. 'What you focus on is what you become. You're gifted at science. You'll go on to one of the top universities. And whatever speciality you choose, I'm sure you'll make a real difference to our world.'

Sister Pierce smiled and Tori could see that she meant every word. That she believed in her, was proud of her. It was a light-bulb moment for Tori. The light soon went out again, but before it did she glimpsed a possible future where every day would be fulfilling. She wouldn't worry about her parents any more. She wouldn't be looking for their love because she would have found her place in the world and be surrounded by like-minded people who wanted to be with her.

And maybe they would even love her.

Chapter Seven

Lynn and Matt arrive just after eight with enough food for four couples. 'We brought Toast along too.' Lynn kisses Anna's cheek. 'We thought he might help cheer you up.'

Toast is their eight-year-old Staffordshire Terrier, the second dog they've owned since Anna met them. He has a strawberry-blond coat and bright blue eyes. The moment he saw Anna it was love at first sight and he immediately falls at her feet, showing his belly. 'Where's my boy?' She makes a fuss of him, then lifts up his firm, warm body and takes him through to Monty, who is unimpressed but tolerates him lying next to him in the roomy basket.

They are unpacking the food containers and spreading them across the kitchen table when John walks in. 'I'll have a quick shower,' he says. His legs are smeared with mud and blood and he has an icepack stuffed into his sock. 'We won,' he adds, grinning.

'Never a week goes by when he isn't hobbling home from football,' Anna says to Matt. 'He's going to end up breaking an ankle or rupturing something unrepairable.'

'Bloodied but unbowed,' Matt says. He pats his small belly. 'Would do me the power of good but I've never been much of a sportsman.' He cracks open a beer and takes a sip before saying, 'Anna, Lynn and I both want you to know that if there's anything we can do, please ask.' He is long-sighted and his eyes are made larger by the corrective lenses. When Isobel was a child she used to describe him as a friendly owl. 'We're completely on your side with this.' Lynn is nodding next to him. 'Completely,' he repeats.

'Thank you. I'm touched.' Anna hugs them both. 'I really appreciate that.'

When John comes downstairs, they sit around the table and she tells them about the phone call from the police. 'It's a voluntary interview.' She looks across at Matt. 'Lynn gave me the number of the firm you use. Patrick Everett will be coming with me.'

Matt nods. 'I know the guy you mean. Don't be put off by the fact that he comes across as a bit of a fool. He's a lot sharper than he seems.'

Matt begins to tell them about a difficult case Patrick Everett won that raised his profile in the firm. And, an hour later, when empty foil containers litter the table and they're on their third bottle of wine, Matt and John go upstairs to the tiny room at the top of the house where John has installed a telescope. Lynn and Anna sit in the living room in front of the woodburner.

'Only the end of September,' Lynn says, 'and already it's freezing.' Lynn would love to move down south but Matt is too much of a Scot. 'I need to start preparing for Pippa's party next week. I was hoping to have it outside but unless the wind drops we'll open up the barn. '

'The barn will be perfect for a party,' Anna says. Toast is lying on her bare feet keeping them warm, his tongue lolling out onto his paw. She reaches down to stroke him. 'You'll love all the visitors, Toasty.'

Lynn invited Anna round for coffee almost immediately after they met. They had recently moved into a house three miles out of town, designed for them by a local architect who specialised in warm, bright spaces that merged with the landscape. Constructed with local timber and slate, and large windows to make the most of the views over the loch, it was utterly idyllic and Anna couldn't help but be impressed. 'It's magnificent,' she said, her eyes taking in the whole space. 'What a view to wake up to!'

'I found it a bit daunting living here at first,' Lynn said. 'Even although it was what we wanted, I'd never lived anywhere with so much space. Growing up, I shared a bedroom with my two sisters.' They sat together on the decking watching the sun go down, the only sound the thrum of white noise from inside the house. 'As my mother said when she came to visit – nobody would hear you scream.'

'Cheerful.'

'Matt has had a security system put in.' She pointed to a couple of cameras on the perimeter. 'And we're getting a dog even though I'm more of a cat person.'

The converted barn was always where the children played when they were younger, train sets and Lego spread out in one corner, with bags of room to cycle or play football when it was too cold outside. Anna spent almost as much time there as she did in her own house.

'She's the first in the year to turn seventeen so she's inviting everyone,' Lynn says.

'Noah mentioned he'd be back for it.' Anna hears a text come in to her mobile. She glances at it, expecting it to be Noah who had been regularly messaging her with words of comfort.

Sister Pierce, it's me, Tori. I need to see you. Will you come to my house? I'm back at my mum's. Or we could meet somewhere else? Please come. Please help me. I have something I need to tell you.

Anna is startled. 'Lynn! Look at this.'

Lynn leans in towards the screen. 'What the fuck?' Her tone is amazed. 'How did she get your mobile number?'

'I've no idea. I didn't give it to her. And it isn't on the school website.'

'Isobel?'

'Maybe, but I've asked her never to give out my number otherwise I'll be at every parent's beck and call.' Anna scratches her head, wonders for half a second whether she should do as Tori asks and go to meet her. 'She could be tricking me, couldn't she?'

'Definitely,' Lynn replies, her eyes wide. 'It might not even be her.'

They both stare at the screen as if expecting something to change.

Sometimes Tori found it hard to separate the lies from the truth but not this time, and she knew she had to tell someone what was going on. Because Sister Pierce had hit her she didn't want that someone to be her, but who else could she tell? Neither of her parents would take her seriously and none of her friends would care. She could tell Mr Pierce but she didn't have his mobile number. She'd got Sister Pierce's number one evening when Isobel had left her mobile on the table, and she memorised it, just in case she needed it in the future.

This was the future. She composed the message, deleting and rewriting until it sounded about right. After she pressed the send button she sat staring at the screen. Hoping. Just hoping.

Anna reaches down to the floor for the wine bottle and pours herself another glass. She could ask Isobel if she gave out her number. She could ask her for Tori's number to see whether the numbers match. But wouldn't meeting Tori just make everything worse? Her solicitor warned her that she should stay away from having any contact with her until the police dropped the case. 'I'm not going to reply.'

'I think that's wise,' Lynn says. 'I can't imagine any good would come from it. She might be feeling apologetic but it's the police she should be speaking to, not you.' She stretches across the back of the sofa and places a hand on Anna's shoulder. 'Don't look so guilty. This isn't your doing. She's sixteen. She should know better.'

'She's only fifteen,' Anna says. 'Remember she was put up a year.'

'Okay, but still. She needs to take responsibility for her actions.'

'You're right,' Anna says, settling her head on a cushion. 'I should tell the police, though, shouldn't I?'

'Probably.'

'I have the number somewhere.' Anna checks back through her recent calls. 'DC Murray said to ring him on this number if anything changed.' She presses the call button. 'Voicemail,' she mouths to Lynn, then says loudly, 'DC Murray, it's Anna Pierce. I'm ringing to tell you that Victoria Carmichael has texted me. I won't reply but I thought you should know.' She ends the call and sits back down on the sofa.

'You've done the right thing,' Lynn says.

'I hope so.' Anna manages to smile. 'So what are you buying Pippa for her birthday?'

Anna sleeps fitfully. She is faintly aware of John coming to bed and then getting up again. She drifts in and out of sleep until, suddenly, she's wide awake, her heart racing. She's out of bed and standing in the middle of the bedroom floor before she has time to think. She feels uneasy, as if a threat is close by. Did she have a nightmare? Or did she hear something?

She waits. She can hear nothing apart from the steady sound of John's breathing. And if she has just experienced a nightmare the details are lost to her.

She glances at the clock: 04.46. It's too early to rise for the day but she's awake now and thirsty. She hauls on sweatpants and a top while Monty does a figure of eight between her ankles. 'Why aren't you outside, guarding your territory?' She lifts him up and speaks into his neck. 'You keeping me company again? What would I do without you, huh?'

She drinks some water from the kitchen tap, then laces up her boots and goes outside, quietly closing the front door behind her. She hesitates on the doorstep, stares up at the windows of the houses either side. Curtains are closed and lights are off. The sunrise won't be long in coming but, for now, the sky is a grey-black and Anna keeps her phone torch close to her right knee as she illuminates the path up towards school. She comes to a stop in the same spot as she stood just days ago with Tori.

The windows at the back of the boarding house are mostly opaque: bathrooms, cupboards and a storeroom. The room Isobel shares with Pippa and Hester is at the other end of the building, facing towards school. The majority of the dorms face the front apart from six, two on each floor at the near and far ends of the building.

She thinks for a moment and is beginning the short walk home when her mobile rings. It's Isobel. Far too early for her to ring. 'Hi Iso–'

'Mum! Mu-um!' She's shouting so loudly Anna has to hold the phone away from her ear. 'Ha-have you …'

'Take a breath, Isobel.'

'To-to-ri Carm-michael,' she sobs.

Anna's heart sinks. So word has got out. She should have warned Isobel that it was Tori who had accused her of assault. *Why didn't she warn her?* 'Isobel. Please. Just—'

'You hit her. Everyone's say-ing that! You hit her.'

'I didn't hit her, Isobel. I know she said as much but—'

'She's dead!'

Chapter Eight

Her scream is so loud that the sound alone makes Anna's heart squeeze with a visceral fear. And then – and then, her brain registers the words. *She's dead.* 'What are you saying?'

'She died a few hours ago. Her mum found her. Everyone's talking about it,' Isobel says, quieter now. 'On social media and in school.'

'Come home,' Anna says, her teeth clenching against the howl in her own throat.

'Now?' Isobel says. 'I can't! Miss Taymere won't let me!'

'I'll get Dad to come for you.'

'Mum—'

Anna drops the phone, scrambles around at her feet to pick it up, her hands grasping at the undergrowth. She is stung by a nettle, feels the skin on the side of her hand bump up and start to throb. Blood flows cold through her joints. Numb feet, legs, hands, she stumbles and falls, scraping the side of her face, not registering the ooze of blood at her temple.

Her vision clouds and clears. She sees her house. Owen is standing at her front door talking to John. They hear her approach and turn to look at her. They both react instantly. John runs, almost pushes, past Owen to reach Anna first. She has collapsed against the wooden bench in their garden, her legs too weak to propel her any further.

John brings her in close, his arm around her waist. 'Let's get you inside, Anna.'

'Is it true?' Anna shouts, staring past John to where Owen has stopped a few feet away. 'Is Tori ... Is she?'

Owen nods and Anna's knees buckle but John antici- pates this and so she doesn't fall. She allows herself to be half walked, half carried across the grass and indoors.

John sits her down on the chair in the hallway. 'You're in shock but you're going to be okay.' He crouches down on the floor in front of her, his hands rubbing at her knees. 'We'll get through this, Anna.'

Their heads touch as she bends to remove her boots but her fingers are still numb and she can't catch hold of the laces.

'Let me help you,' John says.

Anna sits up again, hides her own unhelpful hands under her thighs.

Owen has found a bag of frozen peas in the freezer and wrapped it in a dishtowel. 'For your head.'

She flinches as he touches the bundle against her temple. 'I fell over,' she says. 'When I was trying to get home.'

'It's barely daylight,' John says. 'Why were you out so early?'

'I was trying to clear my head. But tell me, Owen.' Her eyeballs ache as she stares up at him. 'Who called you? Was it one of her parents?'

'No. It was Sadie. She could hear the girls were out of bed and when she went onto the boarding floor to find out what was going on, they told her about Victoria.'

'How did they know?'

'Amanda woke up to go to the loo then checked her phone before she fell back to sleep. She spotted a post on social media.'

'Victoria posted something before she died?' John asks. He has removed Anna's boots and put slippers on her feet. 'Did she commit suicide?'

'It was one of her home friends who posted, and there's no suggestion of suicide.'

'What did she say?'

'RIP my beautiful friend, taken far too soon. That sort of thing.'

Owen's expression is softened by the dim light of the hallway but Anna senses there's more to it than that. 'Isobel called me,' she says. 'She knows I've been accused of hitting Tori. Did the post mention that?'

Owen nods. 'It does say something along those lines, Anna. I'm sorry.'

'But you didn't hit her,' John points out, his voice raised. 'And even if you had, it was days ago, so—'

'A slow bleed,' Anna says, her gaze focused on a spot between both men. 'You can die hours or even days after a blow to the head—' She tries to swallow but her throat is so dry that she can't.

'Surely that's only with serious head injuries where someone is knocked out?' John interrupts. He's still on the floor in front of her. 'Like a car accident or something.'

'Not exclusively.' Anna's forehead is freezing. She reaches up and takes the bag of peas from Owen, places them on the floor at her feet.

'I'm not buying any of this.' John stands up and points at Owen. 'Are you buying this? It sounds far-fetched to me.'

'We don't know the details yet. Her death could be completely unrelated to the accusation,' Owen says. 'The police aren't saying how or when she died, only that she is dead and that the circumstances could be suspicious.'

'You spoke to the police?' Anna asks.

'Briefly.'

Anna's mobile starts to ring. She pulls it from her pocket and glances at the screen – Isobel again. Her hand shakes as she passes the handset to John. 'Could you speak to her?'

John takes the conversation into the kitchen, leaving Owen and Anna alone, not including Monty, who's been watching them from the bottom of the stairs, his front paws tucked neatly underneath his body.

'How could this have happened?' Anna whispers. 'She was only fifteen. She had everything to live for.'

'It's a tragedy,' Owen says, shaking his head. 'Such an awful, awful thing to happen. Her parents will be devastated.'

'Could I have helped her?' A single tear slides down Anna's cheek as she remembers the text from last night: *Please help me.* She tells Owen about the message. 'I should have gone to see her when she asked me.' A shiver passes through her and her teeth chatter. 'She'd still be alive if I'd gone.' She buries her head in her hands, pulling at her hair until it hurts. 'Why didn't I go? Why? *Why?*'

'You didn't go because she'd accused you of hitting her.' He bends down so that their faces are level. 'And you can't say for sure that she'd still be alive. It's important not to speculate.' His gentle tone is meant to calm her but it does the opposite.

'She sent me a text asking for help. I ignored her. And now she's dead. A child *I* cared for is *dead*.' Anna takes a breath; it sounds more like a gasp. 'I've let her down, Owen. I've really let her down.'

'I know this is distressing.' Owen takes hold of her hands. 'But this is not your fault. You need to remember that. Emotions will be running high and you need to be careful not to give them any ammunition.'

Anna's jaw tightens. 'Give who ammunition?'

'Everyone,' he says quietly. 'Your friends and family, the police, the wider school community.'

'I don't understand.' She tries to read his expression. 'Do you mean— Is it because of what her friend posted?'

'Yes.' Owen sighs. 'And several people have already commented. Mostly girls from school. I'll speak to them at assembly about not entering into any sort of dialogue on social media.' He tightens his hold on her hands. 'Anna, this may well get a lot worse before it gets better. If I were you, I would stay offline.'

Anna sits back in her seat, stunned. What girls? What comments? Is she being accused of killing Tori?

John comes back into the hallway, glances at Owen's hands holding Anna's, and hesitates for a moment before he says, 'I'm going to fetch Isobel.' He stares pointedly at Owen. 'You want a lift up to school?'

'I'll go back home to change first.' Owen moves towards the door.

'We'll keep Isobel at home today and tomorrow,' John says, opening the door for him. 'Will you be all right on your own, Anna?' John returns to kiss her. 'I won't be long.'

'I'll be fine.'

Fine. *Fine?* Anna feels as if she'll never be fine again. She stands in front of the mirror to check the wound on her head. It's a long, jagged, mostly superficial scratch. Blood has matted at the edges of her hair and some has dried on her cheek. 'It won't need to be stitched,' she says out loud, and her eyes drop from examining the cut to examining themselves – her pupils are large, glassy, fearful. She flinches and turns away, takes several deep breaths and glances at her watch. Can it only be seven fifteen? She needs to warn Noah but he won't be out of bed yet. Lynn will be though. She's always up early, even on the weekend.

'Morning! You hung over?' Lynn asks.

'No.' Anna closes her eyes. 'Has Pippa been in touch?'

'Not this morning. Why?'

'Lynn, something's happened. Can you come over?'

'What is it?' Lynn says quickly. 'Are the girls okay?'

'Yes, the girls are fine. It's about Tori.'

'Did she send another text?'

'I can't say it over the phone. Please just come.'

'Okay. Sure. I'll be there in ten.'

Anna sits on the third stair from the bottom and Monty immediately climbs onto her knee. She loses her fingers in his fur and tries to let her mind drift on the rise and fall of his breath but it's impossible because Victoria Carmichael is dead and that changes everything. Anna has always known that the worst thing that could happen would be to lose one of the children in her care.

And now it's happened.

She feels sick in her stomach, and in her heart.

Desperate.

Afraid.

And sorry. So very, very sorry.

Chapter Nine

Lynn arrives in a whirlwind of fresh air and anxiety. 'I'm here.' She closes the door behind her and stops in front of Anna. 'What happened to your head? There's blood on your cheek.'

'It's nothing.' Anna stares up at her friend. 'Tori is dead,' she says blankly.

Lynn's mouth drops open and her legs shake. She steadies herself by catching hold of the banister. 'Anna? *What?*'

'She died at some point during the night.'

'How?' Lynn's voice trembles.

'I don't know.'

'Who told you?' Lynn drops onto the stair beside her. 'Are you sure? Are you sure she's dead? This isn't a misunderstanding? Or ...' She frowns as she thinks. 'A sick prank? You know what kids can be like.'

'It's true. Owen was here. He spoke to the police.'

Lynn takes Anna's hand. 'Jesus,' she whispers. 'This is awful.' And then, 'Oh God!' Her tone rises an octave. 'The text. Did you hear back from the police? Did she— Should we have responded?'

'I don't know.' Anna bites her lip. 'Isobel called me just before six saying that—' Anna's voice catches on a sob. 'A friend of Tori's posted something online. I need you to read it to me.'

'Anna, I –' Lynn inhales quickly. 'Where's John?'

'Collecting Isobel.'

Lynn stands up. 'Should I collect Pippa?'

'You don't have to.' Anna pulls Lynn back down beside her. 'He's collecting Isobel because of what it says about me online. I can't look myself because—' She gives an impatient shake of her head. 'Fuck it. I can look myself.' She makes her way upstairs, her foot catching on one of the treads so that she stumbles but doesn't fall. Lynn is behind her.

'Why not wait until John gets back?'

'Isobel's read it.' Her laptop is beside her bed. 'So I need to see it too.'

'Anna, are you sure?' Lynn is wringing her hands, her eyes darting around the room as if trying to find something to grab hold of.

She's out of her depth with this, Anna thinks. And no wonder.

'I'll ring Matt.' She pulls her mobile from her pocket, glad to have found a solution.

Owen's words are at the forefront of Anna's mind as she logs onto Facebook: *this is not your fault … Emotions will be running high … be careful not to give them any ammunition.*

While Lynn calls Matt – 'You need to come over here, straight away. We need you' – Anna types Victoria Carmichael into Facebook and when the page opens, she reads the first post:

Holly Standing

This is awful news, everyone and I'm more than horrified to tell you that Tori passed away during the night. This is a terrible shock! My beautiful friend. Taken too soon. And we don't know what happened yet but we love you and we miss you, Tori #RIPVictoriaCarmichael

*

Reply Amanda Chen
WTF!! I am just reading this and can't believe it. Tori is my roommate at school and we are friends. Please tell me what happened. #RIPVictoriaCarmichael

*

Reply Holly Standing
I don't know the details. I only know she's gone because Tori was texting me and then she went quiet. And I rang her phone a lot then her mum answered and she told me. Her mum thought it might be to do with the fact that a member of staff at your school hit her.

*

Reply Amanda Chen
I know about that. It was Sister Pierce who hit her.

*

Reply Holly Standing
Yeah, and I'm not supposed to say too much but her mum found her at the bottom of the stairs. So if she was still dizzy from being hit then it's the school nurse's fault. I don't know. I'm not a doctor! But the police are there now.

*

Anna turns away from the screen, takes a moment to blink tears from her eyes before looking back. There is a comment from Isobel. She holds a hand to her mouth as she reads it.

Isobel Pierce
Dear Holly, I'm really sorry about Tori – it's a terrible thing and I am very sad for you and for her family but my

mum wouldn't do that. She's never hit anyone. She's
completely non-violent. #RIPVictoriaCarmichael

*

Reply Holly Standing
Of course you take your mother's side! I don't even know
you but I know Tori and she wouldn't lie about something
like that.

*

Reply Isobel Pierce
You need to be careful what you say.

*

Reply Holly Standing
I can say what I like. Tori is DEAD and she was my
FRIEND. She told me about you and your two posh bitch
friends.

Anna is relieved to see that Isobel hasn't replied to this,
but Pippa has also tried to defend her.

Pippa Sykes
I'm so sorry for your loss, Holly, and for all the Carmichael
family but Sister Pierce is one of the nicest, kindest
adults in the whole school. She would never hurt anyone.
#RIPVictoriaCarmichael

*

Reply Holly Standing
Obvs your Isobel's friend. You never liked Tori – you
shouldn't even be on this page!

*

There are several like this and Holly has answered each one with the same I-know-better response. Lynn is reading the comments over Anna's shoulder and when she sees the ones posted by Isobel and Pippa she gasps. 'Good on the girls!'

'It's kind of them to stick up for me but we need to ask them to delete these,' Anna says quietly. She has both hands cupped in front of her middle. The ache is so intense it's as if she has been punched in the stomach.

'What they're saying is true, though, Anna.'

'It doesn't matter. They're better off staying out of it.'

She stumbles into the loo and hangs her head over the basin, dry retching several times until her throat feels as if it's on fire.

Lynn is beside her holding back her hair. 'Matt's on his way,' she says. 'He'll call Everett when he gets here.'

Anna sits down on the edge of the bath and drinks some water straight from the tap. When she raises her head again, she feels the inside of her skull swerve and spin as if she's riding on a not-so-merry-go-round, one that's hell-bent on tipping her onto the floor. Before that happens, she slides down onto the lino and rests her head on her knees, hoping that the dizziness will settle. Lynn has held a flannel under the cold tap and is gently dabbing at her cheek. 'I'll see if I can wipe away some of this blood,' she says. 'Stop me if it hurts.'

It hurts, but Anna doesn't tell her to stop because it's a comfort having her fussing over her like a mother would. She closes her eyes and lets herself be cared for. It's a distraction from the harsh voice of reality that is gripping her stomach in a vice.

Victoria Carmichael is dead.

It's barely eight o'clock in the morning and already Anna is being named and shamed, Tori's accusation treated as if it's a proven fact because the truth is irrelevant. Each and every statement, carries as much weight as the next.

'That's all the blood cleaned away,' Lynn says, rinsing the flannel. 'But you do have quite a bad scrape.'

'I had a look at it in the mirror.' Anna's hand hovers over the wound, then drops back to her side; after all it's the least of her worries. 'It'll be okay.'

'How did it happen?'

'I fell over.' She glances up at Lynn as she says this and imagines she catches a flicker of disbelief in Lynn's eyes. 'When Isobel called. I was so shocked an-and ...' She stutters to a halt. No point in telling Lynn that she was outside the girls' boarding house – doing what? Anna would struggle to explain why she felt she had to go there. Why did she go? She's not even sure herself.

'No wonder.' Lynn kneels on the floor in front of her. 'It has been a terrible shock. But you can get through this.'

She tells her more or less the same things as John said earlier and Anna listens without hope. In moments of crisis we say these things to each other, she thinks, and they are meant to comfort. We are strong. We have right on our side. We can weather the storm.

Anna doesn't believe it. She's been on the wrong side of a tragedy before. It was a long time ago, pre-dating social media. It started out as simple revenge and ended with her mum's death.

Anna hears the squeak of the front door close. 'That's John and Isobel,' she says. Her mouth is painfully dry; she takes another gulp of water from the tap. 'I'd better go down.'

'I'll wait outside for Matt,' Lynn says. 'Give Pippa a

quick ring and see whether she wants to come home for the weekend.'

'Thanks, Lynn.' Anna hugs her friend and tries for a mock salute. 'Unto the breach.'

Chapter Ten

John takes Anna's hand when she comes into the kitchen, holds her in an embrace before saying, 'We should tell Noah.'

'Will you do it?'

He nods, then glances in Isobel's direction. She is sitting at the table, her shoulders pulled up, her jaw tense, her eyes staring down at her feet. 'I'll go through to the living room while you ...' He trails off but it's clear he means for Anna to talk to her.

Anna nods and squeezes his hand before he leaves the room.

As soon as her father has left, Isobel looks up and says, 'Why didn't you tell me it was Tori you hit?'

'I didn't hit her.' Anna sits down on the chair next to her daughter. 'I'm accused of hitting her, that's different.'

'That's not the point and you know it.' Her eyes are grey. In some lights, they are pale as mist rising over water; in others they are warm and soft as doves' wings. But now they are gunmetal grey and her gaze is literally steely. 'You should have told me it was Tori. How do you think I felt when I read that stuff online?'

'I'm sorry.' Anna slumps on the seat, pushes her chin up with her hand, elbow resting on the table. 'I really am.'

'One of my classmates is dead and it looks as if my mother is to blame.' Isobel's tone is ice cold. 'Everyone was asking me about it and I had to say I didn't know anything.'

'Isobel, please.' Anna places a shaky hand over her heart. 'I know I made a mistake by not telling you but I'm trying to handle this as best I can.'

'How can I go back to school? How can I face my friends? How, Mum? *How?*'

'I am sorry, love, but this isn't all about you or me,' she says sadly. 'Tori's death is much more serious than anything you or I might feel.'

'You should be a mother to your own two children instead of scooping up the lost lambs that follow you around bleating for your attention.'

'*What?*' Anna's head jerks back.

'Admit it! You love a sob story. Then you can relive your own dysfunctional childhood. If only you'd had a superhero like yourself on hand to save you.'

Anna takes a second to swallow down her hurt before saying, 'I'm not perfect, but—'

'Nobody expects you to be perfect!'

Anna raises her hand to her face, smooths her fingers across closed eyes.

'You think Tori chose you as a mentor because you're so kind and understanding. But *I* think she chose you because you're easy to manipulate.'

Anna bites her lip. 'I don't know where all this is coming from but what I do know is that I don't have the energy to deal with your anger.' She holds Isobel's steely grey eyes for several seconds, then stands up.

'Victoria Carmichael was a scheming little bitch,' Isobel says quietly, her cheeks reddening. 'You don't know the half of what she got up to. And I've had to carry the burden because you're too blind to see what's going on right in front of your face.'

Anna rocks back. 'Meaning?'

'You and her – both of you – have ruined my life!' Isobel shouts. 'Our whole family's lives! And you don't even care!'

'Of course I care!' Anna shouts back. 'But I don't know what you mean! Tell me, Isobel! Tell me what I've been blind to?'

Anna watches as her daughter wrestles with herself, her mouth opening and then closing, lips bitten, arms crossed over her chest. She gives a terse shake of her head, murmurs something under her breath. When she catches her eye, Anna senses her vulnerability and her fear. She sees the little girl, her little girl, inside the teenager and she steps forward, her arms outstretched, her impulse to make everything better.

'Don't,' Isobel grinds out, but Anna doesn't stop, and when her fingertips make contact with Isobel's upper arms, she is pushed away with so much force that she is sent backward over one of the kitchen chairs. Her arms windmill as she tries to re-establish her balance but her feet are already in the air and there is nothing solid for her to grab onto. She lands heavily, banging her head on the skirting board with a solid crack that echoes off the china in the dresser. She cries out as the scrape on her forehead opens up again and blood trickles down her cheek. Tears fill her eyes. And once she starts crying she finds she can't stop. Sorrow floods through her like heavy rain through a storm drain.

'Isobel!' John is back into the room and rushes over to help Anna up. 'Did you push your mum?'

'Yes.' Her stance is defiant. 'She's fucked up all our lives!'

'She's done no such thing!' John roars across the kitchen. 'Go upstairs to your room!'

'Bu—'

'Now!' John yells. 'Get out of my sight!'

Isobel leaves the room without another word, her footsteps hard and heavy on the stairs as she retreats to her bedroom.

John helps Anna to her feet. 'I'm so sorry, love.' He holds her gently. 'Where does it hurt?' He checks her over with his eyes. 'Your head is bleeding again but hopefully no broken bones, eh?'

Anna has one hand at her hip and the other on her neck but she is unable to speak because she is soul-deep in tears that won't let up. She cries on John's shoulder until her eyes are empty and her ribs ache. Then she splashes her face with cold water, wiping the blood away and easing the heat in her cheeks.

'What possessed Isobel to push you?' John asks as he blots Anna's forehead with a paper towel. 'She hasn't lost her temper like that in years.'

'Apparently I'm all things awful in a mother,' Anna says, her tone flat. 'A fool and a narcissist who has neglected her own children in favour of the ones at school.'

'She said that?' He uses his foot to open the pedal bin and drops the soggy, bloody towel inside. 'Nobody could be a better mother than you. You've done your absolute best for both of them.'

'I'm paraphrasing but …' She takes a clean dishtowel from the drawer and holds it against the wound. 'She pushed me really hard.' She winces against the pain in her head. 'And I get it – she's upset; but we're all upset.'

'I'll have a word with her.' He takes Anna in his arms again. 'She can't get away with behaving like that.' He kisses the top of her head. 'I spoke to Noah. He's worried for you. He'll be home later this afternoon.'

'I don't want him coming home if he misses lectures.'

'It's Saturday,' John says.

'Of course.' She's lost track of what day it is because *a child is dead*. Every time she remembers this, almost every second of every minute, her heart judders like she's running a marathon. Classic anxiety, she tells herself. Just let it go. Do the normal things. Ask the normal questions. 'Does he not have rugby then?'

'He wants to come home, Anna.' John tucks her hair behind her ear. 'You have to let him support you.'

She knows this is something she needs to work on. They've discussed it, husband and wife, over a glass of wine in the evening. They've always tried to recognise their own weaknesses so that they can consciously parent. And sometimes she is too controlling. More often than not, she wants her children to do what she thinks will keep them safe, healthy and purposeful instead of letting them decide for themselves.

'Do you need some ice for your head?' John says.

'I think the bag of peas is still under the chair in the hallway. They won't be cold any more.'

'A bag of sweetcorn instead, then?' John asks. He opens the freezer door, starts rummaging through the drawer and finds three bags to hold up. 'Followed by spinach and cauliflower.'

'No. It's okay.' She gives him a weak smile. 'A cup of tea and some paracetamol would be good, though.'

'I'll bring them up to you,' he says.

Anna nods and climbs the stairs.

'You are a cruel little bitch sometimes, Victoria Carmichael!' her mum shouted.

Tori had been telling her a few home truths. And although what she said was as blindingly obvious as Kim Kardashian's giant arse, her mum had run up the stairs crying.

She'd been dumped again. Fourth time since Tori's dad left her. 'No wonder you can't find a man!' Tori told her. 'Normal men don't swipe left and right. They go out! They join badminton clubs or go to the pub where they don't drink until they're legless and have to pay twice the cab fare for being sick all over the seats!'

Next day when Tori saw Sister Pierce, she told her about what had happened and found herself exaggerating – downright lying, in fact – because Sister Pierce never looked shocked. Sometimes Tori had the sense that she knew her better than she knew herself, that she'd sat in that very same chair.

Tori told her that her mum hit her, and that once she pulled her hair so hard that a chunk of it came out. When Sister Pierce suggested they speak to social services, Tori backtracked. 'I take it all back. She doesn't hit me. She shouts a lot, though, and it's not true what they say about sticks and stones. Words can hurt just as much.'

Chapter Eleven

After Anna's drunk her tea and swallowed a couple of painkillers, John persuades her to have a lie down. Everett will arrive late afternoon, Matt and Lynn will come to add support, and in the meantime she can go back to bed, allow her body to rest after the shock and the injuries.

Miraculously, she falls into a restful sleep. She dreams of the children when they were young, the sounds of their laughter, turning cartwheels on a sandy beach, scrambling up hills to be king or queen of the castle. The sun is shining and Isobel is holding her hand, staring up into her face, love in her eyes.

Anna wakes with that image at the forefront of her mind. Once upon a time they had a mother–daughter relationship that was warm, loving, uncomplicated. Anna's not yet ready to think about what Isobel said to her in the kitchen. Cool, calm Isobel. Words not said in the throes of the temper that came later, but words she had clearly thought about. Words that continue to sting.

She climbs out of bed, wincing as she moves. She is aching all down her right side. She checks herself in the bathroom mirror and sees a mottled purple bruise the size of a fist spread across the top of her hip, and another at the base of her ribcage. The wound on her head seeps tiny droplets of blood and she part-covers it with a dressing from the first-aid box in the cupboard under the sink.

It's almost two in the afternoon and the house is pin-drop quiet. Isobel's bedroom door is closed and there is no one downstairs. Anna makes herself a slice of toast and goes back to sit on her bed. Her laptop is on her bedside table. She glances at it as she chews on her toast. A lot can happen in four hours. The news of Tori's death will be spreading through the school community and through Bishopglen town.

As soon as she's finished eating she goes online and logs onto Facebook. Before she clicks on Tori's page she reads a notification telling her that a newly set up page, 'RIP Victoria Carmichael', might be of interest to her. Anna clicks on the link. There is a photograph of Tori when she was about fourteen, grinning at the camera, her smile wide and sincere. The page has been set up by her father and round about midday he posted:

> It is with great sadness that I have to report the death of my beloved daughter Victoria Jane Carmichael. She passed away during the night, at home with her mother. The reason for her death is unclear but follows very soon after Vic made an accusation against Sister Anna Pierce. I want to assure all of you who loved my daughter that I have spoken with the police and no stone will be left unturned. I will find out how my beautiful daughter died.
> RIP my angel.

'Dear God,' Anna says quietly. 'He believes I was involved in her death.' There are already twenty-three comments and Anna takes a sobering breath before scrolling through them.

John Ingles
Sorry about your lovely daughter, Dave. You must be in bits. What's this about an accusation against the nurse?

*

Reply Dave Carmichael
Vic told us that the nurse hit her. I would show you the photo of the bruise on her face but it's too disturbing.

*

Reply John Ingles
This is truly terrible news. Please let us know if there's anything we can do.

*

Reply Dave Carmichael
Will do.

*

Reply Holly Standing
I'm so sorry, Mr Carmichael! I wish Tori had stayed at our school!! We loved Tori!! She was a good friend to us!! #RIPVictoriaCarmichael

*

And then the floodgates open.

Julia Raeburn
I am so sorry for your loss, Dave. I am a parent in the school and I did not know that your beautiful daughter had been assaulted. And I know I shouldn't say this but I've never been sure of Anna Pierce. There's something about her that doesn't ring true. And it's negligent of the school not to tell us what's been going on. I don't want

my kids anywhere near her. Anything you need, let me know.

*

Reply Dave Carmichael
Thank you for your support, Julia. We have tough days ahead. My fiancée and I, and Vic's mum Saskia, will need help, as I expect you know Vic was there on a full scholarship. My daughter was a very intelligent girl and she had a bright future ahead of her. We don't know much about how the school is run because we are fairly new to the independent sector. We will be looking for answers.

*

Reply Julia Raeburn
You can trust me, Dave. I am on the school parent body and will be happy to speak on your behalf. I'll go in to see Owen Wiseman this afternoon. #RIPVictoriaCarmichael

*

Reply Dave Carmichael
Thank you, Julia. I will PM you my mobile number so that we can stay in close contact.

*

Reply Julia Raeburn
I'll phone you as soon as I've spoken to Owen.

*

Reply Suzy Meeks
So sorry for your loss, Dave. But be careful because Anna Pierce and Owen Wiseman always seem quite friendly to me. #justsaying.

*

Reply Julia Raeburn

Don't worry, Suzy. I'll invite Owen and his wife to dinner. I'll be able to tell if he's bullshitting me. I know most of the governors too so if I'm not happy with what he says to me, I'll take it higher.

*

Reply Dave Carmichael

Cheers Julia. I'm glad you're on our side.

*

Reply Julia Carmichael

*

Mungo Todd

First, my sincere condolences, Dave. We have never met but I am also a parent at Bishopglen and I would like to say that your concerns are completely understandable but we need to remember innocent until proven guilty. My own experience of Sister Pierce is that she is an extremely capable professional, and I am very thankful to her. When my wife died two years ago I was too grief-stricken myself to help my son Alfie grieve. Sister Pierce took him under her wing and helped him through the whole process. He wouldn't have got through losing his mum without her.

*

There's more – much more – some defending Anna, others accusing her. She stops reading and quickly closes the laptop lid before she's tempted to let her fingers do the talking. She knows that replying to any of them is the last thing she should do because it will only add fuel to the fire. But she wants to. She really wants to have her say – first to express her sorrow over Tori's death, and second to assure everyone that she will cooperate with the police inquiry and that there is no suggestion of any negligence or secrecy on the school's part.

But she can't speak out. She'll just have to accept that people will express their opinions and that there will be name-calling.

Her mobile rings – it's Lynn.

'I didn't wake you, did I?'

'No. Have you seen the Facebook page Tori's dad has set up?'

'I was hoping you might not have seen it,' Lynn says. 'Anna, I'm so … This is all so shocking.'

'Julia Raeburn is in her element,' Anna says.

'Sensible people know that she's a gossip and a stirrer,' Lynn replies. 'By teatime people will be singing your praises, just like Mungo Todd has.'

'But I don't want that, I mean …' Anna shakes her head. 'It's not about me or school or anything else. Tori is dead. Her parents need time to grieve and they need answers.'

'You're right,' Lynn says. 'But, unfortunately, there are people who will use this as an opportunity to take sides and spread lies.' She sighs. 'Human nature at its very worst.'

Anna can only agree with this. And she knows with a grim, heartsick certainty that this is just the beginning.

Sister Pierce helped her write an email to her dad and it seemed to work because he arranged to come to take her out for Sunday lunch. She waited for him in the front hall, her heart in her throat, her nerves almost getting the better of her, but she stood her ground, counted down the minutes and then the seconds.

*He was nine minutes and thirty-two seconds late. As soon
as she saw him she had to stop herself from crying because
he looked so different. He was wearing new clothes, had a
fashionable haircut and had lost his belly. All these things
were good, but they happened when he was away from her
and her mum and she knew with painful certainty that his
life was now elsewhere.*

*He took her to a hotel and ordered them both a roast
dinner that she could barely eat because she felt awkward.
It was as if this upgraded version was too different from the
dad she had known and she could no longer be natural with
him. She wasn't sure who to be and she wasn't enough of
an actress to play along. The whole meal was a torture of
questions and silences. It made her feel exposed, threatened
even. And whenever she felt threatened, she lied.*

*She told him she had no friends. (Not true – she and
Amanda really were friends now. She'd even invited her to
Shanghai in the holidays.)*

*She told him that the girls were all snobs. (Also not true
– some of the girls at her old school had been just as bad.)*

*She told him that she was thinking of self-harming. (Lying
was a form of self-harm, or self-sabotage at least, so this was
almost true, but she wasn't about to start cutting or starving
herself. A quarter of the girls did it in a small way.
Occasionally a girl would go too far. One girl was carted
off to the medical centre and then sent home. Her blood was
all over the floor in the showers.)*

*Tori's dad gave her a whole sympathy chat – he knew
how difficult life could be sometimes but he would always
be there for her. 'You do know how much I love you, don't
you?' he said.*

*No, Dad, I don't. (She didn't say that. She didn't say
anything.)*

He dropped her at her mum's because she'd told

Miss Taymere she would be spending the night at his place. As soon as her key was in the lock he drove off. He needn't have worried; her mum wasn't about to come out to greet him. She was lying on the kitchen floor, passed out. She had drunk herself into a stupor. She did this once in a while because, 'I deserve to' and 'Why shouldn't I have fun like that shit of a father of yours?'

Tori stepped over her to heat up a can of soup – Heinz tomato, with a white bread sandwich plopped in the centre of the bowl like a beached whale in a shallow red sea.

She checked her mum was still breathing before she went upstairs.

Chapter Twelve

By four o'clock they are all sitting down at the table: Anna and John, Matt and Lynn, and Patrick Everett, the solicitor. Everett is squat and ruddy-cheeked. He has thick red hair that looks soft to the touch and eyes as beady as a blackbird. He introduces himself to Anna and John, then launches straight in. 'So in light of recent events,' he says, placing a notebook and pen on the table in front of him, 'how are you holding up, Anna?'

Lynn shakes her head at him, her expression making it plain that she thinks his question is crass.

'Not that well,' Anna says, pointing to the dressing on her forehead and her eyes, red from crying.

'Of course it's upsetting,' he says. 'Not only Victoria's death but Matt directed me to the Facebook page that has been set up in Victoria's memory and I've read through the comments.' John has made tea and coffee for everyone and opened a packet of biscuits. Everett helps himself to four biscuits and piles them up next to his mug. 'My advice is don't read anything online – and whatever you do, don't comment.'

'Is there a way for the Facebook page to be taken down?' Matt asks.

'Facebook will take pages down but this one doesn't fit the criteria. The comments, unpleasant as some of them are, are not breaking any laws.'

'But surely some of what's being said is libellous?'

Lynn asks, both hands wrapped tightly around her coffee mug.

'There are laws against libel, whether in print or online. But I don't think any of their comments would be considered libellous.'

'So people can say whatever they want?' John asks.

'No.' Everett puts a whole biscuit into his mouth. Everyone waits while he crunches his way through it. 'Cases have been won at trial for online posts inciting disorder or promoting hate crimes.'

'But that doesn't apply here,' John says with an audible sigh. 'So we just have to put up with it.'

'That's why it's better not to read them.' Everett is unperturbed. 'It's a twenty-first-century problem. See it as background noise. It has no influence on the evidence, or, in this case, lack of it. I'll keep checking the page and if anyone steps over the line then I'll act.' Everett pauses to eat another biscuit. 'The easiest way to have a Facebook page removed is to elicit the support of the person who has set it up.' He glances at each of them in turn. 'I'm not suggesting that any of you should approach Victoria's father, but do you have an acquaintance who could approach him on our behalf?'

John says one of his colleagues is married to Dave Carmichael's brother, Lynn suggests Owen Wiseman, Matt wonders whether Everett could approach Dave or his solicitor directly. And while they discuss the options, Anna thinks 'our' behalf, approach him on *our* behalf. She appreciates that John and her friends are on her side, that they'll see her through this nightmare. A nightmare that has its beginnings some time ago. Because the more Anna thinks about what led up to Tori's accusation, the more convinced she is that something must have happened to her over the long summer holidays.

Something to do with her parents? Other children in
the school?

'Anna?'

It's John who says her name but they're all staring at
her. 'I'm sorry, I drifted off,' she says.

'I spoke to the police this morning,' Everett says. 'And
they told me you agreed to a voluntary interview.'

'I forgot.' Anna shoots to her feet, suddenly panicked.
'I said I'd go there for three thirty.'

'I rearranged it for late Monday morning,' Everett
says, waving her back down. 'Gives us time to prepare.'

He spends the next ten minutes taking notes while
Anna sits on the edge of her seat and tells him about
Tori's accusation, what really happened that night and
what her relationship with Tori was like. Her speech is
slow and stilted and when she finally falters, Lynn says,
'Victoria is – was,' she corrects herself, '... a troubled
girl. It's well documented in her school records.'

Everett nods at Lynn before addressing Anna again.
'At the moment there is no suggestion that you had
anything to do with Victoria's death. The police simply
want to question you about the alleged assault. But while
we're here, I take it you have an alibi for last night?'

'We all had dinner together,' Lynn says. 'We must
have left around midnight. But before that there was
Tori's text.'

'What text?' John asks.

Lynn stares at Anna, wide-eyed with apology. It's clear
that Matt already knows about the text and that's because
they tell each other everything. They call each other
multiple times a day. On occasions Anna has wondered
whether they are capable of operating independently. If
Matt knows something, within an hour Lynn will know
it too. And vice versa. All decisions are taken jointly.

Anna opens the message app on her mobile and passes the handset to John. He reads the message aloud: 'Sister Pierce, it's me, Tori. I need to see you. Will you come to my house? I'm back at my mum's. Or we could meet somewhere else? Please come. Please help me. I have something I need to tell you.'

Hearing the text out loud sends a chill down Anna's spine. This was a child asking for help and she ignored her. Why? *Why?* When that decision goes against everything she stands for. She should have put the accusation to one side and responded to her.

'You didn't reply to this?' Everett asks, leaning across to look at the screen.

'To my shame, I didn't.' She stares down at her hands. John is sitting next to her and she senses that he's shifted his position slightly away from her. 'I called DC Murray to tell him that she'd got in touch. He didn't answer so I left a message on his voicemail.'

'We weren't sure that it was even from Tori,' Lynn adds quickly. 'And with the accusation, we thought the wise move was to tell the police.'

'Sensible,' Everett affirms. 'Do you have any idea what she might have wanted to tell you?'

'No.' Anna shrugs. 'All I know is that since term began she's been behaving out of character.'

'Define out of character,' Everett says.

'Well … last academic year I felt she was open with me. I helped her to write emails to her dad. We talked about the reasons why she stole things and why she told lies, how she needed to develop more positive coping mechanisms when she felt upset or vulnerable. But recently she was more closed off, as if she had a worry or a secret.' Anna raises her eyebrows, feels the skin around her wound tighten. 'Maybe something happened during the summer.' She looks to Lynn for help. 'You haven't got wind of anything?'

'I haven't.' She shakes her head. 'Pippa doesn't tell me everything but I usually have an inkling that something is wrong. At least a dozen of the senior girls regularly use the Wellbeing Centre and they haven't mentioned anything.'

It was Tori's second term at Bishopglen and she was on her way to double maths when she was summoned to the Wellbeing Centre. The walls were painted in several shades, from summer blue to a winter grey, white clouds with writing inside floating across the pretend-sky, posing questions such as: How do you feel today? How do you deal with anxiety? How does your past influence your present?

Tori hadn't spent much time in this room. She preferred to go to Sister Pierce when she felt stressed. Mrs Sykes wasn't like Sister Pierce. She acted as if she cared but Tori didn't trust her. She had a way of smiling that was patently false, and Tori couldn't help but feel it was because she was the scholarship girl and she should be grateful to be at Bishopglen, not causing endless problems.

'I asked you in here because I thought you might welcome the opportunity to talk,' Mrs Sykes said.

Tori dropped her bag on the wooden floor and collapsed into a rainbow-coloured beanbag. 'I'd rather go to my lessons.'

'I understand, but Mr Wiseman has asked me to follow up on a complaint.'

'Why you? Why not Sister Pierce? She's my mentor.'

'I know that.' Mrs Sykes nodded. 'But Sister Pierce is on a course today so I've been asked to speak to you instead.' She gave one of her smiles. 'Is that all right with you?'

Tori shrugged.

'So … I know we haven't had a lot to do with one another

but I want to assure you that anything you say here is confidential—'

'Unless I'm a danger to myself or others. I know this already.'

Mrs Sykes pursed her lips. 'Please correct me if the girl has got it wrong, but word has reached me that a fountain pen is missing and you might have taken it.'

'I don't use fountain pens,' Tori replied.

'Two pupils saw you look inside the girl's bag,' Mrs Sykes said quietly. 'And when you walked away you had something in your hand.'

Tori sighed. 'I was holding my mobile. I didn't take her pen.'

Mrs Sykes's expression was pained. 'I want to believe you, Tori. I really do but this isn't the first time you've been accused of stealing.'

Tori clicked her tongue against the roof of her mouth.

'In fact, it's the third time.'

She stared up at the ceiling. It was painted sunshine yellow. She screwed up her eyes against the brightness of it.

'I'm here to help you, Tori.' Mrs Sykes leaned forward. 'Your feelings are my priority. You can be honest with me.'

Tori opened her mouth to speak, saw Mrs Sykes's eyes widen as she anticipated her confession. 'Can I go now?' she said.

Mrs Sykes leaned back, her lips tightening. She gave one of her 'importance of honesty in a boarding community' speeches and then Tori was allowed to go. She walked along the corridor, gazing through the window towards the bin outside the music block where she'd dumped the pen. Yesterday. The bin had been emptied since then.

'Okay.' Everett points at Matt and Lynn. 'You both left at midnight. And after that?' He looks at John and Anna. 'You went straight to bed?'

'Yes ... well, no,' John says. 'We have a room at the top of the house where I have a telescope. It was a clear night so I stayed up there for half an hour or so. When I got into bed, Anna was already asleep.'

Everett writes this down, crunching on the third biscuit as he does so. This is everyday business to him, Anna thinks. It's a straightforward case. A girl is dead but Anna hasn't killed her, and as for the accusation? Where's the proof?

He's confident he's got this.

'So.' Everett rubs his hands together. 'At the moment, the police are treating her death as suspicious. They won't issue further clarification until after the post-mortem and it will be at least forty-eight hours before the results are through.'

'According to what her friend Holly Standing said, her body was found at the bottom of the stairs,' Anna says.

'That's correct.'

Anna lifts her eyes to meet the others around the table. 'So when the police say suspicious, does that mean they think she could have died as a result of her original injury?'

'I saw her at school,' Lynn adds. 'She had a bruise on her cheek.'

'Or does suspicious mean something else?' Anna asks.

'If she died from a slow bleed in her brain,' Everett says, 'then her death could be linked to what happened on Wednesday.'

'How does that work, then?' Lynn asks, looking at Anna.

'If someone has a slow bleed they will gradually feel unwell and then lose consciousness,' Anna replies. 'It could have happened when she was at the top of the stairs.'

'Bit of a coincidence, no?' Matt asks.

'Bad luck.' Everett shrugs. 'It happens. And if not, and the police believe the fall wasn't an accident, then her mother has to be prime suspect. She was in the house all evening. And she has been brought to the police's attention before.'

'How come?' Anna asks.

'Domestic violence. Fuelled by alcohol. Before the couple were divorced David Carmichael called the police on three separate occasions. Twice he needed hospital treatment for injuries to his head and back but in the end he never pressed charges.'

'Jesus,' Anna says quietly. From what Tori has told her, she's not altogether surprised but still, she feels a chill pass through her. 'Killing her daughter, even by mistake, that's—' She bites her lip and shakes her head. 'That's something else altogether.'

When Tori was fourteen, she and her friend Holly were inseparable. Every weekend they got Holly's older brother to buy them a bottle of vodka and they would hang out at the skate park. At first she loved the drunken feeling because nothing mattered. There were no consequences, she could say and do exactly what she wanted, no holds barred, because other people's feelings were just that – other people's.

And gradually, she began to catch a glimpse of the reason why her mother drank. It was an anaesthetic. It stopped her from feeling anything. Tori realised that her mother's anger began with fear. Fear and grief, because losing the man you loved – and hated – was too much to bear. She wasn't a bad person. She was emotionally battered. And she was alone.

No wonder she lashed out sometimes.

Anna shifts in her chair. A pulse of pain shoots down her leg and another spreads through her neck and head, wrapping itself around her skull like a too-tight swimcap. She remembers her own parents' divorce was an ugly, protracted affair. There was aggression on both sides. Anna, aged twelve, took refuge under the stairs.

'Anna?'

'Sorry?'

'I'm wondering whether Tori ever told you that her mum hit her? Because if she did you would have recorded it, wouldn't you?' Lynn asks.

'Yes, she did tell me and I did record it.' Anna rubs her eyes. 'I remember very clearly. It was back in May. She told me her mum had slapped her and pulled her hair but when I suggested we do something about it, she completely changed her story, said she'd made it all up.' Anna twists in her seat, flinches against the discomfort over her ribcage.

'You okay, hun?' Lynn reaches for her hand and Anna gives her a weak smile.

'She showed no signs of bruising, and she was a full boarder so she was in school almost all the time, but still I reported what she'd told me to social services just in case anything came of it.'

'And now it has,' Matt says.

'Perhaps,' Everett replies. 'Okay, let's leave things here for the time being.'

He packs his papers into his briefcase and then Anna sees him to the door. 'Thank you for coming out so quickly,' she says. 'And on a Saturday.' In a rush she adds, 'What will the police make of me not answering her text?'

'Anna.' His eyes are gentle. 'Victoria has lied about you hitting her. She's initiated a police investigation that has had you suspended from work. You received a pleading text from a number you didn't recognise. You passed this message onto the police.' He pauses. 'Your behaviour is straight and true. Try not to worry.' He gives her a sympathetic smile. 'I'll see you very soon.'

She watches as he drives off in an MG Midget that's been lovingly polished, the chrome wheels gleaming in the afternoon light.

When she closes the door behind him Lynn approaches. 'Did you see the way he stuffed those biscuits into his mouth?' she says to Anna. 'In a one-er.'

'I don't think he'd had any lunch,' Anna says. 'And actually, he was very kind to me just now.' Not that it lessens the guilt she's feeling but she can see that not replying to the text was the rational, sensible thing to do.

'He's the sort of man only a mother could love,' Lynn says.

She goes on to describe Everett's personality in a way that proves her point but Anna is only half listening because her ears are straining to tune in to the conversation Matt is having with John: '... worry about the bill ...' Matt is saying, '... happy to help.'

'... not necessary ...' John replies and adds something else Anna doesn't catch. Anna knows that John won't want financial help but if they don't accept Matt's offer then she has no idea how they will pay for all this legal work. They have very little savings. Like most people with school-age children, they are only a couple of missed pay cheques away from insolvency.

When Lynn and Matt drive off to collect Pippa from school, Anna is left alone in the kitchen with John. He's standing with his arms folded, brooding.

'What?' she says. If he's spoiling for an argument then they might as well get it over with.

'Why didn't you tell me about the text?'

Straight to the point. 'I forgot.'

'You forgot? You're accused of hitting a child and you forget to tell me she texted you? And now she's dead.'

'You make it sound like those events are linked! She'd still be dead if I'd told you.'

'Not necessarily.' His head shake is decisive. 'We could have gone over there together, listened to her, sorted it out.'

'You're right, we could have.' She takes a short breath. 'And believe me, I feel bad about not answering her. Really fucking bad. Because in case you've forgotten, John, I'm in the business of helping children, not ignoring them.' He turns his face away so that she can't see his expression. They've been married a long time. They know each other's tricks and tics. She can tell he wants to push her to explain herself but is holding back because their situation is difficult enough without a full-blown argument.

'I'm sorry I didn't tell you.' She takes his arm. 'I discussed it with Lynn and we decided it was best not to reply. I'd drunk half a bottle of wine. I was knackered! And like you said, when Matt and Lynn left, you went back upstairs to look at the stars again.'

'Well, now I wish I hadn't.'

She throws up her arms. 'I don't know what else to say! This whole situation is shit. It's appalling and worrying and I feel very, very sad.' Her eyes fill again. 'How can I have any tears left!' she says angrily, grabbing for a towel to bury her face in.

'Your tear ducts are on overtime.' John touches her shoulder. 'I'm sorry too.' He twirls a strand of her hair around his finger. 'I don't want to make you feel any worse than you already do. I just wish I'd known.'

Anna lifts her eyes to look at him. 'What was Matt saying to you before he left?'

'He offered to cover your legal fees. But I don't want to mix money with friendship so I've said that for now it's a no.'

Anna notices John says 'your' legal fees rather than simply 'the' legal fees, and why couldn't he have said to Matt, I'll discuss it with Anna? Since when have they been the sort of couple where the man makes a decision that will affect their whole family on his own?

It's enough to open a wound.

'John, we have to accept the money from Matt. We have no savings.' Their eyes meet. She doesn't have to spell it out. *'No one's fault.'*

They should have money saved. They've been living rent-free for five years but they still have tens of thousands of pounds' worth of debt to pay off. They must be the only people in the UK to have bought a house that ended up worth substantially less than they paid for it. She wanted to buy a modest property and rent it out to cover the mortgage – almost all her live-in colleagues do this – but John's brother had a deal in mind. A sure thing. Except it wasn't a sure thing. It was an expensive disaster of a building that was rotten at the core, sucked the money from their bank accounts and forced them to take out a loan so that they could afford to shore up the foundations before selling it on to a developer.

She can't blame John because she agreed to the purchase – albeit reluctantly, not wanting to miss their opportunity to buy a property they could retire to when the time came. So they took the risk and it didn't pay off.

'I don't want to accept the money,' John repeats.

'Well, we have nothing to sell,' Anna says lightly. 'We have no money in the bank. And I need a solicitor. So what should we do, John? How do you suggest we fix it?'

'Like you've fixed things before?'

'What does that mean?' Her expression is cold.

'When you were promoted.'

'Why then?' she says. She knows what he's itching to say. The accusation hovers between them like a malevolent piñata just waiting for the swipe of a baseball bat. 'Why, John?'

He doesn't reply. He takes what she knows he will consider to be the high ground and walks away.

'Not today, then,' she says under her breath.

Chapter Thirteen

It's Monday morning and Isobel has refused to go to school. She's spent most of the weekend in her room, and apart from toilet breaks, came out just the once to talk to Noah. Anna couldn't hear their conversation but she spent five minutes talking to her brother and when Anna called them for Sunday breakfast she went back into her room. No amount of persuasion from John or Noah could bring her out again. 'It's me she doesn't want to see,' Anna said. 'I could go round to Lynn's—'

'No!' John and Noah said in unison.

'None of this is your fault, Mum,' Noah said. 'Iso needs to accept that.'

'And she needs to apologise to you,' John added. 'She can't be allowed to get away with pushing you the way she did.'

In principle Anna agreed with this but as time ticked by she wanted to just forget it and move on. She wants them all to be united, one family, all for one and one for all. They're stronger that way.

Noah bolstered Anna's spirits and did his best to stand between her and the online trolling. 'You shouldn't look, Mum,' he said. 'I can check for you.'

'I don't want you reading it either.'

'It's something I can do for you,' he said.

She gave in, and he read out the supportive comments – 'great nurse', 'really good person', 'one of the reasons

I sent my children to Bishopglen' – and glossed over the rest. When Anna asked him to read out Julia Raeburn's latest comments, she watched his eyes move across the screen, scrolling down several times before he got to the end of it. 'She's nuts, Mum,' he said. 'Don't dignify her with attention.'

It's when Ed Wiseman comes to collect Noah, and Anna's standing outside waving them goodbye that Geraldine's front door opens. Anna stiffens, briefly considers scuttling back indoors, but she knows how that would look and while Geraldine isn't a gossip, Anna feels the need to stand her ground.

The noise from the car engine fades into the distance and Geraldine says, 'Was that Noah home?'

'Just for a wee while.'

'Is Isobel going in to lessons today?'

'No, she's …' Anna can't help but glance up at Isobel's bedroom window and as she does so she sees Miranda, her neighbour on the other side, wave from one of her upstairs rooms. She returns her wave and says to Geraldine, 'With what's been happening, Isobel's anxious about going in.'

'I expect it will be hard for her.'

Anna is grateful to be living on the school grounds – she never forgets how much it cost them to run their own home – but at tough times like this she feels the lack of privacy like a spotlight on her naked body. She takes a breath and turns to look Geraldine in the eye. 'Have you seen the Facebook page?'

'Julia Raeburn is a menace,' Geraldine states flatly. 'Mr Carmichael would do well to ignore her.'

'She's been the bane of my life for a few years now.'

'All that fuss about head lice,' Geraldine says. 'And no scientific basis for any of her half-baked solutions.

As if we haven't already tried everything that's worth trying.'

Anna smiles. 'God save us from the mothers who know best.'

They both laugh and Anna's reminded how loyal Geraldine is. For all she might be gruff and a little short sometimes, she is a team player.

'And while I hate to speak ill of the dead, Anna,' Geraldine says. 'We both know that Victoria was a troubled lass.'

'She was,' Anna says. 'I feel so sad, though. She wasn't an easy girl but she had so much potential. And she was really trying to change, to stop lying and take responsibility for her actions. I can't believe she's dead.' She shakes her head. 'It's so awful.'

'It's a tragedy and no mistake,' Geraldine affirms. 'Only last week when I was on break duty I gave her a good mark for being so helpful with the younger ones. I should think Lois is very upset.'

'You're right.' Anna has forgotten about this connection. 'I must ask Lynn how Lois is coping.'

They both glance down at Monty, who is weaving between Geraldine's ankles and then Anna's as if reinforcing their unexpected rapport.

'How's work?' Anna asks.

'Everything's going fine,' Geraldine replies. 'We've not been too busy. I'm planning to crack on with the HPV vaccinations today. The form teachers will take it in turns to cover your Sex and Relationships lessons.' She coughs into her hand. 'If Isobel wants someone to walk in to school with her then please let her know I'm happy to do that.'

'I will,' Anna says, both grateful and doubting that Isobel would be willing to take her up on the offer.

'And by the way, Anna,' Geraldine says as she walks back to her own doorstep. 'There but for the grace of God go all of us. I don't believe you could ever hit anyone.'

Tears spring into Anna's eyes. 'Thank you, Geraldine,' she says, her voice a whisper.

'While we might not always see eye to eye,' Geraldine adds, 'you're an excellent nurse and I would be happy to testify to your character in court if it should come to that.'

The door closes behind her before Anna has the chance to hug her.

It was June and unusually warm so the class were taking a while to settle. Anna stood at the front and watched them nudge each other and swap places, move closer to the open windows, fan themselves with their books. When they were all finally facing the front she said, 'Each group should write down examples of the following.' She pointed to the topics on the whiteboard:

> *Peer on peer abuse*
> *Coercive control*
> *Cyber bullying – e.g. sexting*
> *Hazing – initiation to join a gang*

Tori was in a group with Isobel, Pippa and three of the boys.

'I'll take notes,' said Pippa, setting her pad and fountain pen on the desk in front of her. 'Peer on peer abuse – examples anyone?'

'It's a form of bullying,' one of the boys said. 'If someone keeps saying something to you, you start to believe that it's true.'

'It's basic programming. It's the way the brain works,'

Isobel said. 'Your face is fat. Your face is fat. Your face is fat. Eventually when you look in the mirror you see a fat face.'

Pippa was busy writing this down when Tori said, 'You're a virgin, you wouldn't understand.'

Pippa had said these exact words to Tori just twelve hours before. Now she gave her a dead-eyed look, something she was particularly good at. 'That's peer pressure, not peer abuse,' she said flatly, then turned to smile at one of the boys, who had taken her water bottle from her bag and was holding it up, a questioning expression on his face. 'Help yourself,' she said.

Tori's cheeks flushed. The boys had heard what she said and were nudging each other, grinning. She toyed with the idea of telling Pippa, of telling them all, that she wasn't a virgin. She'd got that out of the way several months ago, down in the skate park, her head turning away from the push of the boy's tongue in her mouth, tolerating his cock as it drove into her with all the finesse of a rhino. The following week he expected to repeat the experience and she told him, 'No, thanks. You've turned me into a lesbian.' She ran off with Holly, both of them giggling as they swallowed some pills they'd bought from Holly's brother.

'Tori, will you come with me to the toilet?' Isobel asked, her voice quiet in Tori's ear.

'Why?' Tori asked and then she clocked Isobel's expression – she felt sorry for her. The mighty Isobel was showing some empathy. 'I'm okay,' she said, and Isobel gave her a small smile, a smile that said – I see you. I'm on your side.

Tori thought it about it later as she lay in bed trying to fall asleep through the sound of Amanda's snoring. Maybe Isobel had more of her mother in her than Tori had given her credit for.

Or maybe not.

Chapter Fourteen

Anna is in the police station. The room is strip-lit and has clearly seen better days. The paintwork is chipped. The table has one leg slightly shorter than the others and wobbles when leaned on, and there's a kick-dent in the door. Patrick Everett is sitting beside her, notebook open, pen poised. His other hand is resting on his knee, part-ways under the table. He gives her a thumbs up and she tries to smile an acknowledgement but she is sick to her stomach. Sick and terrified.

'I appreciate your cooperation in coming here today,' DC Murray says, sitting down opposite them. He is clean-cut, hair in a side parting, a smattering of freckles over his nose. He looks about twenty.

'Before we start.' Anna takes a breath. 'I'd like to say how incredibly sad I am that Tori is dead.' Her fingers are gripping the edge of the table as she speaks. 'And I'd like to express my condolences to her parents but I haven't been able to for obvious reasons.'

'Noted,' Murray says curtly. 'I received the voicemail you left about Victoria's text. Unfortunately, I didn't listen to it until Saturday morning.'

'Should I have called the station instead?' Anna asks. 'I wanted to do the right thing. I hope I did.'

'You called the number I gave you,' he states.

Anna wonders what the rules are – should he have answered it? Should he have given her another number to call if he wasn't available? Is he in trouble, now? If so, then perhaps he'll better understand her position. Police officers and nurses – their roles aren't dissimilar. Both professions come with a responsibility to the public, both operate within a strict code of ethics and protocols. Public expectations are high but neither police officers nor nurses are infallible.

'Any sign of the post-mortem results?' Everett asks.

'Delays have meant that we're looking at possibly Wednesday, more likely Thursday.' Murray clears his throat. 'We've asked you here, Mrs Pierce, because before Victoria Carmichael's death, she accused you of assault.'

He pauses and Everett fills the space with a question. 'When was this alleged assault supposed to have taken place?'

'Victoria Carmichael told us that she met you' – he regards Anna with serious eyes – 'on Wednesday at around 10 p.m., in the grounds of Bishopglen Independent School, between the two boarding houses where the path enters the woods. Are you familiar with this location?'

'Yes,' Anna says. A nerve jumps in her cheek and she lifts a hand to press against it. 'That's the way I walk home.'

'And did you meet Victoria Carmichael there on Wednesday at 10 p.m.?'

'No, I did not.'

He pushes two photographs across the table and before Anna glances at them she has a horrible feeling that they will show Tori dead at the bottom of the stairs. Her hands grip the table tighter as she glances down, relieved to see Tori alive. Both photos are A5 sized and Tori's face fills the frame. In one she is staring directly at the camera; in the other she is sideways on. The photographs are well lit and show a palm-sized red mark on her cheek. There are no scratches, but a hefty bruise is just beginning to bloom across her cheekbone.

'Do you recognise her?' Murray asks.

Anna nods. 'I do.'

'Did you cause these injuries?'

'No.' She winces. 'Of course not.'

'And you did not meet her on Wednesday as you were walking home?'

'No, I didn't,' Anna says, and then she frowns. 'Wait! I didn't *meet* her but I did *see* her. She was standing about ten metres away and I called out to her to go inside. I leave after curfew and she should have been in the girls' boarding house.'

There was a chill in the air and Anna was rushing. The day had been long and tiring and she was desperate for a bite to eat and then straight to bed. She'd worked a fourteen-hour shift, her feet were throbbing and a tension headache tightened at the base of her skull. She hadn't had a moment to herself all day. Normally she could grab a few minutes after lunch but she was too busy for those few minutes, let alone lunch itself, where she managed to swallow two mouthfuls of soup before she was called to deal with a pre-prepper who had fallen off the climbing frame. The medical centre had been non-stop and when she wasn't caring for the children, she was teaching lessons or pulled into meetings.

Her eyes were on the ground as she hurried along the path so she was startled when a voice called her name. 'Sister Pierce!' Her head jerked upward and she saw Tori standing on the path ahead of her. 'I have to talk to you.'

'Is everything okay?' Anna asked.

'I want to tell you about my dad.'

'Let's talk in the morning, Tori,' Anna called back. She could see it wasn't an emergency. Tori wasn't in tears, nor was she agitated. 'Go inside now before you catch cold.'

'She said that you talked for at least five minutes.'

Anna raises her eyebrows at this. 'No. That's not true.'

'Less than five minutes or more than five minutes?'

'About thirty seconds at most.'

'Why would she say it was five minutes?'

'I've no idea.'

Anna looks to Everett for help. He is scribbling by her side. His notepaper makes a crackling sound as the pen scratches across the surface. He glances up, focuses his eyes on Anna then Murray. 'It would be inappropriate for my client to offer an opinion as to what might be going on in Victoria's mind.' His tone is crisp but Murray doesn't retreat.

'Victoria reported that she was crying and wanted to talk to you about her father, but you told her you didn't have time.'

'I wouldn't have said that.' Anna is on solid ground with this. It's well known that she stays late if a child needs her. 'If she'd been crying, I would have taken her into the boarding house or the medical centre and spent time talking the problem through.'

'You told her to go back inside and when she wouldn't, you slapped her face with enough force and aggression to lead to a significant injury to her cheek.'

'No!' Anna's voice is strong, almost a shout. 'That's not what happened!'

DC Murray holds eye contact. Anna blinks. She wants to stare him down but finds she can't. There's so much confusion pinballing around inside her. She feels angry and embarrassed, afraid and ashamed that she is there, sitting in a police station being questioned about hitting a child. A child who is now dead.

Everett gives Anna a sympathetic look before saying, 'Do you have any further questions for my client, DC Murray?'

'A few, yes.' Murray takes his time before saying, 'How did you sustain the injury to your head?'

'I fell over. Slipped.' Anna's hand rises reflexively. 'Scraped my head on some rough ground.'

Murray's eyebrows twitch at this explanation; Anna has the distinct impression he doesn't believe her and is ready to defend her corner when he says, 'What was your opinion of Victoria Carmichael, Mrs Pierce?'

'I liked her,' Anna says slowly.

He waits for more.

'Her life wasn't easy. Her dad left her mum a couple of years ago and her mum is also absent, if not physically then emotionally.'

'I hear your husband recommended her to Bishopglen?'

'Yes, but …' Anna frowns again. 'I'm not sure why that's relevant.'

'We're building a picture, Mrs Pierce. We need to establish how well you and your family knew Victoria.' He smiles. His teeth are white. His eyes are blank. 'I'm keen to understand Victoria's connection to you all.'

John worked in the local school, Davison High, and it was when Tori was in S3 that John started teaching her. Within a couple of weeks he identified that she was gifted. 'I'm going to suggest that she applies for one of Bishopglen's scholarships,' he told Anna. 'She's got loads of potential. Bishopglen has the resources to really nurture her talent.'

'Doesn't that go against your socialist principles?' Anna

teased him. John had never wanted to work in Bishopglen.
He was a staunch believer in state education.

'*Tori's the exception that proves the rule,' he replied.*

'*I've never understood what that expression means,' Anna*
said. 'You don't see any apples rising from the ground to
disprove gravity, do you?'

'*That's a physical law,' he replied, kissing the top of her*
head. 'Rules, on the other hand, are there to be broken.'

The memory is a sweet one and it allows Anna's
breathing to settle. Thinking of John always helps her to
relax, feel safe, feel optimistic. His very existence helps
her make sense of the world.

'I see. Well … Tori was extremely bright. She was
gifted in science and maths. But her English language
was also excellent. And yes, my husband put her forward
for the scholarship, gave her extra tuition after school—'

'Did he coach her in your home or hers?' Murray
interrupts.

'Neither. He coached her in Davison High, in a room
with a glass panel in the door, in full view of anyone
walking along the corridor. As is consistent with child
safeguarding regulations,' Anna says coldly. She doesn't
like the suggestion that John might have done anything
unprofessional. 'But the bulk of effort was Tori's. She
needed the full scholarship and she achieved it. She
joined in S4 and was with us for just over a year.'

'So your husband was instrumental in her joining
Bishopglen. And you?' His stare is unyielding and Anna
feels her breath catch again. 'Did you see much of her?'

'She came to the medical centre fairly regularly.' Anna
briefly explains her role as school nurse. 'As well as that,
I teach Sex and Relationships Education, and I also
mentor several students. Tori was one of them.'

He glances up, interested. 'And how did that come about?'

'What do you mean?'

'Did you become her mentor because of her connection to your husband?'

'No.'

'So how are mentors chosen?'

'It depends. Sometimes the head of pastoral care chooses a child for us based on interests, for example if the child is a keen musician and the mentor is also a musician.' She stops, swallows. Her mouth is dry. She reaches for the small bottle of water Everett has placed in front of her but her hand shakes as she tries to unscrew the top. She immediately stops trying, catches Murray's eye as he registers her anxiety.

'You were telling me how mentors are chosen,' Murray says, no let-up.

'I … The …' Everett has unscrewed the top and passes the open bottle to her. *Do not shake.* She lifts it to her lips, gripping it tight enough to bend the plastic. *Do not shake.* She drinks the full bottle, the water cooling her mouth and giving her confidence a temporary boost. 'I often mentor the children who have long-term medical conditions because I have knowledge of their illness and am able to facilitate any reasonable adjustments they might require.'

'Are children able to choose their own mentors?'

Anna nods. 'They can request a particular adult.'

'In fact, Victoria requested you as her mentor,' Murray states. 'Didn't she?'

Anna's mouth shuts tight. She feels a rush of stupidity. He's forcing her to tell him what he already knows, checking her story against Tori's.

'Why do you think Victoria chose you as her mentor?'

'Because …' Anna shrugs. 'She was new to the school.
The medical centre is a safe space.' She keeps her tone
deliberately flat. 'And yes, I think the fact that she knew
John, that he had taken a professional interest in her,
probably contributed to her choosing me.'

Silence.

Again.

Apart from the scratch of Everett's pen and the sound
of him breathing.

He's in no rush, DC Murray. It makes Anna's skin
itch and she begins scratching at her wrist, her fingers
probing under her watch strap, nails tearing at the soft
skin. What else did Tori tell him? How much of it is
made up? All this talk of John. *Did she say something
about John?* Mixing truth and lies until they blend into
a convincing tale.

'How often did you meet?' Murray says at last.

Anna stills her hand and looks up to the right, thinking.
'Usually once a week, sometimes less, occasionally more.'

'Would you say you had a rapport?'

'Yes, I think so. She seems – or seemed – to find it
easy to open up to me.'

'But you maintain she was lying about the assault?'

Assault. The word alone makes Anna's nerves jump.
'I've been a school nurse for more than twenty years.'
She presses her palms together under the table. 'And if
there's one thing I know for sure – children and young
adults lie.'

He nods as if considering this before changing tack.
'Victoria visited your home?'

'Yes, but only because she was in the same year as
my daughter.' Everett's eyes are burning a hole in the
side of Anna's face so she adds, 'I understand where the
boundaries lie.'

'And where is that?'

'I am an adult in a position of trust. She was fifteen, in the eyes of the law still a child. Whenever we met for a mentoring session, it was in the medical centre. There were always colleagues in adjacent rooms.'

'And what did you talk about?'

'Her family life, or lack of it. Her hopes for the future. Whatever was on her mind.'

'For example?'

'Peer pressure, boys, her relationship with her parents.'

'Did you talk about her mother?'

'Yes.' Murray's eyes encourage more. 'She didn't have an easy time with her mum but that's not unusual with teenagers,' Anna says slowly. 'A single parent and an only child – the relationship can be intense.'

'Do you know her parents well?' Murray asks.

'No. I've met her mum once. Tori was ill and she came to collect her. Mr Carmichael and I haven't met at all.'

'I spoke with someone at social services this morning,' Murray says, looking down at the papers in front of him. 'Last May you alerted them to the fact that Victoria's mum might have been physically abusive.'

'That's true.' Anna's hands move onto her lap, fingers twisting together. If Tori's mother is responsible for her death, if, God forbid, she pushed her down the stairs, then there would surely have been other acts of violence. Should Anna have encouraged Tori to open up about her mother? Is this something else for her conscience to grapple with?

Murray's hand rests underneath his chin as if he is thinking. 'So … scholarship girl goes to posh school … that has to throw up a few issues.'

'In what way?' asks Anna.

'In a fish-out-of-water kind of a way.'

'Do you mean for Tori? Or her parents?' If he wants to make this about class then he's barking up the wrong tree.

'Let's start with Victoria.'

'Well … members of staff's children attend Bishopglen at a reduced rate. There are at least twenty of them, my own daughter included. And there are more than two dozen scholarships in the upper school.' She stops to take a breath. All this talking. All this anxiety. She's beginning to feel dizzy. 'Most of our parents are neither posh nor rich,' she continues, her tone soft. 'They make huge sacrifices to send their children to Bishopglen. They live in very modest homes and don't have any money left over for expensive trainers or the latest phones.'

'So Bishopglen isn't all rich kids with trust funds?'

'Far from it.'

'And yet from what Tori told me before she *died*' – he stresses the last word, his eyes fixed on Anna's face – 'aside from Amanda Chen, she struggled to make friends.'

'That wasn't because of her parents' earning power. It was because of her character,' Anna says. She rubs a hand across her forehead. The dizziness is increasing. 'Could I have some more water, please?' she asks Murray.

'Of course.'

'You're doing well, Anna,' Everett tells her when Murray leaves the room.

'Am I? I feel sick.' She takes a laboured breath. 'Hopeless.'

'That's perfectly normal.'

'Here we are.' Murray comes back into the room and places a plastic cup three-quarters full of water on the table in front of Anna. Holding the cup with both hands, she lifts it to her lips and drinks the water down in one long thirsty gulp.

'You were talking about Victoria's character,' Murray reminds her.

'Yes.' Anna thinks for a moment. 'She wasn't always truthful. She was suspected of stealing on several occasions. She was working on both these aspects of her nature but ...' She trails off. It feels unkind, worse, deceitful, to speak of Tori like this when she was in no position to defend herself.

Murray is staring at her, waiting for her to say more, so Anna chooses her words more carefully. 'Moving school at fourteen isn't easy. Friendships in the mid to late teens are well established. Even the most socially adept children have difficulty making inroads. At first Tori spent break times either on her own or she would come to the medical centre to chat to me. It was a safe space for her.'

More nodding from Murray. 'And her parents, did they make friends, mix with other parents?'

From what Tori told her, Anna knows that if her mother was asked what subjects her daughter was studying, she would be hard pushed to get it right. 'I don't think they'd managed to make friends yet,' Anna says. 'It's easier when your children are younger because you have to organise play dates and so on. Teenagers make most of their own arrangements.'

'Okay.' DC Murray seems satisfied with this and changes direction. 'Let's go through your statement again.' He smiles at her. It's a professional smile, one without warmth or kindness. 'Remind me exactly what happened on Wednesday evening.'

The dizziness has receded but still Anna feels as if she's hanging on by a thread. She goes through it again, her voice a monotone. She was on her way home. She saw Tori on the path. She asked her to go inside. That was it.

'You still maintain that you didn't have a conversation with her?'

'A few words, and then she went into the boarding house and I went home.'

There's a silence while DC Murray checks through the papers in front of him. Everett seems to be holding his breath and then he says, 'Any more questions for my client?'

'Not at the moment, no.' DC Murray looks up from his reading. 'Thank you for your cooperation, Mrs Pierce. We'll be in touch.'

'So what happens now?' Anna says. 'Am I allowed to return to work?'

'Not until we've taken witness statements and presented our findings to the Procurator Fiscal.'

'What witnesses?' Everett asks.

'One of the other girls has come forward,' Murray replies. 'She saw what happened.'

Chapter Fifteen

It's just after three when Anna arrives home. She doesn't take off her coat. She feels as if she can't quite catch her breath, as if her lungs won't fully inflate. Witnesses? What witnesses? What girl?

She opens a pouch of tuna for a purring Monty and changes from her flats into her walking boots. She can't stay home. She needs to walk off this anxiety, try to bring some order to her thoughts.

The school sits at the northern edge of four hundred acres of water and woodland, and fifty metres through the trees is the headmaster's house where Owen lives with his wife Katia and their children. As long as there are no special events, during afternoon break Owen walks their dog around the loch. Anna knows there's nothing on the school calendar so there's a good chance she will bump into him.

She sets off downhill. The path leads her through a dense forest of trees, away from school towards the water's edge. Lynn and Matt's house is positioned high up the bank on the other side of the loch, glass windows gleaming like a beacon on the hillside. It's not long before Owen's spaniel Molly finds Anna, briefly sniffing her leg then rushing off into the undergrowth, her tail wagging.

'I'm sorry to ambush you like this,' Anna says to Owen as he walks towards her along the stony beach. 'I was hoping for a quick chat.'

'Of course.' He stops in front of her. 'How are you holding up?'

'I'm okay.' She points to his hand. 'You vaping now?'

'Replacing one vice with another,' he says, glancing down at the vape resting in the palm of his right hand.

'Well, it is better for you,' Anna says. 'As far as we know.'

'When I turned fifty, Katia made me go for a health check.' They walk side by side towards the treeline. 'Everything's too high – cholesterol, blood pressure, HD something. I blame the endless parent–governor dinners.' He stops in front of a tired oak tree, branches dragging on the ground. 'So.' He leans his back against the trunk and his eyes narrow with sympathy. 'Tell me how you really are.'

Anna straightens her spine and breathes deeply, deter-mined not to let go to tears. 'I was interviewed by the police just now,' she says.

'How did it go?'

'It was really intense.' She stares down at the boggy earth. 'I can see why people end up agreeing to anything just to get out of the room.'

'That bad?'

'This on my head.' She points to the dressing on her forehead. 'Didn't help either. Automatically makes me look guilty of fighting with someone.' She bites her thumbnail. 'Maybe it's just me, but police stations? They freak me out.'

'Hospitals do that to me,' Owen says.

'His questions jogged my memory.'

'How so?'

'I remembered that I saw Tori when I was walking home.' She explains what happened, from looking at the police photographs, to details about her mentoring sessions with Tori. While she talks, Owen doesn't break eye contact. She sees the flecks of grey in the blue of his iris, the infinity in his pupils. 'She told the police that she wanted to talk to me about her dad but I wouldn't listen.' She rubs her fingers across her forehead. 'You know me, Owen. I wouldn't do that. I leave work late more often than I leave on time.'

He nods. 'And it's not the story she told me.'

'About seeing me after supper?'

'Exactly.'

'So our paths crossed for about thirty seconds,' Anna finishes. 'And she turned it into a conversation that ends with me slapping her.'

'I'm so sorry.' His expression is solemn.

'And apparently there are witnesses. I don't know how that's possible because there was no one else there and the school lights stop a good twenty metres away from where I saw her.'

'But maybe it would be better if someone had seen you? It would prove your innocence'

'Maybe.'

'You're not convinced?'

'You know what kids are like. They might side with her especially now that she's—' Anna bites her lip.

'She wasn't particularly popular, though, was she?' he says with a sigh. 'I don't think anyone would lie for her.'

'That's true,' Anna acknowledges. 'Apart from maybe Amanda.'

'I've been catching up with the minutes from recent pastoral care meetings. Sounds like her parents' divorce was acrimonious.'

'It was. And recently Tori was worried that he was going to marry the woman he lives with.' Tori had expressed to Anna her quiet hope that her mum and dad would get back together. 'Do you think that's why she accused me?' Anna asks, frowning.

'To get her father's attention?' He raises his eyebrows. 'I wouldn't be surprised. She was a complicated girl.'

'My teenage years weren't dissimilar to hers,' Anna says. 'Getting my dad's attention was important to me too, but I wouldn't have lied about something like this. The odd sore stomach maybe, so that he would have to come to the house on a weeknight to see me. But not like this.' As she says this, she is reminded of one glaring exception, one monumental lie that wreaked havoc on her whole world. She stamps her feet on the cold, damp ground, feels her toes wake up. 'Everything okay in the med centre today?'

'Yup. Geraldine pulled her finger out.'

'Her last hurrah before she becomes a full-time granny.'

A silence falls between them as they stare out over the loch to where a flock of geese are taking flight, white bellies and orange beaks standing out against the variegated grey of their wings.

'I never tire of this landscape,' Owen says, his tone soft.

'Me neither.' She folds her arms against the nearness of him, the sharing of this moment.

He puts his vape in his right-hand pocket and pulls a joint and a lighter out of his left. 'Birthday present from my brother. It's been in my coat for six weeks.'

Anna laughs. 'One of my friends carries a condom in her purse but she has no intention of ever cheating on her husband.' Lynn. Lynn is that friend.

Owen gives her a half smile. 'So we don't have to smoke it?'

'We definitely shouldn't smoke it!' Anna says. 'It's

reckless behaviour – exactly what we warn teenagers against. And it's illegal. I give lessons on the dangers of drug-taking. Speaking of which, did the policeman come in today?'

'He did. Gave a sobering lecture on drug use to the senior school. I had lunch with him afterwards. It's like you hear on the news. Glasgow is flooded with drugs and so the dealers are crossing county lines, selling to kids in the countryside. God knows where it will end.'

A gust of wind lifts Anna's hair and sends a chill down her spine. She glances over her shoulder, sees only trees, branches, leaves swaying in the breeze. 'You busy this evening?'

'Katia and I are going to an early dinner at the Raeburns'.'

Anna's eyes widen. 'Rather you than me.'

'My way of keeping her onside.'

'She's been giving me the evil eye for years now.' Anna relaxes back against a thick tree trunk. 'She wanted the children who had head lice to be named and shamed in the school newsletter.'

'As if.'

'She needs to get a job. That's the problem with the car park mafia – too much time on their hands.' She gives a short laugh. 'And by the way, if ever head lice become a carrier for disease, I'm handing in my notice.'

'You and me both.' A shadow falls across his face. 'I fantasise about handing in my notice.'

'What? You're doing a great job!'

'Maybe. But sometimes I'd like not to have to hold on so hard. I could be a fisherman,' he says, his eyes bright. 'Buy myself a boat. Catch mackerel.' He glances at his watch and sighs. 'I should get going.' He kisses her lightly on either cheek. 'Stay strong, Anna. Don't let the bastards grind you down.'

'I'll keep that in mind when they slap on the hand-cuffs.'

He checks her expression before laughing. 'Stay in touch.' As he walks off he calls out, 'I've told you before, you need to get a dog!'

'Too much hassle!' she shouts, her eyes fixed on his retreating back. 'And it would be the end of me,' she adds, her whisper swallowed into the collar of her coat.

When she gets home, she paces up and down the kitchen, her thoughts leading her in one direction and then another before landing on Isobel. Isobel's outburst after she found out Tori was dead. What was that all about?

The physical pain of being pushed is fading and now Anna's just worried about her daughter, worried about their relationship, worried about what Isobel might know. *What she might have done?* No. She slaps that thought away. Isobel won't have done anything wrong.

She goes upstairs and taps on Isobel's bedroom door. 'Are you awake, love?'

No reply.

She taps again, louder. 'Isobel! Will you talk to me, please?'

Still no reply.

'I'm worried, darling. Please. We need to talk.'

Still no reply so she turns the handle and opens the door. The curtains are closed and an Isobel-shaped bundle lies under the covers. Anna steps over discarded school uniform, shoes, books and a tray with a dried-up, half-eaten omelette on a plate. She gently shakes her daughter. But it's not her daughter. It's two pillows laid lengthways to imitate a body. Anna starts back, shocked.

Where is she? She looks under the bed and inside the wardrobe as if she could be hiding in either of these places. She was definitely home when Anna left for the police station but that was hours ago.

She opens the curtains and looks down on the flat roof, which is a short drop outside the window. Isobel and Noah would sometimes climb out of her bedroom window to lie on the roof during the summer months but they haven't done that for a while.

And why the mound of pillows? Why pretend she's in bed when she isn't?

Anna takes her mobile from her pocket, then hesitates. Isobel's most likely gone up through the woods to school. In all likelihood she won't answer when she sees 'Mum' on the screen so really there's no point calling her. Better to leave it. Better to let her think that no one's noticed she's gone.

Julia Raeburn
Just so everyone is aware, I spoke with Owen Wiseman, head of Bishopglen, this evening. He told me the school is fully cooperating with police inquiries and that Sister Pierce is on leave in the meantime. On leave? He made it sound as if she was taking a holiday. 😟

I also met with Victoria's dad and he is grieving deeply. His only child has been taken from him. We will keep you posted. #RIPVictoriaCarmichael. #theywontgetawaywithit

*

Reply Steve Mulberry
Whoever hurt this girl deserves to rot in jail.

*

Reply Mary Schofield
I second that #RIPVictoriaCarmichael
Let's use the hashtag, folks, and get
#RIPVictoriaCarmichael trending on twitter.

*

Reply Sandra Barry
We're on Facebook.

*

Reply Mary Schofield
Most people's accounts are linked.

*

Reply Steve Mulberry
Let's get this trending. #schoolnurserotinjail

*

Bob Whitlock
You lot need to think about what you're writing. Julia, you
need to stop adding fuel to the fire. Dave, I'm truly sorry
for your loss but you need to be careful not to be drawn
into other people's agendas. Steve – really? What gives
you the right to come up with a # like that?

*

Reply Julia Raeburn
You've always tried to patronise me, Bob. We all know the
real reason. I suggest that you stay off this page unless
you're willing to be supportive. #RIPVictoriaCarmichael

*

Reply Steve Mulberry
What's the real reason? #schoolnurserotinjail

*

Reply Julia Raeburn
He's a mouthpiece for the school. Works as the groundsman.
He's married to Geraldine, one of the other nurses.

*

Reply Steve Mulberry
Bob I'll use whatever # I want. #schoolnurserotinjail

*

Reply Mary Schofield
His wife is good with the kids, so I hear.

*

Reply Julia Raeburn
Anyone's an improvement on Anna Pierce!!
#schoolnurserotinjail

*

Suzy Meeks
I just saw Anna Pierce coming out of the police station.
Her head was down but I know it was her. She looked like
she'd been crying.

*

Reply Steve Mulberry
Was she in handcuffs? #schoolnurserotinjail

*

Reply Suzy Meeks
No. As I said she was coming out. They must have been
questioning her. And she had a man with her, not her
husband. I know what he looks like. He's a chemistry
teacher in the high school. #RIPVictoriaCarmichael

*

Reply Steve Mulberry
Poor bastard, married to her. #schoolnurserotinjail

*

Reply Julia Raeburn
Probably her solicitor. Take a picture of them both next time.

*

Reply Steve Mulberry
If you get a photo of her going in send it to us ASAP so that we can go there and wait for her to come out. #schoolnurserotinjail

*

Reply Suzy Meeks
I live opposite the police station. I'll keep an eye out.

*

Reply Andy Durham
The police were at Bishopglen today searching the girls' boarding house. Anyone know what they're looking for?

*

Reply Suzy Meeks
Evidence?

*

Reply Andy Durham
Obvs. Makes me think it's a murder inquiry.

*

Holly Standing
I'm really missing my friend. And I've been to see her mum. She's not doing so great. 😨 I hope

you're okay, Mr Carmichael? We are going to have a
memorial service for Tori at school. I know she left for
Bishopglen but we still remember her. I saw her a lot
through the summer holidays. We had loads of fun! I'll
post some pictures. She really loved you and missed
you BTW.

*

Reply Dave Carmichael
Thank you, Holly. I appreciate that. I'm okay thanks. Just
trying to get through each day.

*

'You coming to bed, love?'

Anna slams the laptop shut. 'Yup.'

John's expression is serious. 'Tell me you weren't on
that Facebook page?'

'No.' She tries to smile but after what she's been
reading her face is stiff with anxiety. 'I was just forwarding
my school emails on to Geraldine.' She follows him to
the stairs. 'Isobel disappeared this afternoon. She left a
pillow lump in her bed to make it look like she was
asleep.'

'She was here for tea, though.'

'I know.' Isobel sat through tea, managing to completely avoid looking at Anna for the whole ten minutes
before she said goodnight to John and went back upstairs
to her room. 'But she didn't come back through the
front or back doors. She climbed in through her
bedroom window.'

'What?' John screws up his face. 'Are you sure?'

'I was in the kitchen the whole time. I would have
seen her.'

They're in front of her bedroom door now; their voices dropped to a whisper. 'Why would she do that?'

'I've no idea.'

'She's in now, though?'

'Unless she's sneaked out again.'

John locks eyes with Anna and she nods. He knocks on the door. 'Isobel? We're off to bed!' No reply. 'Isobel?' he repeats, firmer this time. 'Could you answer me, please?'

'O-*kay*!'

John widens his eyes at Anna. 'Well at least she's in there now,' he says, his voice low. 'I suppose she went up to school.'

'That was my guess too but— ' Anna shrugs. 'Who knows?'

When they're both in bed Anna cuddles into John's side. He's asleep in twenty seconds flat. She's always envied him his ability to drop off no matter what is going on in their lives. She gives it another five minutes until his breathing deepens, and then she goes back downstairs. She sits at the kitchen table and reads through the rest of the comments. There's more of the same. And several people want to know when she's being questioned again so that they can be outside the police station. Anna makes a mental note to mention this to Everett, then she logs onto Twitter and types in the hashtag #schoolnurserotinjail. There are eighty-three users who have tweeted and used the tag. She reads every one of them. The best of a very bad bunch is:

@M65naked
Leave her alone you fucks! In this country you're guilty until proven innocent. #schoolnurserotinjail

The worst ones are so vile that her only response is to close her eyes and curl herself into a ball, pray that none of the things they say they want to do to her will ever come to pass.

Chapter Sixteen

It's eleven o'clock in the morning and Anna is pacing the floor, her heart and mind churning between sadness and anxiety. Before John left for work he mentioned the memorial service. 'I want to come,' Anna said, grabbing her shoes, but John held her arm, not speaking, his eyes regretful. 'I can't go, can I?' Anna said, truth dawning. She wouldn't be welcome. If she were to show up, everyone would stare. Her motives would be questioned and she would be a target for the social media brigade. There would be whispering, confrontation even. She would become the focus of the event, not Tori, who deserved to be remembered by her friends and teachers without any distractions.

John kissed her forehead, told her he was sorry. She watched him drive away and after that the pacing began. She considered going for a walk but Geraldine's husband Bob was working in the garden. Having read his Facebook post, she knows that he's on her side. She should go out and thank him. And she will. When she knows she's not about to burst into tears, when her heart feels less heavy and the pulse in her ears less urgent.

She empties out the kitchen cupboards, checks the sell-by dates on all the jars and packets, then wipes the cupboard down and puts all the in-date items back. When she sees tears drop onto the cloth she moves to the oven and scrubs it with enough vigour to keep all her attention in her muscles.

She's pacing again when the doorbell rings. She thinks it will be Bob. She opens it at once. 'Bob, I—'

It isn't Bob. There's a young woman she doesn't recognise on her doorstep. 'Hello! I'm from the *Bishopglen Courier*.' She smiles, wide and bright as a crescent moon. 'I wonder whether you'd be willing to answer a few questions?'

'I'd rather not.'

'I understand.' The woman tilts her head in sympathy. 'But we thought, as we're a local newspaper with your best interests at heart, you might like the opportunity to air your side of the story with us.'

Anna frowns. 'It's not a story. It's real life. And honestly this is not a good time—'

'I went to the memorial assembly at Davison High this morning,' she interrupts. 'Such a loving atmosphere. All the things her friends and family said. It was so touching.'

Anna hesitates. 'Were Tori's parents there?' she blurts out.

'They were and they looked …' She pauses as she thinks of the right word. 'Gutted.'

Anna leans against the doorframe and briefly closes her eyes.

'I can see you're upset. I'm sure you're aware that you're taking a beating on social media.' Her eyes are pained. 'This would give you the chance to redress the balance a little bit.'

'That's not a game I want to play,' Anna says tiredly. She begins to close the door.

'You don't remember me, do you?'

Anna pauses to stare at the young woman more closely.

In truth, she has barely registered her face because her mind is too full of worries to input any more information. She concentrates now on her features and within seconds catches hold of a connection. 'Flora Manson?'

'Yup.' She smiles, her cheeks dimpling.

'Of course I remember you. I'm sorry. I'm not myself at the moment.'

'That's understandable,' she says. 'You must be having a terrible time.'

Flora and her sister Molly must both be in their twenties now, Anna thinks, but she remembers them well, the memory linked to what brought them to surgery. Flora was a frequent monthly visitor – she suffered from intense period pains until she was prescribed the pill and the discomfort settled down. Her sister Molly only came to Anna's attention once – she fell down the music block stairs and broke her leg in two places, a significant injury that kept her off games for three months.

'Molly sends her best wishes,' Flora says. 'We're both really concerned about what's happening to you.'

'Thank you, Flora, but I'm sure you understand that for me to talk to the press would most likely add fuel to the fire.'

'If we handle it correctly,' Flora replies, 'your words could put the fire out. People have only heard one side of the story and will keep slagging you off unless they have something else to go on.' She delves into her shoulder bag. 'I've brought a couple of examples of the sort of piece I would write.' She holds the clippings out to Anna. 'You would get to see my draft before it goes to print and if there was anything you didn't approve of, we would change it.'

Anna feels herself being swayed. 'I hear what you're saying but I'll need to speak to my solicitor first.' She takes the clippings and opens the door wider. 'Do you want to come inside and wait?'

'Cool.' Flora follows Anna into the kitchen. 'I appreciate this, Sister Pierce.'

'Call me Anna. Take a seat; I'll just be a minute.'

Anna finds her mobile in the living room and calls Everett. While she waits to be connected, she reads the clippings. One is about a man who knocked over a child on a zebra crossing. The other is about a care worker who gave an elderly woman the wrong dose of medication. The articles are broadly sympathetic but in both cases the people admitted guilt. When she gets through to Everett, she tells him about Flora. 'She's an ex-pupil of the school who now works for the *Bishopglen Courier*.'

'Never trust a journalist.'

'She was always a sweet girl but …'

'Anna.' His tone is loud and firm. 'Ask her to leave. Now.'

'Okay.' She ends the phone call and takes a slow, deep breath. When she returns to the kitchen Flora is sitting at the kitchen table, writing in a notebook. 'I'm really sorry, Flora, but my solicitor has advised against it.'

Flora nods her head. 'I thought he might.' She gives Anna a crisp smile. 'You know this just makes you look guilty?'

'No,' Anna says calmly. 'I think it just makes me look careful.'

'Did you hurt her?' Flora says. She stands up, pushing the chair back with her foot so that it screeches on the floor tiles. 'Did you push her down the stairs?'

'No, I didn't.' Anna's face hardens. 'I'd like you to leave now, Flora.'

'When I was at school, lots of the girls liked you, but not everyone did. Not me.' She's staring into Anna's face. 'I thought you lacked empathy. I thought you were a fake.'

'Leave my house, please. Right now.' She wants to take her by the elbow and steer her to the door but she resists. And she won't shout either, because she might be recording this. 'Now, please.'

Flora lifts her bag off the table with an exaggerated flourish and taps her notebook with her pen. 'I think I have quite enough here anyway.' She smiles. 'You have a good day now.'

Anna closes the door behind her and stands with her back against it, eyes smarting. She feels humiliated. And hurt. And it's her own fault. Ex-pupils are no safer to talk to than someone she's never met. Well, she won't make that mistake again. Her impulse is to ring John to pour out her feelings to him but she knows he'll be mid-lesson. She glances at her watch – Lynn will be on her break about now. Anna calls her instead.

'Hello, how's it going?' Lynn asks.

'Well, not that great, considering I've just been doorstepped by a journalist.' She tells her about Flora. 'Her attitude when she left was really off. She switched from supportive to snide and insulting.'

'Cheeky little madam!' Lynn says. 'Her mother was a pain. I remember her complaining because her girls never dried their hair after swimming. Somehow I got involved. I told her there were hairdryers for them to use, and plenty of time to do it in, but her girls were always too busy talking. She made a formal complaint against me.'

'I'd forgotten about that,' Anna says. 'You got time for a coffee? Lunch?'

'I'll be down in two ticks.'

*   *   *

Lynn starts chopping the vegetables for a salad while Anna paces up and down. 'I feel like a pariah! I wish I could have gone to the memorial assembly at the high school today but I couldn't. The online brigade are letting rip. Have you seen the hashtag?'

Lynn bites her lip. 'You really shouldn't read the crap those morons are posting—'

'I can't help it! I think not knowing would be worse!' She pauses to breathe. 'Do people at school think I could have been involved?'

Lynn pauses, knife in the air. 'In Tori's death?' Anna nods. 'Jesus, Anna! Of course not!' She drops the knife on the chopping board and comes across to hug her friend. 'I get that you must be feeling paranoid. Who wouldn't? With all that shite on the Internet. But no one with a functioning brain believes that you hurt Tori. Not the initial assault nor whatever happened to cause her death.'

'Thank you.' Anna takes a step back, her breathing easier as she lets Lynn's common sense take root. 'That helps.'

'Owen is organising a memorial service in the school chapel and we've planned something for Pippa's party on Saturday. I've got some candles and several of the senior girls have put together a speech to honour Tori. You're more than welcome to come to both of those events.'

'Cheers. I will come. I'll keep a low profile, sit in an alcove, stay out of the way of her parents.'

'You've nothing to be ashamed of, Anna.' Lynn tips the vegetables into a bowl. 'Nothing at all.'

Anna takes some ingredients from the cupboard to whisk up a salad dressing. 'How's Lois?' she asks, suddenly remembering that this isn't all about her. Other people are hurting too.

'She's …' Lynn's sigh speaks volumes. 'She doesn't

get it, Anna. She cried on and off all weekend. It was awful. She was completely inconsolable.'

They bring the food to the table and sit down. Lynn tells her about their weekend and how difficult it was. 'Even Pippa taking a special interest in Lois, something she never does, didn't help.'

At the mention of Pippa, Anna remembers the other worry that's been playing on her mind. 'Do you know what's going on with Isobel?'

Lynn sits stock still for a second as if she's been caught with her hand in Anna's purse. 'What do you mean?'

'I can tell by your face that you know what I mean.' She lays down her fork. 'I know there's something going on but she won't tell me what it is.'

'Almost all the seniors are stressed, Anna, especially the girls,' Lynn says. 'I've timetabled sessions for them to come to talk to me. And, of course, Isobel is particularly upset because of … your involvement.' She frowns and then almost immediately her voice brightens. 'Hopefully, after today she'll be in a better frame of mind.'

Isobel was persuaded into school that morning by Pippa and Hester, who came to the house and escorted her there, one either side, like female henchmen. Anna hasn't heard how her day is going but as Isobel still isn't talking to her that's hardly a surprise.

'Tori's death aside, I feel like Isobel's not herself,' Anna says, spearing spinach and tomato with her fork. 'Almost since term began she's been quieter than normal and more tense than I've ever seen her.' She gives Lynn a significant look. 'I can't help her unless I find out what's going on.'

'Didn't we always say we wouldn't share the information in our own children's files?' Lynn says.

'So you do know something?'

'Not exactly.' Lynn purses her lips.

'This is no time for keeping secrets.'

'Anna.' Lynn sighs. 'Of course if there was anything really worrying, then to hell with the rules! I would let you know. But ...' She hesitates. 'It's really just normal girl stuff. I can't break confidentiality.' She screws up her face. 'Or Isobel's trust.'

'Says the woman who used her daughter's thumbprint to access her phone.' Anna's tone is light and she smiles as she says this but the undercurrent is there.

Lynn finishes a mouthful of food before saying, 'Is that why you asked about the scratches?'

'What scratches?' Anna asks. She has genuinely forgotten. 'When?'

'When I told you I'd seen Tori with a pile of books being collected by her dad and you asked me if her face was scratched.'

Anna slowly chews and swallows a forkful of salad.

'Did you suspect Isobel of hitting Tori?' Lynn asks. 'Because I would understand if you did.' She puts down her fork and lays a hand on Anna's forearm. 'For what it's worth, I don't think it was Isobel who hit Tori. I think that behaviour is a long way behind her now.'

When Isobel was just eleven she was given a five-day exclusion from school for scratching a boy's face. She said he kicked her but three other children who witnessed the attack said that wasn't true. The scratches were deep and almost six inches long but, fortunately, they healed without incident. His parents took a 'these things happen' approach but Anna and John were shocked that their daughter could be so aggressive. They took her to see a child psychologist, and after a couple of sessions he told them that she was reacting to her parents' troubles. They had just lost the money on the house, Anna had yet to be promoted and they were living in rented accommodation with a short-term lease and no idea where they would live next. Their outgoings were sky-high and their income fell well short of covering the debt. 'Your daughter is anxious because you are anxious,' the psychologist told them. 'For her behaviour to improve you need to talk to her, spend more time together as a family, alleviate her fears.'

So that's what they did. They pulled together, focused on family time, and then good fortune beckoned and Anna was promoted. They saw a way through their debts. They moved into the school grounds where they could breathe again.

'I wasn't thinking about that time,' Anna says. 'It never occurred to me that Isobel could be involved in hurting Tori.'

A lie, and she guesses that Lynn knows it. But she's not ready to confide in Lynn yet because to do that might be to betray Isobel. Also, Anna feels strangely let down by her friend. She has no justification for this – not really – she would probably do the same if the boot were on the other foot. Confidentiality is the pillar that supports both their roles in the school.

'I'm sorry,' Lynn says. 'I don't mean to upset you, Anna. I just thought it made a twisted sort of sense.'

'Isobel hits Tori and Tori accuses me instead of her?'

Lynn nods. 'I'm not saying that's what *I* think happened but I could understand if it were to have crossed your mind.'

Sister Pierce was a good mentor. She made a point of looking out for her. She visited the boarding house in the evening to chat to the girls but Tori knew she mostly visited to make

sure she was okay. She was there for Tori, not for Isobel or
Pippa or Hester, the three girls who popped up everywhere
– from orchestra to hockey, theatre productions to maths club.
They pedalled hard to stay in the top academic sets, studied
violin or piano to Grade Six, signed up for Duke of Edinburgh
gold award.

Hester was Tori's partner for the first few weeks. She was
supposed to introduce her to students and teachers, and help
her find her way around. She played the role dutifully and
was as polite and friendly as she needed to be. No more, no
less.

Pippa had privilege sewn into every stitch of her designer
jeans and her highlighted hair. If she wasn't talking about
her exotic holidays or her new clothes she was talking about
boys. She spoke about them constantly. She was one of those
girls who needed to be liked by everyone. And that simply
isn't possible. Not if you were true to yourself.

Isobel was the best of the three. What you saw was what
you got. She didn't manipulate the boys and didn't talk
behind the other girls' backs. Tori didn't think they would
ever be friends but at least they weren't enemies.

Chapter Seventeen

Anna wakes in the middle of the night and her first thought is: Tori is dead. She feels the familiar lurch of her heart and race of her pulse and then she has her second thought: she still has her keys to the surgery. She latches onto this thought. She understands Lynn's reluctance to give her any information about Isobel's pastoral care records, but Anna knows that she will be able to access them through the school Intranet.

Her daughter is still refusing to talk to her and Anna can't get her last unguarded outburst out of her mind: *Victoria Carmichael was a scheming little bitch. You don't know the half of what she got up to. And I've had to carry the burden because you're too blind to see what's going on right in front of your face.* She needs to know whether the girls had an argument or a falling out and, if they did, there's a good chance Isobel has said something in one of her mentoring sessions. If there is something to be uncovered, Anna's instincts tell her she needs to find out what it is before the police start digging. That way she will be prepared.

Geraldine is on duty in the medical centre overnight on a Tuesday, but unless there is a child in sick bay, she'll be asleep in the on-call room. Anna doesn't know whether there's a child in sick bay or not – chances are there won't be because it's only the end of September; the cold and flu season is still a few weeks away. But

she'll be taking a risk. If she's caught she'll almost
certainly lose her job.

She pulls on trousers, a sweatshirt and boots, deliberately choosing dark colours. She doesn't expect anyone
to be out at this time of night but it would be foolish
not to make herself as invisible as she can. There are no
security personnel working at the school. Between eleven
and six, a locked gate secures the driveway, and every
outside door (there are twenty-four of them) is either
alarmed or has a door code that changes termly.

She wears a head torch switched to low light as she
moves through the woods. To her left, an owl hoots, and
there is a breeze whispering through the leaves but apart
from that, the only sounds are her footsteps on the
ground.

She reaches the path between the boarding houses
and looks towards the end of the building where Isobel
sleeps, wishing they were on better terms, wishing she
didn't feel the necessity to do this, to break the confidentiality she promised both her children when she was
promoted to senior nurse. 'We'll have no privacy!' Isobel
moaned. 'You'll be in all the staff meetings, you'll know
everything about us.' So Anna made a solemn promise
and, up to now, she has never broken it.

She's careful to stay close to the buildings so that she
doesn't trip the automatic lights. A fox crosses her path
several metres ahead, taking no notice of Anna, his attention focused on his own nocturnal hunt. It takes her less
than a minute to reach the medical centre. There are no
lights on in the office or the surgery and this is reassuring. The centre is alarmed but luckily the panel is
some distance away from where Geraldine will be
sleeping. When the beeping starts, Anna keys in the
four-digit code. The beeping stops at once but Anna

waits. She listens. She's ready to run if she hears footsteps approaching. She counts to one hundred. Nothing. She dares to open the door into the waiting area. Night-lights prevent the corridor from being pitch-black. She looks in each direction and tiptoes quietly to the office, unlocking it with her key and closing it quietly behind her.

She takes a breath and surveys the room. The first thing she notices is that Isobel's name is on the doctor's list for next week. The whiteboard is covered in three neat rows of names: children who are due for vaccinations, children who are off games and children on the doctor's list: James Moorfoot, Polly Maclean and Isobel Pierce.

She's about to log onto the computer with her own log-in when she remembers that Geraldine keeps a copy of her password in the drawer. As with the door codes, they have to change their passwords termly and they're not allowed simple words and a couple of numbers – their passwords have to be a random ten digits. And as one term inevitably blends into the next, that makes them difficult to keep track of. Anna stores hers in her phone; Geraldine writes hers on a piece of paper that she keeps in the drawer.

Anna logs on as Geraldine, who, like Anna, has access to all the medical and pastoral care files. Anna types in Isobel Pierce and is surprised to see that, in total, Isobel's files run to more than thirty pages. She turns on the printer and waits as it chugs its way through the job. Her fingers are crossed behind her back, hoping the phone doesn't suddenly ring to report a sick child in one of the boarding houses. She would be horrified to meet Geraldine in the corridor.

She's lucky; she's not disturbed. The printer finishes

the job and she stuffs the pages inside her sweatshirt, switches off the machines, makes sure everything is as she found it, locks the office door behind her and resets the alarm. She is retracing her steps back towards home when she sees two figures come out of the girls' boarding house. They trigger the light and immediately cleave together, arms clinging, suppressing giggles as they run across the lower quad and down the hill. Anna is blind-sided. For several seconds all she can do is stand and stare as Pippa and Isobel pass less than three metres in front of her, so caught up in their own antics that they are oblivious to her presence. It's three o'clock in the morning and they have managed to get out without triggering the door alarms inside the girls' boarding house. How? And where are they going?

Anna follows them. They run past the front of the chapel and stop at the side door. Both girls are in the choir so they know where the key is hidden. Pippa looks behind her before reaching up and taking it from the hiding place above the lintel. Anna watches from the shadow of the music block as another figure approaches from further down the hill. She already suspects the figure, tall and broad-shouldered, is male. Isobel shines a light in his direction and walks forward to take his hand and then kiss him. They go inside the chapel and Pippa waits outside, keeping guard.

Anna stands there for at least five minutes, in two minds about whether to confront them. Both girls are breaking school rules. But Isobel could say the same of her. Anna is banned from school until she is given the all-clear to return. So what would she say? Why would she be in the school at this time of night if it wasn't for exactly the same reason as them – so that she could move around unseen and not be caught doing something she shouldn't?

Isobel isn't in any danger. She'd like her daughter to avoid sex until she's old enough to handle the emotions that go with it but she's almost seventeen and if she is having sex with this boy – in the chapel? What is she thinking! – then Anna can only hope all the SRE lessons she's had means that she's on the pill and using condoms. Anna hugs the printed sheets closer to her chest; the information will be in the medical files.

Pippa is scrolling through her phone, glancing up occasionally to make sure no one is approaching. She is as good a friend to Isobel as Lynn is to Anna. Anna will tell Lynn about this – about how the girls have each other's backs in much the same way as they do – but she won't tell her today, probably not tomorrow either. She'll save it for when this is all over.

Amanda was distracting Miss Taymere so that Tori could slip out and catch Sister Pierce on her way home. Tori knew her shift pattern; she usually worked till late on a Wednesday and took a short cut home through the woods.

All the girls knew the code to deactivate the alarm. At the beginning of each term, one of the girls would hide on the stairs and watch Miss Taymere key in the numbers. Within a matter of days, it would be whispered between them so that they could all get in and out of the building un-detected.

Tori sneaked out just after ten and waited on the path. When she saw her coming, she called out, 'Sister Pierce, I need to talk to you.'

'I'll speak to you tomorrow, Tori,' she said, her tone weary. 'Go back inside now.'

Chapter Eighteen

Anna makes herself some tea before sitting down to read through Isobel's pastoral records. She's just about to begin when there's a quiet knocking on the front door and then a voice calls through her letterbox. 'I'm sorry to bother you in the middle of the night, Anna, but I saw your light on.' Anna recognises the voice as Miranda from next door. 'Could you help me, please?' Her voice cracks. 'Peter's away. His mum's been taken into hospital so he's gone to Yorkshire. And I'm really worried about Charlotte.'

Anna slides the pages under the sofa and opens the door. Miranda is standing on the doorstep, a desperate look in her eyes. Her daughter Charlotte is bundled up inside a green tartan blanket. Anna can just see the top of her head; soft, blonde hair standing on end as if alive with static electricity. She is squirming in her mother's arms, her feet pushing into Miranda's stomach, short legs bent at the knee as she uses her weight to try to break free.

'She's got really bad croup and I'm just not sure …' Miranda holds the toddler out towards Anna and, right on cue, Charlotte gives a cough that sounds more like a sea lion's bark.

Anna balances Charlotte on her hip and pulls the blanket back from her face. Her plump baby cheeks are flushed, her eyes wet with tears. 'Are you not well,

Charlie?' she asks, touching the back of her hand against her forehead.

Charlotte's eyes are fixed on Anna's face as her chest contorts with a spasm of coughing.

'I'm overanxious, I know that,' Miranda says, wringing her hands. 'It's just that, when it's anything to do with their breathing, I panic.'

'That's completely understandable,' Anna says. 'It's really frightening when they're so wee. Let's take her back to your house.' She slides her feet into her shoes. 'Have you tried turning on the shower?'

'I thought that advice was redundant now?'

'Moist air helps,' Anna says. She follows Miranda across the gravel path that divides their cottages. The front door is wide open; the smell of burned toast greets them as they step over the threshold. Lego is scattered across the floor and a wooden train set blocks the bottom of the stairs. Miranda pushes the pieces aside with her foot and they all go up to the family bathroom. The bath is three-quarters full of water, soap scum and plastic toys bobbing on the surface in happy harmony.

'I'm sorry. I haven't had a chance to …' Miranda leans across and pulls out the plug.

'Don't apologise,' Anna says, adjusting Charlotte on her hip. She has almost forgotten the weight of a toddler. 'You're a mother of young children. Getting through the day without losing your rag, or even worse your sanity, is victory enough. A tidy house is optional.' Charlotte finishes a bout of coughing and lets out a loud, anguished wail that sets off a buzzing in Anna's ear. She reaches past Miranda and takes hold of a wide-mouthed hippo with comedy teeth. She shakes off the water and passes it to Charlotte. 'Look!'

Charlotte pushes it away, her expression disgusted.

She points downwards and catches her breath for long enough to say, 'Fog.'

A frog circles above the plughole and Anna catches it with her free hand. She winds up the mechanism on the side and Charlotte stares, mesmerised, as the legs kick into the air. Miranda turns on the shower and the room begins to fill with steam. Anna lets the blanket fall away from Charlotte's shoulders and sits down on the lid of the toilet seat while Miranda perches on the edge of the bath. The steam gradually works its magic and Charlotte begins to breathe more easily. Anna rubs her back and sings a quiet 'Twinkle Twinkle, Little Star' close to her ear. Her eyes grow heavy, her long lashes blinking in slow motion, putting Anna in mind of an overfed Monty.

Charlotte relaxes into the contours of Anna's arms, her body twitching with the occasional sniff or hiccup before she gives in to the power of sleep. Miranda turns off the shower and leads the way to her own bedroom, where she arranges the pillows so that Anna is able to prop Charlotte up in the centre of the king-size bed. Both women stare down at her.

'There's nothing quite as satisfying as the sight of a sleeping child,' Anna whispers. 'I used to tiptoe backwards out of Isobel's room when she was this age. She was very difficult to settle.'

'Harry was a tyrant,' Miranda says. 'He's been much better since he turned five.'

They go downstairs and Anna's hand is reaching for the door when Miranda says, 'Thank you for helping me with Charlotte.' She squeezes Anna's arm. 'And by the way, I'm so sorry about what you're going through.'

'It's a difficult time,' Anna acknowledges, opening the door. 'And very sad.' Her breath catches. 'Tori had such a bright future ahead of her.'

'I bumped into John earlier and he mentioned the memorial they had at Davison High.'

Anna nods. John had told her about it when he came home. Several children had stood up to talk about Tori and, at the end, her parents also said a few words. 'Her dad was very composed,' John said. 'But I think her mum had been drinking. She was slurring her words and had to be helped off the stage.'

'I think if something happened to Noah or Isobel I'd spend the rest of my life drunk,' Anna had replied.

'It must be hard on you all,' Miranda adds. 'How are the kids coping?'

'Noah's once removed being off at uni but Isobel's struggling a bit. It's not easy when your mum's under the spotlight.'

'She's such a fantastic girl. I'm sure she'll get through this.'

'I hope so,' Anna acknowledges.

'She's done so well to be head of year. You and John must be so proud of her.'

'We are,' Anna says. She knows how hard Isobel works to stay in the top academic sets, as well as hockey team captain, violin lessons, Duke of Edinburgh. That is her public face. Climbing out of her bedroom window when she's pretending to be asleep, sneaking out of dorm in the middle of the night to have a rendezvous with a boy in the chapel is her private one.

'Peter feels really bad that he isn't here,' Miranda says. 'It's a comfort to him to know that Lynn is helping with the grief counselling.'

'She'll do a good job,' Anna says. She steps outside and looks back at Miranda. 'The children trust her.'

'I hadn't realised she was joining the senior management team,' Miranda says, yawning.

'Fingers crossed Charlotte will stay asleep.' Anna gives her a quick hug. 'See you tomorrow.' She goes inside her own house, closes the door behind her and stands there, thinking. It's odd that Lynn didn't tell her she'd applied for senior management. And then when she got the job. It was a reason to celebrate – it makes no sense that she'd keep news like that to herself.

Anna sits down on the living room floor and pulls the sheets out from under the sofa, trying to distract herself from the question now playing on her mind. *Lynn wouldn't say anything to the police about Isobel, would she? Mark her out as a suspect?*

'Of course she wouldn't,' Anna says to the empty room. 'We're all friends. She'd never do something like that.'

Chapter Nineteen

Anna starts with the medical files. The first few pages are from Isobel's childhood. She had three consecutive winters with asthma, hay fever in the summer months, throat infections that became so frequent and debilitating that she had her tonsils out aged ten. The last time Anna took her to the doctor was when she was referred to the child psychologist for scratching her classmate.

The first time Isobel took herself to the school doctor was when she was fifteen – and on a Tuesday, Anna's day off. She's been to Dr Mary Dalton six times over the past couple of years, always on a Tuesday. Anna's not expecting to read anything upsetting. She believes she knows her daughter well. Of course she'll have secrets but Anna expects them to be, like Lynn said, the usual stuff of teenage girls – worries about boys and school work and gaining weight.

12.10.18
Isobel was brought in by her housemistress, Miss Taymere. She has been cutting herself with a maths protractor. One-centimetre, superficial cuts on the inside of her thighs that heal quickly and are not at risk of infection. Isobel would like to stop cutting herself but describes it as a 'coping mechanism'. She reports that several of her friends also do this. I encouraged her to discuss this with her parents. She says

she doesn't want them to know. I consider her to be Gillick Competent in this regard – she understands what she is doing, she has sought help, she wishes to stop self-harming. We discussed her joining the mindfulness classes but she doesn't want to because her mum runs these classes. She has promised to discuss other ways of coping with head of pastoral care, Lynn Sykes, who is Isobel's mentor. Follow up 1/52.

19.10.18
Follow up after last week's consultation: Isobel has seen Mrs Sykes and has not self-harmed this week. She feels Mrs Sykes understands her personal circumstances and is the best person to help her. Isobel has told her dad and intends to tell her mum soon.

As Anna reads these two entries, her stomach drops to her boots. Isobel has been self-harming. Her daughter has been self-harming and she had no idea because Isobel never told her. And while Anna can accept Lynn not telling her – Pippa has come to surgery on several occasions and Anna has not shared the information with Lynn – but *John*? John knew their daughter was self-harming and he didn't tell her. What gave him the right to do that? Didn't he know that she wouldn't let on to Isobel, but that having the information would allow her to support their daughter?

Her chest simmers as she continues reading. There are two entries that aren't concerning and then:

02.02.19
Isobel asked for a consult because she is already anxious about her GCSEs. She feels under pressure to perform. I understand from Mrs Sykes that as long as

she continues to work hard she will easily meet her predicted grades. Thus far she is managing not to resort to self-harm and she is reluctant to take medication. She has not had suicidal thoughts but promises to return should she experience them. She has not seen Mrs Sykes since before Christmas and has requested a meeting with her this week.

05.05.19

Isobel has started a relationship and would like a prescription for the contraceptive pill. She recently turned sixteen. The boy is also sixteen. She shows maturity and awareness of both the law and the adult nature of a sexual relationship. I am starting her on Microgynon and will review in four weeks. Have advised her of side effects.

Anna puts the medical files to one side. Her breathing is as rapid as if she'd been running. She's not concerned about Isobel being on the pill, in fact she's pleased that she's taking the risk of pregnancy seriously.

What concerns her far more is that Isobel has been self-harming.

And John knew about it.

These two statements are neon-lit inside Anna's brain. And there is an ache in her chest. She is both angry and hurt. Hurt and angry. She spins between the two emotions, her eyes filling, her jaw tightening.

Hurt that Isobel felt unable to tell her. Angry that John kept it from her.

Angry that Isobel felt unable to tell her. Hurt that John kept it from her.

No good ever comes from spying. Her mother's words from long ago when she was caught reading a letter her dad had sent to her mum, a letter that made everything clear: *Anna needs to realise that I have moved on. She is rude to Angela and refuses to share a room with Vivien. She won't be able to stay again until she behaves herself.* Anna's mother told her that her dad was a wanker and that she should forget him. But Anna couldn't. He was her dad, and her heart was broken.

Anna lays the medical pages to one side and begins to read the pastoral care records. She knows the details will not make easy reading; there may be more shocks to come because having read her medical records, Anna now knows that her daughter – and her husband – are very good at keeping secrets.

14.10.18

This is my first mentoring session with Isobel Pierce since she was in S1. She is now aged fifteen and in S4. Isobel is a high-achieving, popular girl with good friends, a full school life and the responsibilities that go with that. She has been self-harming and has seen Dr Dalton, who has agreed that Isobel is Gillick Competent so her parents will not be informed. Isobel's reason for self-harming is that she feels under pressure because no matter how hard she works, she never feels good enough. Furthermore, she feels that she's not exciting to boys. She said, 'I try my best at everything but that means I'm not good fun. I don't have money to buy make-up or fashionable clothes. My parents won't let me go to music festivals.' We discussed expectations for young women today and what it means to be true to herself.

We have agreed that she will continue to meet with me weekly for the next month. She is downloading a mindfulness app that will help her relax in the evening and she has made me a promise to seek me out if she is tempted to self-harm.

Lynn Sykes

21.10.18

Isobel is having trouble with another one of the girls who is new to the year group. 'My dad thinks she's a chemistry genius. And my mum's her mentor. They want me to be friends with her and I've tried but she's a liar. She is a majorly compulsive liar. And I can't be friends with someone like that.'

We discussed what it means to be a good friend and why it's important to be tolerant with others without feeling we have to allow them into our lives.

Lynn Sykes

07.11.18

Isobel is doing extremely well. She is not self-harming and she feels she is better able to handle herself and others. She would like to find it easier to talk to her mum. 'It's like I have an angel on one shoulder and a devil on the other,' she said. 'And my mum is just so annoying! She always brings out the worst in me. My dad doesn't.'

We discussed what happens to teenage brains as they develop, why it's necessary to grow up and away from our parents while remembering that they love us and want the best for us even although it might not always feel like that.

Lynn Sykes

Anna is forced to stop reading because there are tears in her eyes. She sees how much Lynn has been helping Isobel, without Anna having any idea that this was going on. Does she really bring out the worst in Isobel? She doesn't think so. Sure, Isobel is moody with her, but don't all teenage girls hate their mothers at some point? Anna's always felt that because Isobel is so good, so 'perfect' at school, it's only to be expected she will play up at home sometimes.

Perhaps she should be questioning her mothering but she's not going to go down that road. Not yet. Maybe later when all this is over she'll have a heart-to-heart with Isobel. She'll talk it through with Lynn and John first, make sure she gets it right. But for now she has to focus on the connection between Isobel and Tori.

Anna continues reading and sees that in May, soon after Isobel started on the pill, she changed her mentor, moved from Lynn to Geraldine – *Geraldine?* Why? Her mind immediately throws up options: a) because her mother and Geraldine are barely on speaking terms; b) because she suspected that Lynn told Anna something she shared in one of their mentoring sessions; c) because Pippa guessed that her mum had accessed her phone to warn off the boy who was harassing her and she told Isobel that neither of their mothers could be trusted.

'Anna?'

Anna jumps guiltily. It's John's voice. She hears the creaking floorboards as he descends the stairs. Anna pushes the pages underneath the sofa, makes sure there are no edges showing. When John comes into the room she is lifting the cold cup of tea to her lips.

'What are you doing up?' He's wearing boxers and a T-shirt. His hand is inside his T-shirt scratching at his chest. 'You're dressed?'

'Miranda needed help with Charlotte.' She can't look at him. 'She was shouting through the letterbox so I went next door with her.'

'I didn't hear her shouting.'

'Well, I did,' she says lightly. 'I'm not exactly sleeping soundly at the moment.'

He stands there, waiting for her to say more. She still hasn't looked at him.

'Something wrong?' he says.

'I don't know, John. Is there?' She looks up then and locks her eyes onto his. His expression is at first unguarded, but within seconds it has hardened to match hers.

'I'm trying to support you, Anna, but I can't do that when you're like this.' He turns away. 'I'm going back to bed. I hope you'll join me there.'

'Not on your life,' Anna murmurs, her heartbeat racing as she imagines shouting: *You bastard! You knew our daughter was self-harming and you didn't tell me?* She waits until he's climbed the stairs and her breathing settles and then she returns to the pages.

Chapter Twenty

Isobel's first session with Geraldine.

08.05.19

Isobel Pierce asked me to mentor her. In the interest of full disclosure, I told Isobel that although her mum runs the medical centre, anything Isobel discusses with me is confidential. I know Isobel has a history of self-harm but she has not done that now for several months. We discussed the fact that Isobel has recently become sexually active with a boy named Andrew Dyson who goes to the local comprehensive and is the year above her. She is keeping him a secret because, 'My mum and dad will act like they approve but they won't really. They have higher standards for their own children than they do for other people's. So even though my dad works in the school Andrew goes to, they won't think he's right for me because he doesn't go to Bishopglen and he's not applying to university.'

I tell her that I'm sure her parents only want what's best for her and that their main concern will be that she is safe from pregnancy and STIs. Isobel assures me that she is taking the pill and that they are also using condoms. I suggest that the timing is also tricky because she is in the middle of GCSEs. 'I'm happy,' she said. 'So I'm not even nervous about my exams.'

I encourage her to think about introducing Andrew

to the family. She says that when her brother Noah returns from his gap year she will get Andrew and him together. 'My brother's great. I really miss him. And he knows what our parents are like. My dad's okay most of the time but he's usually out at football or watching the stars, and my mum – I'm not saying she isn't nice, that would be stupid because everyone knows she's nice – the problem is she always knows best. I want to make my own choices and Andrew is better than any of the boys here who're mostly full of themselves.'

    Geraldine Whitlock

Anna stops reading to give her thoughts time to catch up with what she's discovering. Geraldine has been giving Isobel sound advice; Isobel's boyfriend is called Andrew Dyson and he goes to Davison High – John will know him; Isobel's opinion of John is harsh to say the least. Like Lynn, Geraldine's style of note-taking means that she always quotes the children directly and Anna can hear her daughter saying these things, but from an objective standpoint it simply isn't true. John helps her with her science coursework, provides a taxi service for her and her friends, and has recently begun taking her out on weekends to visit universities. Isobel needs a reality check. She's no idea what it's like to have a dad who's not around. It's one of the gifts Anna's been able to give her children.

    A single page remains to be read. Anna takes a breath and dives in.

09.09.19

Isobel had an enjoyable summer but she is worried about someone. She says this 'someone' (she wouldn't say who) has done something that, if found out, could ruin their life. I tried to ascertain what this 'some-thing' could be but she said she couldn't tell me because I might have to report it. She's unable to speak to anyone about it because she doesn't want it coming out into the open and the person doesn't even know they've done it. I asked her how this was possible if it's something so serious and she said, 'It's complicated.' She became quite tearful at this point and said, 'And it's my fault they did it! I got them involved without even knowing it! And now their life could be over.'

I helped calm her down and tried to reassure her. I suggested she try not to worry as most things work themselves out. She said she would try.

Geraldine Whitlock

15.09.19

I caught up with Isobel today and asked her whether she'd resolved the issue. She said no but she's dealing with it. She hopes it won't come to anything. Before she left the room she also mentioned that, 'One of the girls knows about it, by the way, and that's what makes it a ticking time bomb.' I asked her the name of the girl and she said, 'Victoria Carmichael.'

Geraldine Whitlock

Less than one week ago, Isobel had another session with Geraldine.

23.09.19

Isobel came in today looking quite anxious and upset. 'I'm feeling a bit depressed because Noah's off at uni now and Andrew doesn't really get what I'm going through. I can't tell him about the big problem because I can't tell anyone. Not even Pippa. And Andrew knows I'm keeping something from him.'

I asked Isobel again whether she could be more specific. 'I know what happens when you tell someone a secret,' she said. 'They tell one person who tells another person and before long everyone knows. I can't risk that.'

I asked her about VC's part in all of this and she said, 'She hasn't told anyone yet. She said she won't but she can't be trusted because she lies.'

Geraldine Whitlock

Anna places this final page on the floor and stands up. Her legs are stiff from sitting for so long and she stretches them out as she walks to the log pile beside the back door. She gathers logs and kindling and begins to build a fire in the living room woodburner. She scrunches up every one of the pages, pushing them underneath the kindling so that they will catch fire first. She strikes a match and sets light to the paper, watches it burn and blacken, and fall to ash.

Her breathing is shallow. Her heart is sore. She was hoping to find nothing much, perhaps an argument over a boy, a power struggle with friends or disappointment with one of the teachers who believed Tori when they should have believed her.

But this is so much more than that.

Isobel had been going out with Andrew for five months and every week they grew closer. They texted each other between lessons and met up most evenings. They were planning on spending the October half term week together. She just had to get her parents onside first. She would speak to her dad, get him to broach it with her mum.

'Isobel!' Tori was several metres behind her. 'Wait a minute!'

Isobel stopped to give Tori time to catch up. 'I'm resigning from the school newsletter,' she said to Tori, thinking this was why she wanted to talk. 'I'm going to recommend you for editor.'

'It's not that,' Tori said. 'I have something to show you.' She held her mobile out. 'Watch this video.'

'Now?' Tori nodded and Isobel sighed but took the mobile and pressed play. 'We can't be late for double English because we—' Her mouth dropped open; she was frowning and then her hands began to shake. 'What is this?' Her eyes were wide, her face pale.

Tori grabbed the mobile and slipped it into her pocket. 'I'm proving a point,' she said.

'What point?' Isobel's tone was incredulous.

'You challenged me,' Tori said.

'Challenged you to do this?' Her voice broke. 'I would never challenge you to do this!'

And then she remembered a lesson last term, the last lesson before the long summer holidays. She stared at Tori, her expression horrified. 'You did this because of what I said in a lesson?'

Tori's tone was silky smooth when she replied, 'You asked for it.'

Isobel turned and bolted along the corridor, through the lower quad and down towards the chapel where she paused for breath, her mind spinning. Should she call him? Warn him? What should she do? Her stomach heaved and she vomited onto the grass.

When the teacher asked why Isobel didn't show up to double English, Tori said, 'She wasn't feeling well, miss.' And then she smiled.

Chapter Twenty-One

If you can deceive those closest to you, what does that say about you? That you don't love them enough? That you love them too much? That you love yourself and your secrets more than you love them? That you lack what it takes to really commit to others? Or is it simply that you take charge in order to protect your loved ones because you understand that we all teeter on the edge of a chasm: of death, of neglect, of one small step in the wrong direction that leads us into a wasteland. Sometimes it's not even a step. Sometimes the scenery on life's stage crashes to the floor, knocks the breadwinner off the stage, the food from your hand. And then you're left on the stage by yourself. Lonely and alone.

Isobel.

Somehow Isobel understands this. Anna doesn't know how, but after reading her school records she has gained insight into her daughter's character. Isobel is scared. Someone she cares about has unwittingly done something that she feels is her fault. Anna can't even begin to get a grasp of what it could be.

She's wary of putting two and two together and making five but the connection is obvious.

Tori knew about this 'something'.

Isobel told Geraldine she was 'dealing with it'.

Tori is dead.

Anna fears that these events are linked. Her fear is so

visceral that she can barely register the thought, never mind speak it out loud. At breakfast she says nothing to John about what she's read. Because where would she start? I sneaked into the medical centre and printed off Isobel's confidential records. I'm hurt because you knew Isobel was self-harming and you didn't tell me. Isobel is bunking off during the night to have sex in the chapel. She has had a boyfriend for almost five months that she didn't feel she could tell us about.

Oh! And by the way, I've found out that someone Isobel cares for could be in serious trouble – I have no idea who or what for, but Tori knew about it and it's been sending Isobel into a spin.

She's reluctant to tell him about Isobel's disclosures for two reasons: first, because they're both stressed and so any conversation where it's possible to form opposing opinions will quickly degenerate into an argument; and second, she wants to control this herself. She doesn't trust him not to react instinctively, without thinking it through. He'll question Isobel, force the truth out of her and that will backfire on Anna because she brought the secrets out into the open.

But worse than that – the truth could be life-destroying.

So she acts her conciliatory self at breakfast. She makes them both porridge, apologises for her grumpiness last night, smiles, strokes his hair, kisses him on the lips when he leaves.

And when she closes the door behind him, for a split second, she sees herself – her duplicity – clearly, and she shudders.

Her daughter has two faces.

And so does she.

*   *   *

Anna sits down at the kitchen table, her laptop in front of her. She believes in process. She believes in thinking things through, making lists and plans, approaching problems with her head engaged. She needs to know two things: who the person is that Isobel is worried about and what this person has done.

First, there is the who. She searches her own behaviour over the last few months but can come up with nothing she has done that could be remotely concerning. They went to St Ives on holiday for two weeks but otherwise they stayed at home, gardening, seeing friends. At the end of August, school started up again. Since then there has been a procession of normal days.

And John? What could John have done? He is the most equable, easy-going of men. She's never had to worry about him being sexually inappropriate; he doesn't drive when drunk and he doesn't take drugs. He plays football, watches the stars, is involved in family life.

And Noah? Has he got a girl pregnant? That would be upsetting but it's hardly a crime. Cheated on his exams? He had no need to. Has Isobel found out about something he did on his gap year, something she encouraged him to do, that could potentially blow his life apart?

And then there are possibilities that she considers to be so 'out there' that they're non-starters: John could be a child molester, Noah could be a Class A drug dealer, she could be a murderer.

She's getting nowhere. She opens her laptop and logs onto Facebook. The very sight of the blue bar at the top of the page makes her stomach turn. She ignores the notification 'Julia Raeburn, Holly Standing and twenty-four others have posted in RIP Victoria Carmichael' and types 'Andrew Dyson' into search. She might as well see whether she can find out anything about Isobel's boyfriend. It's not an uncommon name and she has to click on more than twenty Andrew Dysons before she comes to the conclusion he isn't on Facebook. Nor Instagram, nor any other social media website that she's heard of. Noah isn't on social media either. When he was sixteen he dismissed the whole thing as time-wasting. Andrew must be of similar mind.

She types 'Andrew Dyson Bishopglen town' into Google and finds that he plays in the local football team. There are several references to him scoring goals and one game last year when he was red-carded. In 2015 there is a death notice in the town newspaper: 'Kevin Dyson, peacefully in his sleep, leaves his wife Jenna and three children, Andrew, Parker and Huw.'

'He lost his dad,' she says out loud and, as if in reply, a text sounds on her mobile. She jumps in alarm, slams the laptop lid closed before glancing at the message. It's from Owen.

I have some time off this morning – join me for a walk?

They agree to meet at the edge of the loch. She pulls on her walking boots and coat and closes the door behind her. Miranda is just driving away in her car and they have a quick conversation about Charlotte before Anna heads off through the trees. The sky is bright blue above her as she follows a barely trodden path down to the water. It took her a while to get used to being surrounded by trees. She was every bit a townie before they moved here. One hundred yards beyond her door was a parade of shops, everything you could want from a post office to a very decent curry house. But now she sees this place as her home. The shades of green, the ever-changing sky above, the brown earth below, insects busy with purpose, birds singing to each other. It feeds her soul in a way that the town never did.

Owen is waiting for her at the water's edge. 'How are you?' He hugs her hard, and when he lets her go she rocks back on her heels.

'I think I'm just about ready to smoke that joint.'

He smiles. 'I'll assume you're joking.' He takes some pages out of his coat pocket and passes them to her. 'I printed out the supportive messages that you're getting on Facebook and Twitter.'

'That's thoughtful of you.' Anna takes the papers and has a quick look at the first few lines.

Thank you for everything you've done for Hunter. Be strong. We believe in you! Sophie Wade

Mia would never have made it through school so successfully without your help. We want you back! Brian Marks

Both my children are really missing you! Please come back soon. The Ackerman family

Pages and pages of support; Anna's heart lifts in her chest. 'This is so kind of people.'

'Yesterday Mungo Todd set up a Facebook page in support of you. Did he tell you?'

Anna shakes her head. She hasn't been answering emails or phone calls unless from those close to her.

'There are dozens of comments already. All of them singing your praises.'

Anna manages a smile. 'I've only been reading the ones on Twitter or the Facebook page set up by Tori's dad. "Hashtag school nurse rot in hell".'

'Anna.' Owen frowns. 'Don't torment yourself. Stay

away from that page. They're morons. Julia Raeburn is in her element but she'll burn out soon enough.'

'I haven't been able to stop myself from reading the comments. In fact, I think it would be stupid not to read them. I now know that next time I go to the police station, there will be people ready to photograph me when I come out.' She looks at Owen with a resigned expression. 'I'm hoping they have a back door.'

'I'm so sorry. But surely the police will protect you from any trouble. Have you told them about what's being said?'

'Not the latest barrage.' She lifts her shoulders and blows out a breath. 'Anyway.' She smiles. 'I hear Lynn has been promoted to SMT.'

'She has.' He raises his eyebrows. 'It's not been announced yet.' He stares out over the loch. The wind is blowing towards them, lifting small drops off the water's surface so that the air is wet.

Anna licks her lips. She senses that Owen has something on his mind. 'What?' she asks him. 'I can tell you want to say something.' She tries for a laugh. 'You're not going to sack me, are you?'

'No, no. No, of course not.' He gives her weak smile. 'But while we're on the subject of printouts, Geraldine called me. Someone used her log-in details during the night.'

Anna is surprised that Geraldine noticed so quickly but she manages not to show it. 'And you think it was me?' She frowns. 'I can't access the school Intranet from home. And even if I could, I don't know Geraldine's password.'

'The reason I'm asking you is because when Geraldine checked the files accessed – they were Isobel's.'

Anna folds her arms. 'You're not really suggesting I crept into school in the middle of the night, went into the medical centre and accessed Isobel's records, printed them out then sneaked off home again?'

'I didn't say they were printed out,' he says quietly.

'You did! You said – while we're on the subject of printouts.'

'Well, if you didn't do it, Anna, then who did?'

'Geraldine has never liked me. I don't know why. I've tried my best with her but she has a chip on her shoulder.' Anna experiences a heavy dollop of guilt as she says this. 'She wanted that promotion. And five years on, she hasn't forgiven me for getting it ahead of her.'

Owen stares out over the loch again and she watches the tension in his jaw increase. 'Passwords throughout the school will have to be changed. I'll have to inform the governors and I'll have to question Isobel and her friends in case they were involved.'

This hadn't occurred to Anna. And, as it happens, Isobel and Pippa were out of bed at almost exactly the same time as Anna was accessing the files. If anyone saw them ... 'Why would Isobel want to steal her own files when all she has to do is ask for them? She's entitled to see everything that's written about her.'

When he looks back at her his expression is unforgiving. 'Anna, let's be clear – I'm on your side. But I'm also Bishopglen's head teacher and the buck stops with me. Geraldine hasn't made this up, and I would bet my right arm that you did it.' She holds his eyes because to look away at that point would be an admission of guilt and she's not going to do that. 'I didn't take your keys from you because I thought I could trust you. Geraldine is genuinely concerned. She is Isobel's mentor and has promised her confidentiality.'

'Why would I have taken them?' she says flatly.

'I don't know.' He shrugs. 'But I can only assume that you think there is a link with Tori's death.'

'How?' She manages a surprised laugh. 'How could Isobel's records be linked to Tori's death?'

'How could they not?' he snaps back. 'Two out-of-the ordinary events happen one after the other, linked by the same person.'

'Me?' Her tone is staggered.

'Yes, you,' he confirms.

'Well.' She shakes her head as if everything he is saying is completely beyond her ken. 'I'm sorry I can't help you, Owen.' She tries to work up some righteous anger. 'I will, however, hand in my keys. I won't come up to school, of course, because I'm not allowed to, but I'll ask John to drop them off on his way to work tomorrow.' She begins to power-walk away, briefly glancing back to say, 'Thank you for your support.'

Chapter Twenty-Two

As soon as she's out of Owen's sightline, she slows down. She feels embarrassed and ashamed to have been caught out so quickly. She's known Owen for a long time and it feels wrong to blatantly lie to him. Should she have confided in him? She desperately wants to confide in someone but there is a downside to everyone she thinks of: Owen's made it clear his loyalty lies with the school; Lynn would feel compelled to tell Matt, who would most likely tell John; and John? John is the obvious person because he is Isobel's father. If she could only be sure that he wouldn't fly off the handle. But then she managed to stop him going to Tori's house when she first told him about the accusation. If, before she tells him, she makes him promise not to go it alone then it could work, couldn't it?

Her chance to unburden herself comes sooner than she thought because when she arrives home John is in the kitchen. 'What's happened?' Anna says. 'Are you okay?'

'Unexpected free periods,' he says. 'Community police are running a workshop on the dangers of drug-taking.' He widens his eyes. 'I thought I'd give it a miss and come home to you instead.' He strokes her hair. 'Where were you?'

'Owen texted me. He wanted to give me these.' She pulls the pages out of her pocket. 'Mungo Todd set up a

Facebook page for people to make supportive comments. You know I helped his son Alfie after his wife died?'

John glances at the pages. 'This is great, Anna. Must help you feel a wee bit better?'

'It does.' She leans into him and his arms automatically encircle her. She closes her eyes and lets her mind drift back to the moment they met. John was brought into Accident and Emergency suffering from a football injury and they chatted while he waited for an X-ray. 'I'm off down the pub for a drink,' he said when he was leaving, and as soon as her shift finished she followed him there as if pulled by an invisible thread because he was quite simply the most handsome, confident, warm-hearted man she'd ever met. He exuded good humour. She could see that he trusted other people. He wasn't like her. He didn't look over his shoulder and think, Is that cannonball headed towards me?

'Penny for them?'

She looks up into his face. 'You know it was love at first sight for me,' she tells him.

'And me,' he says, his eyes softening.

He's reading her expression. And she's reading his. The look on his face tells her why he's come home. They've done this many times before, stolen hours for themselves, squeezed in between work and school. Secret kisses that made them both feel less like parents and more like the man and woman who got together in the first place. She takes his hand and leads him upstairs. She feels bruised inside, betrayed by the secret he has kept from her, but she is willing to park that for now. She would have liked a shot of vodka for instant relaxation, but she'll have to manage without, hope that if he senses the tension in her, he'll assume it's because of Tori's death.

It isn't the best sex they've ever had but it's better than good enough. Within seconds of him coming, she fakes an orgasm, and then they lie together, limbs wrapped around each other, relaxed to the bone.

After a few minutes, John says, 'Let's go out for lunch.'

'What if we bump into people we know?' Anna screws up her face. 'Or even worse, the online trolls. They've seen me go into the police station and are planning on photographing me next time I have to go there.'

'You can't let them dictate your movements.' His tone is gentle. 'And they're never going to be brave enough to say anything to your face. You know that's the marker of these people – they're cowards.'

She sighs. 'I feel like I've been lucky all my life and suddenly the luck has run out.'

'But you haven't been lucky all your life.'

She gives a short laugh. 'You're right, I haven't.' She rolls onto his chest. 'But since I met you, I've been lucky. We've been blessed as a family, haven't we?'

'We have.'

They smile at each other, and love burrows deeper before their tranquillity is interrupted by the sound of the doorbell. John climbs out of bed and glances through the window. 'It's Miranda,' he says.

'Bloody hell.' Anna grabs her underwear and starts to dress. 'Maybe it's Charlotte again.'

The bell sounds a second time. 'She's not got Charlotte with her. She is carrying something, though. Looks like flowers.'

'Must be as a thank you,' Anna says. She pulls on trousers and a T-shirt. 'Not that she needed to.'

'She'll leave them on the doorstep.' He climbs back into the bed and reaches for Anna. 'Let's stay here a bit longer.'

'She knows we're in here,' Anna says, kissing his hand. The doorbell chimes a third time. 'She won't stop.'

'Living in school.' John sighs. 'It's such a goldfish bowl.'

Anna kisses his lips. 'Yes, but just think about how much money it saves us.'

She goes downstairs and when she opens the door Miranda is smiling. 'These are for you.'

'You shouldn't have,' Anna says. She adjusts her bra strap and takes hold of a bouquet of roses and a six-pack of lager. 'I love little Charlotte. I was happy to help.'

'The lager's for John. Is he home?'

'He is.' Anna gestures vaguely behind her.

'It's a double thank you.'

'What has he done to deserve the lager?' she says, laughing, so that when the answer comes her face remains frozen in a smile.

'I hope he wasn't pissed off with me the other night.'

'When was that?' Anna asks.

'Friday night. I was trying to get Charlotte to settle and I thought the bunny might pacify her. It was on the back seat of my car. I must have given him a fright, suddenly appearing like that when he pulled into the drive.'

'What time was it again?' Anna says. She hears her own voice, slightly high-pitched, just a little bit tense.

'It was about one, I think.' Charlotte cries out from her car seat and Miranda's head immediately jerks towards the sound. 'I'd better get going. She's hungry for her lunch.'

'Thank you for these,' Anna says. 'You're too kind.' She closes the door and goes into the kitchen. She lays the roses beside the sink and drags one of the kitchen chairs across to the high shelf where she keeps the vases.

Her mind is racing. Friday night. John went out in the car on *Friday night*. The night Tori died. Everett asked them about that night and John said he'd gone upstairs to watch the stars before coming to bed. He didn't mention that he'd gone out in the car. He lied to Everett. *John lied to her solicitor.* This shocks her, floods her head with cold, clear water.

John would never drive when he was drunk. She'd had that thought less than three hours ago. But on Friday night when Miranda saw him he was definitely drunk.

John is always strong and true – this is her belief.

Except that he isn't – and she's wrong.

Is it John that Isobel is worried about? Has John done something? And when he went to see Tori he was intending to make it right but instead, she ended up dead?

She cuts several of the stems shorter by a few centimetres and arranges the roses in the vase. She sets the vase on the windowsill, stares at it for a few seconds and moves it to the centre of the table. That's not right either so she moves it back to the windowsill again. Then she stops, stands completely still and lets herself breathe. She's making a mountain out of a molehill. Except that, you think you know someone. You're *sure* you know the man you've lived with for twenty-five years. And you know he doesn't keep secrets – but it turns out that he does. And you know he doesn't lie – but it turns out that he does that too.

You're overreacting!

You're not.

Mr Pierce was the sort of man who was happy being a dad and a husband. He didn't look at teenage girls to assess their shagging potential. He would never congratulate his son on how fit his girlfriend was. Tori missed him when she moved to Bishopglen. She didn't miss his lessons – he wasn't as good a teacher as Mr Bradshaw – but just having him around made everything better. She could see why Sister Pierce married him. She hoped to marry a man like him one day.

That's why she stopped short when she was walking past the music block and she saw Mr Wiseman talking to Sister Pierce. When they finished and she was walking away, his eyes followed her. Not like a headmaster's eyes normally would.

Tori wondered if Mr P knew?

Chapter Twenty-Three

John comes into the kitchen. His hair is wet. He's wearing his good jeans and the shirt she bought him for his birthday. His hips bump up against hers as he gets himself a glass of water. 'I thought we could go to the new Thai place for lunch. Their set menu is good, so I hear.' He tells her about someone at the football club who's been there. 'I don't have to be back at work until two thirty. If we get our skates on we have a good couple of hours.'

'Did you go out in the car on Friday night?' The words come out of her mouth before she's aware of speaking them, her tone interested rather than accusing.

John shakes his head as if there's water in his ears. 'No.'

'Miranda says you did.' She reaches for the lagers and holds them out towards him. 'Exhibit A. This is a present for you because apparently she gave you a fright.'

He takes the lagers and lays them on the counter. His eyes flicker. She witnesses this expression often in children – they're caught out in a lie and have to think their way out of it, usually by piling one fabrication on top of another until they're lost in a tangle of spaghetti wires that leads them further and further from the truth.

'I went outside. Sure. But I didn't drive off.'

… *when he pulled into the drive*. 'Where did you go?'

'I didn't go anywhere! I just told you that!'

She feels their closeness dissipate and her heart harden, quite literally, as if anger actually changes the texture of her heart's muscle, from soft, malleable putty to a hard, unyielding stone.

'I would never drive when I'd been drinking.' He's frowning at her. 'You know that.'

And yet you did, she thinks, but she doesn't say that. Instead she says, 'Why didn't you tell me Isobel was self-harming?'

'What?' He's shaking his head again, tiny movements from side to side, his eyes popping, almost comically, as if her sudden change in topic is so ridiculously left-field that he can't keep up.

'Please be honest,' she tells him. Her arms are folded. She knows all about closed and open body language but for the life of her she can't, won't, unfold her arms.

'What is this, Anna?' He moves towards her and she pulls back against the work surface, watches him flinch as he registers her resistance. 'What's going on? Why are you doing this?'

'I want to tell you something. I want to talk to you. But I'm not sure I can trust you.'

'And this is based on *what*?' He throws out an arm towards the front door. 'Our sleep-deprived neighbour who's up most of the night because her kids are sick, telling you that I was out in the car when I wasn't?'

'Why would she make that up?'

'She's confused!'

'Were you out in the car, John?' Her tone is stern and she spots the briefest of hesitations flit across his face. 'You were!' she shouts. It's the first time she's raised her voice.

'I drove to the end of the drive before I acknowledged I was over the limit and shouldn't be driving,' he bites back. 'I turned the car around. I didn't even leave the school grounds.'

'Where were you going?'

'Where do you think?' He slams his fist into the palm of his hand. 'I was going to confront Tori. It was a mad idea, hence the reason I didn't go.'

His explanation makes sense but when people are angry it's more difficult to tell whether they are lying or not. This is a life lesson that's lodged deep in the marrow of Anna's bones and she feels a slip in time that makes her catch her breath.

She was hiding under the stairs, trying not to listen to her parents arguing. When she took her hands away from her ears she heard her father denying all knowledge of this woman called Angela with whom he'd been spotted. His tone was indignant as he shouted, 'How can you accuse me of this! What makes you believe other people before me?'

He sounded so plausible.

When Anna came out from her hiding place her mum said, 'Everything is fine, Anna. Daddy isn't having an affair.'

Anna's cheeks hurt as she tried to smile. She had seen him with Angela. She knew he was lying.

She turns away from her memories, away from John, away from his words and his anger, and stares into the garden, where Monty has got himself into the apple tree. She can see his face poking out in between branches heavy with fruit. He won't be able to get down again and he'll wait patiently until one of the family passes by before giving a meow to attract their attention. Then he'll be lifted down, cuddled, cosseted, fed. Cats have so much to teach us about life, Anna thinks: how to take risks but how to know when the time comes to ask for help; how to attract love, and how to return it. How to leave home and how to find our way back.

Anna closes her eyes tight and then opens them again, blinking. 'Just explain to me,' she says slowly, 'why you didn't tell me about Isobel.'

She's still staring through the window so she doesn't see his face as he replies but she can hear his breathing, the fast inhale, the sigh on the exhale. 'Because she was upset and I promised her.' His tone is a shrug, as if what he did is of no consequence. 'It was a trade-off. She told me that she wouldn't do it again as long as I didn't tell you.'

'You could have told me in confidence.'

'And broken *her* confidence? I had to respect her request. Are you saying you wouldn't have done the same for Noah?'

She takes a moment to ask herself this question but almost immediately decides that she would not have kept details of Noah's mental health from John. She would have told him in private, having sworn him to secrecy, so that he could act on the insight, not mention it to Noah, but modify his behaviour when speaking to him. If she had known about Isobel, she would have made herself more available, kept an eye out for signs that she might be slipping.

Information has a way of dividing people and she doesn't believe parents should ever be divided when it comes to their children. She's seen this happen so many times: one parent says something, knows something, the other parent is on a different page and the child can either exploit the points of difference or swim in the insecure waters that exists between the two viewpoints.

It never ends well.

She swivels back round to face him. 'Do you know a boy called Andrew Dyson?'

'Andrew? He's in my chemistry class. And he plays football at the club. Why?'

'I heard that he and Isobel are seeing each other.'

'Heard from whom? Lynn?'

'No, not Lynn.'

'Who then? Owen?'

'Does it matter who?' she says impatiently. 'Is that really the question you should be asking? The point is, I want to make sure that he's a decent lad. Not involved with the police or—'

'Why would Isobel be going out with someone who was involved with the police?' He is flabbergasted. 'What are you driving at here, Anna?'

'Okay, please.' Her hands are stretched out in front of her, palms facing him. 'The other day before Isobel pushed me, she said' – she pauses to recall her exact words – 'Victoria Carmichael was a scheming little bitch. You don't know the half of what she got up to. And I've had to carry the burden because you're too blind to see what's going on right in front of your face.' Anna gives John a significant look, waits for a shocked expression or frown of concern but the words appear to have no impact. 'I am genuinely afraid that she might know something about what happened to Tori.'

John is staring at Anna as if he doesn't know who she is. 'So, correct me if I'm wrong,' he says, 'but only five minutes ago, you thought I secretly drove out of here on Friday night to talk to, possibly kill' – he raises his eyebrows –'Tori?'

'I never said that—'

'And now, because our daughter, whom we both know to be melodramatic, made some wild statement about

Tori, when really you were the person she was having a problem with, you've decided that she and Andrew Dyson must be involved in her death?'

'No!' she shouts. 'I'm not suggesting anything of the sort! But I feel it, John.' She places her hand over her chest. 'In my heart, in my bones, there is something not right.' *And Isobel's pastoral care record is further evidence.* She should say this but she doesn't because with the mood he's in she doesn't trust him not to spin off. 'Isobel knows something,' she says. 'I'm sure of it.'

'You know what I think, Anna?' He moves closer. 'I think that feeling in your bones says more about you than it does about Isobel. The person you should be interrogating is yourself.' He walks away a few paces then turns back to add, 'Don't judge the rest of us by your own shabby idea of what constitutes the truth.'

She gasps. 'Fuck you, John.'

'You want people to tell you the truth?' He's approaching her again. 'Why not lead by example?' He's in her face now. 'Why not tell the truth about what happened five years ago?'

'Fuck you,' she repeats quietly, and then she does what he normally does – she walks away. She grabs her phone, her shoes, the car keys and leaves the house, slamming the door behind her.

Chapter Twenty-Four

She drives into Bishopglen, through the town and out the other side. She's aware of the countryside thickening, spaces between houses increasing, arable and cattle farms on either side of the road, crops being harvested. Tractors hauling heavily laden trailers trundle ahead of her, their width making them almost impossible to pass.

She's in no hurry. When she's driven for almost an hour she stops at one of the scenic points in the Trossachs National Park. She doesn't get out of the car. She watches people, mostly older couples, pulling on their walking boots, taking photographs on their phones, making sure they have bottles of water before they set off on their walk.

Watching the stuff of ordinary lives is calming but it doesn't take away the sour taste in her mouth from what's just happened with John. So much for thinking she could share the truth with him. She didn't even get as far as talking about Isobel's pastoral care record. She hoped she could, hoped that he would understand why she effectively broke into the medical centre to steal their daughter's file.

But no. She's on her own with this. Because, as usual, he is preoccupied with her promotion. John is convinced she has questions to answer and she can't deny him his right to intuition, she's just tired of having to sidestep his jibes because he never quite gets to the point. He never asks her outright; he expects her to fill in those blanks for him. And she never has because she naively imagined that with every sunrise and sunset the questions would be buried under more recent events, concealed ever deeper until there was no trace.

And anyway, how could he know?

Anna had never been more nervous. She knew she wasn't the strongest candidate. Her CV lacked two key features: Bishopglen was the only school she had ever worked in and she could show barely any evidence of leadership qualities. She hoped she made up for her lack of other school experience by the fact that she was a known quantity. Her rapport with children, staff and parents spoke for itself. And although she had never run a medical department, she had been in charge for two months when the lead nurse was off sick.

The interview panel was made up of three people: Owen Wiseman and two of the school governors. As she sat down in front of them, Owen's eyes were encouraging and it gave her the confidence to speak with authority about the role and what she could bring to it.

When, only two days later, she heard that she'd been successful she cried with relief. They would be given a home to live in and a huge reduction in school fees, but more than that, she felt they could now breathe easy again as a family, and as a couple. John was as happy as she was. 'You must have impressed them,' he said. 'Good for you.' He hugged her hard and then called the children, 'Kids! Come and hear what your mum's done! We need to celebrate.'

Anna sits for over an hour, her limbs stiffening, her neck beginning to hurt. She needs a hot drink. She remembers driving past a café a few miles back and she starts the engine, heads back along the road. It's as she's parking that her mobile rings. For a few mad seconds she imagines it will be John, apologising, saying that she's right to be concerned about what Isobel might know, telling her that he'll keep an eye out for Andrew Dyson, see whether he can suss anything out.

But it isn't John; it's Patrick Everett. He's just spoken with Murray and the post-mortem results are in. Anna should meet him at the police station at four o'clock and they can go over the findings. 'Did he tell you what the findings are?' Anna asks.

'All he would say is that Victoria's death is suspicious.' He pauses to allow Anna to say something. She remains silent. 'See you at three.'

Anna forgets about the tea. Her mouth is dry but she knows that she won't be able to hold a cup, never mind swallow liquid. Her hands are shaking and her stomach churns. She grips the steering wheel tightly and drives to Bishopglen town centre. As the car eats up the miles, Isobel slips to the back of her mind and the comments on the Facebook page push to the front. The trolls will be looking out for her. If they spot her, she'll be photographed, and however she looks – sad, confident, nervous, normal, anxious, carefree – it will be used against her. If she looks upset that will be because she's guilty and has been caught out. If she looks confident, that won't be because she's innocent – it will be because she doesn't care.

To make matters worse, there are no free parking spaces close to the police station and she has to park over one hundred metres down the road. She's wearing jeans and a plain jacket – nothing that would make her stand out – but it's rare for her to come to town and not bump into someone she knows. So many children have been through Bishopglen and most of them still live in the area. Parents, grandparents, people who worked in the school – she'll be lucky not to be spotted by someone who knows her.

She keeps her head down as she walks towards the building, almost scuttling the last few metres as she runs up the steps and into the reception, where Everett is sitting waiting for her. 'Perfect timing,' he says, standing up. 'Murray's just poked his head around the door. He's waiting for us along the hallway.'

The desk sergeant buzzes them through and they walk along a corridor that smells of cabbage. Someone is shouting in the room at the end, swear words turning the air blue. They go into a room halfway along and find Murray seated at the table waiting for them. As soon as they sit down he starts the tape, names the people in the room and begins with his questions.

'Did you know that Victoria wrote a diary?'

'Yes.' Anna nods, feels her heart skip a beat. *Where is this going?* 'She told me that she liked to write things down. It helped her make sense of everything in her head.'

'It was where she wrote down all her secrets?'

'I believe so, yes. That's normal for teenage girls.' Anna waits for him to tell her that one of the entries in Tori's diary mentions Anna assaulting her but he doesn't.

'We've searched her school dorm and her locker, and her bedrooms in both her father's and mother's homes, but we've been unable to find it. Do you have any idea where it might be?'

Anna shakes her head. 'I'm sorry. I never saw the diary. I have no idea where it is.'

'Her mother tells us the book is A5 in size, more than an inch thick, red in colour.' He holds a book out to

Anna. 'Exactly like this one, in fact. Would you like to have a look at it?'

Anna takes the book and opens it in several places. It's brand new and completely blank. 'I'm sorry, that doesn't help me remember. I really haven't seen it before.'

'She didn't have it in her school bag when she came to see you for mentoring sessions?'

'Her bag was normally closed. It had a flap that came over the top.' She moves her hands to illustrate. 'If I'm remembering correctly, it's a greeny-brown colour and has an all-over camouflage pattern.'

'We have found her bag,' he affirms. 'So she never went into her bag when she was with you? Say, for example, to find a pen?'

'No.'

Showing you some of her school work, perhaps?'

'No.'

'I think my client has answered this question, DC Murray,' Everett says. 'Would you be good enough to share with us the results of the post-mortem?'

Murray takes time to shuffle through papers before passing one to Everett. 'This is the preliminary report. Further tests are yet to be completed.'

Anna doesn't look at the page. She's expecting the worst. She's expecting it to say that Victoria Carmichael died from a bleed in her brain, this the result of a historic injury – the assault she sustained forty-eight hours earlier.

Anna is holding her breath.

'Toxicology?' Everett says.

'Nothing of note. No drugs. No alcohol,' Murray says. He pauses the tape and stands up. 'I expect you want five minutes to discuss the findings with your client?'

'Thank you.' Everett gives a perfunctory bow of his head before turning to Anna. 'It's what I was expecting

– there's insufficient evidence to be clear about exactly what took place.' He seems pleased with this. 'She was found at the bottom of the stairs and sustained a serious fracture to the base of her skull. An injury that would have killed her almost instantly.' He pauses before saying quietly, 'There are four partial fingerprints on the back of Victoria's T-shirt, a suggestion that she might have been pushed.'

Anna recoils, frowning. 'Someone pushed her down the stairs?'

'Possibly.'

'Jesus.' Anna's hand goes over her mouth. Everett passes her a bottle of water and she lifts it to her lips, her hands shaking so much that some spills down her front.

'You're in the clear, Anna,' Everett says. 'You can begin to relax again.'

Anna stares down at the bottle in her lap. How can she be in the clear if the post-mortem is inconclusive?

'I know this has been extremely difficult for you,' Everett acknowledges. He is eating a muesli bar, happily munching through it as he takes notes on his yellow legal pad. 'But it won't be long until you're out the other side and you can get on with your life.'

Chapter Twenty-Five

When DC Murray comes back into the room, Everett glances up from his writing to say, 'I would have thought my client was free to go, Detective. Bearing in mind her husband will give her an alibi for the night of Victoria's death.'

'Mrs Pierce remains a suspect with regards to the assault.'

'Alleged assault,' Everett interjects quickly.

'And bearing in mind the fact that Victoria may have died as a result of the assault—'

'There is no assertion in the post-mortem that Victoria died as a result of the injury she sustained last Wednesday evening,' Everett states. 'In fact, the fingerprints on the back of the T-shirt are a clear indication that Victoria was pushed.'

Murray ignores this. 'We were hoping you might help us with a couple of further points,' he says, staring directly at Anna.

Inside Anna is screaming 'No!' but what comes out of her mouth is, 'Of course.' It makes her think about her mother, who always said that she should have an outside and an inside face. It was one of the things that drove her dad away, that constant pretence in front of others.

Murray shuffles his papers again, moving the one at the bottom of the pile to the top. 'So, Victoria's mother,

Saskia Wilson, has given us a statement detailing what happened on the night Victoria died. Ms Wilson checked on her daughter at around ten. She said Victoria was lying on her bed writing in her diary. She said hello to her mum, seemed in good spirits, and then Ms Wilson retired to bed. At twenty past one, she woke to the sound of voices coming from Victoria's bedroom.'

Twenty past one, Anna thinks. Miranda saw John coming back at one so he couldn't have been there, could he? Not unless he went back. *Stop thinking like this!* John wouldn't hurt anyone. It's just not in his nature.

'Ms Wilson thought that Victoria was watching something online,' Murray is saying. 'She was going to ask her to turn the volume down but she nodded off again. Five minutes later, she heard a loud thump, followed almost immediately by the front door slamming. She got out of bed and found her daughter at the bottom of the stairs. She called an ambulance then attempted CPR. The ambulance arrived ten minutes later and the paramedics took over but unfortunately Victoria was pronounced dead on her arrival at the hospital.' He looks up from his notes and says to Anna. 'Do you know anyone who would have reason to kill Victoria, Mrs Pierce?'

'No.' Anna feels hollow inside. She doesn't want to imagine what she would feel – the panic, the shock, the overwhelming grief – if she found her daughter at the bottom of the stairs, not breathing, her skull fractured.

Isobel. She doesn't suspect her of pushing Tori. Not really. But suppose she went there to reason with her? She's clearly capable of sneaking out of the dorm at night. She could have gone there with Andrew. At first to talk to Tori but the talking turned into shouting and then the push – it could have been an accident, Or not. Anna shudders.

'Are you all right, Mrs Pierce?'

'Yes, thank you.' She clears her throat. 'This is all very difficult to process.'

Murray nods. She imagines she sees genuine empathy in his eyes. 'I'm sure Mr Everett has mentioned that on the back of Victoria's T-shirt there is evidence of four partial fingerprints?'

'He has.'

'I wonder whether you would agree to us taking your prints? For the purpose of exclusion,' he adds quickly.

'There is no legal requirement for you to do this, Anna,' Everett says. He's sitting back with his arms folded across his chest.

'Of course I'm willing,' Anna says. 'I want to help.' I always want to help, she thinks. I'm one of those people who steps up, volunteers, puts her money where her mouth is.

'Thank you.' Murray gives her a brief smile. 'The sooner we can expedite matters for you, the better. There's just one more thing.' Murray holds up a finger. 'The witness. From the night of the assault,' he adds. 'We have video footage that was taken on one of the girls' phones.'

Drops of ice land on Anna's spine. She shivers.

'Are you sure you're all right, Mrs Pierce?'

'I'm just a bit cold.' She senses Everett giving her a side-eye look. She pulls at her cardigan so that it tightens around her ribcage.

'Are you ready to watch the video?' Murray asks.

Anna nods, sits forward in her seat, her eyes on the laptop computer. An image of the school woods appears on screen. Two figures are barely visible in the distance. One of the figures has a light but it's shining down towards the ground. There is an argument taking place, voices are raised but the words are indistinct. The voices sound like female but it's hard to be completely sure. Anna can make out the odd word, 'don't care', 'my dad' and what sounds like 'Mr P'.

After a couple of minutes, it looks as if one figure lunges towards the other and there is a high-pitched scream. A girl comes running towards the camera, clutching at her cheek. The security light is triggered and the girl looks up. It's Victoria Carmichael. When the camera pans back towards the wood, the other figure has gone. The video ends there.

'Before we go any further, DC Murray,' Everett says, holding up his hand. 'I would like to have a private word with my client.'

'There's more,' Murray says. 'Would you like to see that before you advise your client?'

'Yes, please,' says Everett.

The next video is taken in Tori's dorm. She is sitting on the bed, her face wet with tears. An angry, red mark covers one of her cheeks. Anna's hand goes up to her mouth, shocked to see Tori up close like this. This is Tori, injured, but still very much alive. 'Tell everyone what happened,' says a voice Anna recognises as Amanda's, Tori's dorm mate.

'I wanted to talk to Sister Pierce about my dad,' Tori says. She holds a piece of paper towards the camera. Amanda zooms in on the page and the words come into focus. Anna manages to read: *I hope you'll be happy for us—* And then the camera moves up to focus on Tori's face. 'I waited for her outside because I knew she'd be walking home that way.' She pauses, and Amanda moves in closer so that her blue eyes almost fill the frame. 'I tried to talk to her but she got really mad and then she hit me.' She turns sideways so that the camera focuses on her red cheek.

'Does it hurt?' Amanda asks.

'Yes.' She starts to cry again, a stream of tears wetting her cheeks. 'Not that much but …' She sniffs and wipes the back of her hand across her face. 'It's more hurtful that she wouldn't speak to me.'

'Because she's your mentor!' Amanda says, her tone indignant.

'I know.' Tori stares at the camera, her expression a mixture of anger and pain. Then she lifts her hand and covers the lens with a finger. 'Turn it off now,' she says quietly.

The screen goes blank.

Anna's head is down as DC Murray stands up. 'Five minutes enough?'

'Thank you,' Everett replies.

'And just so you know.' He stands at the door and looks back at them. 'Our forensic technicians are working to make the sound and image clearer.'

The door closes behind him and Everett says, 'Anna? Talk to me.'

Anna raises her head. Her eyes are wet with tears. 'I don't know what to say.'

'Start with the truth. Anything you tell me is privileged, and I'm in a far better position to defend you if I know the truth.'

'It wasn't me.' She grits her teeth. 'I didn't hit her.'

'Bearing in mind they might be able to improve the video quality?'

'I didn't hit her,' Anna repeats. 'Do you think it looked like me?' She starts back frowning. 'Did you?'

'No,' Everett concedes. 'It's impossible to tell who it is.' He rummages in his pocket and pulls out another muesli bar. 'Would you like some?'

'No, thank you.' Anna stares at the chipped paintwork

on the door surround as if she'll find some answers there. Staring and staring, trying to focus on the wood and not the look in Tori's eyes when she faced the camera, her expression so pained, so emotionally wounded.

But so alive.

And now she's dead.

Let down by an adult who wouldn't stop to speak to her. Wouldn't answer her text pleading for help. An adult who is trained in child safeguarding. Who was genuinely fond of this girl, wanted her to succeed, wanted her to go on to live a happy, fulfilled life.

And that adult is me, Anna thinks.

How could I have let this happen?

She was pissed off when Sister Pierce didn't give her permission to miss swimming. She spent the whole lesson in a sulk and then went to the library. Her dad's email pinged into her inbox just after four o'clock. She read it several times, then printed it out and put it in her pocket. When she returned to the boarding house, Isobel and Pippa were in the front hall. Isobel said hello but Tori ignored her and went up to her room. Her pin-board was covered in photographs and in every single one she was with her dad. She grabbed them off the board, twice stabbing her finger with the drawing pins, enough to draw blood that stained their smiling faces. She didn't wipe off the blood. She stared at each of the happy memories: swimming in Loch Fyne, a day trip to Edinburgh Castle, eating burgers from a fast food van after seeing Celtic beat Rangers, a holiday in the Algarve, half term at Center Parcs.

Her hands moved quickly as she tore up each of the photographs and cast the pieces out of the window. She watched as the wind lifted up the fragments of smiles and sky, and carried them off into the woods.

After supper she went to the medical centre to talk to Sister Pierce but she held up her hand and mouthed, 'Not right now.' Okay, so she was calling an ambulance and Tori should have felt sympathetic, if only she could have found one ounce of sympathy for a child who was clearly faking it.

She read the email again:

Dear Tori

   Mandy and I are getting married in spring next year. I'll hope you'll be happy for us! Mandy is really looking forward to meeting you. She's suggested you could be a bridesmaid! She also has a sixteen-year-old daughter. We think you'll really get on. You can be bridesmaids together.

   Lots of love

   Dad xx

She should feel happy for him, shouldn't she? But there were three things wrong. First, she knew Mandy's daughter from inter-school netball. All she could talk about was the most shaggable boys on Love Island. *How could her dad think she would get on with her? Second, he didn't even know how old she was. She's not sixteen till October. And third, why was he calling her Tori? He never called her that, always Vic, after his mother.*

It was as if he didn't know her at all.

The door opens and DC Murray comes back in. He's whistling tunelessly and jiggling the coins in his pocket. It makes a change from the silence but it grates on Anna's nerves; makes her itch to blurt out whatever he wants to hear so that she can get the interview over with and leave the room. How to indirectly break the suspect. No words required, just irritating mannerisms and noises.

'So, where were we?' he asks, knowing full well.

'The videos,' Everett says.

'Of course. Mrs Pierce?' She lifts her head. 'Did you want to change your statement?'

'No.'

'Despite Victoria's speech to camera and the video of the argument outside?'

'As I've already explained, Tori was known for telling lies.'

'You're sure that wasn't you in the woods?'

'DC Murray, I have dozens, sometimes hundreds, of interactions every day,' Anna says flatly. 'I'd been on shift since eight in the morning, taught three lessons, attended two meetings, had to call an ambulance and in between all of that, at least thirty children came to the medical centre, but I still know that wasn't me.'

'She was outside after curfew. She was a girl you mentored, a girl with whom you had a close relationship. From what you've told me about yourself, I think it's extremely likely you would have stopped to talk to her for longer than you've previously stated.'

'I thought she'd gone straight back inside. And, as I said, I was tired. Perhaps I was—' She stops.

'Perhaps you were …?' he prompts.

'Look, I regret not stopping to speak to her, to help her.' Everett taps the table with his pen. Anna ignores him. 'I wish I had. Then quite possibly none of this would have happened. And I have to live with that.' She presses a fist to her chest. 'For the rest of my life I'll know that I had two opportunities to help this girl, once on that night and again when she texted me.' Everett's tapping increases in volume and she turns to him. 'I have to say this.' She takes a breath, stares down at the table as she thinks through her next few words. 'I made an error of judgement and I hold my hands up to that. But the rest of it? It wasn't me.'

DC Murray sits back in his seat, a frown line deepening between his eyes. 'But what I don't understand is why Victoria would say it was you if it wasn't?'

'All I know is that there was something going on in the last couple of weeks and it affected her behaviour. I think it most likely concerned her dad.' Anna points towards the laptop. 'What was in the letter that she held up to camera? There wasn't time to read more than a line.'

DC Murray doesn't answer her. Instead he says, 'So you admit that you saw Victoria as you left school, at exactly the time this incident outside was filmed, but you maintain that it wasn't you she was arguing with at the entrance to the woods?'

'My interaction with Victoria was over in thirty seconds or less.'

'So she met someone else immediately after you left?'

Anna shrugs. 'She must have.'

'Do you have any idea who that might have been?'

'None,' Anna says, her eyes sliding from his to her hands under the table, her knuckles white and bloodless.

'When I spoke to your husband earlier, he thought that Mr P could be referring to him as his pupils often shorten his name. Victoria would be likely to call him Mr Pierce when talking to anyone other than you, don't you agree?'

'You spoke to my husband?' Anna's eyes sting so that when she looks at Everett for clarification her face is painfully screwed up.

'I showed him the video a couple of hours ago,' Murray says.

Everett raises his eyebrows. Anna takes that to mean he didn't know John was being questioned. Murray must have called John just after their argument.

'He confirmed your alibi for the time of death, Mrs Pierce.' Murray's eyes probe hers. She looks away. 'Your husband reports that you were home all night.'

Anna frowns down at her shoes. She wonders if this makes her look guilty but there's nothing she can do about it. She is unable to lift her head because she is suffering another time slip. The world has looped back on itself and she has a sudden clear image of the policeman who spoke to her when she was fifteen. His name was William Dick, which would normally have made her giggle, had it not been for the fact that she was sick with anxiety.

'We won't be long, Anna,' PC Dick said to her. 'We're just checking to see where your mum is.'

She nodded, unable to speak, unable to even breathe because she knew something had happened to her mum. She'd heard the tail end of a whisper from the corridor '... told her about her mum?' And the answer, ' ... waiting for a WPC ...' She'd strained her ears to hear more but couldn't make out the rest of it.

'Would you like to watch the video again?' Murray asks.

Anna has been holding her breath and she gulps in some air. 'No. I find it upsetting.'

'Because she's telling the truth?' he says gently. He leans his elbows on the table. 'I understand how hard it must be to admit to something like this. You are a good person, an upstanding member of the community, well respected in your school.' His voice is persuasive. 'But there's no shame in losing your temper, Anna. She was a difficult girl. Everyone says so.' He shrugs. 'You were pushed to your limits, it was late in the evening and there she was, waiting for you—'

'I find it upsetting because she's dead,' Anna interrupts. 'I've said all along that, first, I felt her behaviour changed over the last few weeks, perhaps because of her dad's new woman, and second she is – she was – a girl who frequently lied.' Anna pauses, feels tears spring into her eyes. 'I sound harsh but I don't mean to. Young people make mistakes and I'm sure that had she lived, she would have grown out of the lie-telling but the fact remains that she did lie.' She takes a tissue from her pocket and holds it in her hand. 'I would like to return to work, DC Murray, before my career is damaged beyond repair.'

Murray nods. 'As the PM is inconclusive as to cause of death we are obliged to continue with our investigations. With no blood or alcohol in her body, it's unlikely she would have fallen downstairs. So either she was pushed or she fell, perhaps after a blackout linked to the original head injury.'

'Is there any proof of a blackout?' Everett asks.

'Not at the moment, no. But further tests could indicate as much.'

'I was hoping the post-mortem report would put an end to all the speculation about me being involved in her death,' Anna says, panic rising. 'Not only am I worried about my job but there are some vicious comments about me on social media. And I was doorstepped by a journalist from the local paper.'

'Did you give the journalist a statement?'

'No.' Anna shakes her head. 'I didn't get the feeling she was particularly interested in the truth.'

'The justice system is our tool for punishment, not

social or print media, and my client has neither been arrested nor charged,' Everett says, sounding as if he's making a speech to the crowd. 'The ubiquitous outraged who hide their own transgressions while targeting others should be unmasked.'

Murray stares at him, expressionless. 'We are monitoring the online comments but, as the law stands, the commentators are not breaking any.'

'Could I at least leave the station through the back door?' Anna asks.

'Of course.' They all stand up. 'Let's take your prints and then you can get off home.'

Taking prints is a speedy process. The palms of her hands are placed on a computer screen and the trace memorised. Five minutes later she's outside the back door with Everett.

'John didn't tell you he'd been questioned?' Everett asks.

'No.' She sighs. 'We had an argument ...' She trails off. 'I was out driving when you called me.' She bites her lip. 'John and I, we don't fight often but this is putting a strain on things.' She tries to laugh. 'To put it mildly.'

'Hang tough, Anna. We're almost through this,' Everett says, clapping a hand on her shoulder. 'I spoke with Lynn this morning. She mentioned that Murray will be questioning Victoria's classmates tomorrow. Lynn will be accompanying them.'

'That's good,' Anna says. She hasn't spoken to Lynn today. Now that she is being promoted to the SMT, Anna knows her loyalties will be pulled in opposing directions. She hopes their friendship will survive the strain.

Anna watches Everett drive off in his MG. The street is empty of people apart from two children at the far end kicking a football against the wall. The quickest route back to the car park would take her past the front of the station. Hugging the side of the building, she peeks around the corner and then sharply pulls her head back in. A man and a woman are waiting outside; both of them are on their mobiles. She doesn't know what Suzy Meeks or Steve Mulberry look like. These two people might have nothing to do with the Facebook page but she doesn't want to risk it.

She hurries along the street that runs parallel, keeping her head down. She's barely taken a dozen steps before a voice calls out, 'Sister Pierce! Wait!'

She quickens her step, her heart in her throat, hears the voice calling out again. And then the hand on her arm.

Chapter Twenty-Six

She shakes the hand off her arm, her head flooding with an extended second of panic before her eyes focus and she recognises Mungo Todd and his son Alfie.

Mungo grabs her in a crushing hug. 'Am I glad to have bumped into you!' he says. 'I've been wanting to get in touch but was afraid of intruding.'

'It's good to see you, Mungo,' she says, her smile tight as her heartbeat slows. She thanks him for setting up the Facebook page. 'I really appreciate the support.'

'It was the least I could do, the very least. Nobody has helped Alfie as much as you have.' He places a large hand on his son's head. 'Say hello to Sister Pierce, Alfie.' Alfie says hello, then takes the opportunity to pull his dad's phone out of his pocket to find a game to play. 'I'm getting a petition together. I've spoken to Mr Wiseman and he's all for it,' Mungo says. 'I've also asked him to tackle Julia Raeburn. She's far and away the worst.' He puts his hands over his son's ears. 'You've not been reading any of that shite, have you? Excuse my French.'

'I have.' She bites her lip. 'It's nasty ... scary stuff.'

'We'll fight them, Anna.' Concern puckers his forehead. 'Lynn Sykes is helping, and so are over a dozen of the teachers and parents.'

'Well, hopefully it'll all be over soon.' She mentions the post-mortem results. 'It's horrible to think of her dying like that.'

'Poor kid,' Mungo agrees. 'And a very clever girl by all accounts?'

Anna tells him about John's reaction when he first started teaching her and how proud he was when she won the academic scholarship. It feels good to praise her. So much has been said about her lying. Anna doesn't want her to be remembered that way. She wants her to be remembered as a girl with huge potential who was funny, articulate and intelligent.

Anna says goodbye to Mungo and Alfie and takes a short cut through the churchyard. This was a route they often took when Noah and Isobel were young. They would practise their word skills by reading the gravestone inscriptions, Anna helping with the tricky ones that were difficult to make out, the stone worn smooth by time and weather. They would imagine the people's lives, tell each other stories about how they might have lived and died. The children soon knew the names by heart and would always pause with a thoughtful reverence at the gravestones of three young siblings who died in a house fire more than one hundred years ago.

Anna sits down on a bench surrounded by the dead. She has nothing to rush home for – there's a conversation to be had with John, but for now it can wait. When she closes her eyes, she sees her children, one on a scooter and the other on a bike, giggling as they race each other. 'Not too fast now!' she shouts, and they slow down for a couple of seconds before speeding up again.

Between nine and thirteen are the best ages, Anna thinks. They can walk for miles, are excited by everything and love being with their parents. Younger than nine and there might still be tantrums, tiredness and an urgent need for food and drink. Older than thirteen, and hormones have raised their ugly heads, sneaking into the bloodstream to wreak their own particular havoc – does he love me, does he not, am I big enough, strong enough, fast enough. There's moodiness and secretiveness, and spending time with parents ceases to be their first choice.

When Noah was twelve and Isobel had just turned ten, they went to Florida for a holiday. John had been cramming in some chemistry tuition during the Easter holidays and so they had money to spare. Three days in Disneyland and then upstate to the Kennedy Space Center. They were all in awe of the size of the Saturn V moon rocket and the science behind space travel. And then they spent several days canoeing along a river close to Gainesville – Anna and Noah were in one canoe, Isobel and John in the other. 'From the future to the past,' Noah had said. 'From space travel to canoeing along an ancient American river!'

Looking back on it now, Anna sees that this was when they reached their peak of closeness and enjoyment as a family. They didn't realise it at the time, of course, but such is the cruelty of hindsight.

When she arrives back home she doesn't climb out of the car immediately but stares straight ahead at the row of three houses: Miranda and Peter on one side, Geraldine and Bob on the other. Bob's car isn't there because he goes to practise bowls most evenings before the light fades. Geraldine will likely be home, though, because it's her day off. Anna thinks back to her conversation with Owen. It seems like days ago, now, but it was only this morning. This is one thing she might be able to make better.

She knocks on Geraldine's door and waits. No reply so she goes through the side gate and sees her colleague at the bottom of the garden weeding the vegetable beds. Anna walks towards her and Geraldine turns at the sound of her steps, stands up and removes her gardening gloves.

'I'm sorry,' Anna calls out. 'I've come to apologise.'

'For what?'

'For logging in as you.'

Geraldine stares briefly at the sky then gestures towards the house. 'Let's go inside.'

She makes them both a mug of tea and then they sit down at the dining table. Geraldine's house is neater than Anna's, the tablecloth pressed, the view through the window unobscured by books, letters, candles – just some of the things that end up on the family's window-sills for weeks on end.

'I …' Anna stalls. 'I did it because …' She shakes her head. 'Because I needed to see Isobel's records.'

'A double deceit.' Geraldine's lips are tight. 'You log on as me and you break confidentiality.'

'I know. I—'

'Why?' Geraldine's tone says it all. She's not just angry; she's also disappointed. 'Why did you want to see her records?'

Anna tells her about the argument, about Isobel pushing her and what she said about Tori. 'I was turning myself inside out, and I still had my keys and—' She sighs. 'It was wrong. It was an abuse of your trust and hers.'

Anna has Geraldine's full attention and she feels brave enough, tired enough, desperate enough, to hold eye contact until her armour falls away, piece by shiny piece. Underneath there is a naked honesty. She takes a quick breath before she says, 'I'm worried, Geraldine. I think that Isobel is in trouble and that this could be history repeating itself, that this will be the moment our family implodes and there is no stopping it. I know that you've been good enough never to remind me of the time when you found me drunk and … '

'This is about your mum?' Geraldine states, her expression softening.

It was eight o'clock in the evening, the anniversary of her mum's death, and the ghost of her own mistake rose up to taunt her. She was trying to drown that ghost in alcohol when the doorbell rang. She squinted against the June sunshine, surprised by the light when she was neck deep in her own darkness. Geraldine was standing on the doorstep carrying a bag of home-grown produce: a dozen eggs, spinach and courgettes. 'We have a glut,' she said.

Anna barely knew Geraldine. She had been working at Bishopglen for less than a term and they had exchanged information relating to their job but little else. Anna didn't remember inviting her in, but somehow she ended up sitting at Anna's kitchen table. It turned out that she was a good listener. She was wise; her advice was direct. And she was as close-mouthed as a priest. As far as Anna knew, she told no one about her confession, for that was what it was – an unburdening of the part she played in her mother's death. 'You were a child,' Geraldine told her. 'We all make mistakes as children but most of us are lucky enough to get away with it.'

'I've always been afraid that one of my children might make the kind of mistake that I made,' Anna says. Her voice trembles. 'I can't shake the feeling that, somehow, Isobel is involved in Tori's death.'

'Have you spoken to her about it?'

'Well, I can't because I'm not supposed to know any of this.' She rubs her hip where the bruise still lingers. 'I think … I haven't been a good enough mother. Or not the sort of mother Isobel needs. She told me that I neglect her and Noah in favour of the children at school.'

'Anna.' Geraldine dismisses this with a snort. 'That's nonsense!'

Anna rubs at her forehead. 'That's what I'm hoping but I can't deny her her feelings.'

'It seems to me that you have to get past all this and speak to her. Get John onside first.'

Anna's forehead puckers in a frown. 'We're not on best terms at the moment.'

Geraldine leans across the table and takes Anna's hand. 'Talk to John. And then you can both talk to Isobel. For what it's worth, I don't think Isobel could be involved in assaulting Tori or in her death.'

'Did she – I shouldn't ask – but did she say any more than you wrote in the notes?'

'No, Anna. And I have no idea what was bothering her. If I did I would urge her to tell you.' She stands up. 'Come on, now. Go back home. Speak to both your children. Get everyone talking. And I'll leave you to tell Mr Wiseman!' she calls after her.

Anna takes Geraldine's advice. As soon as the front door closes behind her, she calls Noah. He replies almost at once. 'How are you, Mum? What's happening?'

She tells him about the post-mortem and the fact that she has his dad as an alibi for the time of Tori's death. 'My solicitor reckons it will all be over in a day or two. For me, at least.'

'Good news, Mum!'

'And without wanting to tempt fate, I wondered whether you were free to come home on Friday? I'll ask Isobel too and we'll have a meal together.'

'Definitely. I was coming back for Pippa's party

anyway.' Of course, the party on Saturday, and Anna
promised to help Lynn with the preparations. 'Love you,
Mum.' She hears someone in the background call his
name. 'See you Friday.'

Next, she texts Isobel.

Hi Isobel, I'd like you to please come home on Friday
for a family supper. I know I've let you down recently but I
want to make it up to you. Noah will be home. I promise to
be the best mum I can be. Lots of love xxx

She doesn't wait for a reply – she'll be lucky to get one
– but immediately calls Lynn, who answers after five rings.

'Hi. How's it going?' Lynn's tone is hushed.

'The post-mortem results are in. It looks like Tori
might have been pushed down the stairs.'

'Really?' Lynn keeps her voice low. 'Do the police
have any idea who might have done it?'

'If they do, they're not telling me,' Anna says. She
hears the click of a door closing. 'Sorry, are you busy?'

'Owen's here. And Peter's just back from Yorkshire.
He's here too,' Lynn says, her voice louder now. 'His
mum's been sick.'

'I heard.'

'I'm not going to ask you anything about Isobel's
records, Anna.' She pauses. 'Because I know that Owen
has already spoken to you.'

'The security breach.'

'Exactly.' She takes a breath. 'Listen, I want us to
separate out what happens at school and home. We're
friends, and that's more important to me than anything.'

Anna smiles into the handset, relief and happiness in
equal measure. 'Sounds good to me. And I hear you're
on the SMT now.'

'I know! Me? Senior management? Can you imagine?'

They both start laughing. 'But they asked me, and with so much focus on young people's mental wellbeing I thought – why not?'

'You'll be great. You'll bring a unique perspective. Shake them up a bit.'

'I hope so. I also want to involve myself more in the school's drug-taking policy. I think we could do better in terms of education and support.'

'Sadie's often suspicious that drugs are getting into the girls' boarding house.'

'I'll speak to her about it.' Her voice quickens. 'I'd better go, Anna. But I'll call you tomorrow. We could meet for a coffee?'

'Any time,' Anna says.

It's past ten o'clock and John isn't anywhere to be seen. She's disappointed because after talking to Geraldine she feels ready to answer his questions as honestly as she can. He can ask her anything. No more tiptoeing around the sleeping lion. 'Let's wake the lion up and see how sharp its claws are,' she says out loud, staring down at Monty, who is trailing around her ankles, meowing his enthusiasm for something to eat. She opens a tin of his favourite tuna, grabs a handful of crackers and a hunk of cheese for herself, and sits down with her laptop. She opens the Facebook page and three words jump out at her: **bitch**, **killer**, **video**. She gets herself a glass of wine and takes two generous mouthfuls before reading the comments.

Dave Carmichael
Sorry I've been silent, folks. Emotional couple of days.
I went to Bishopglen yesterday evening to collect Vic's belongings. The girls in her year had made a card for me and her mother. They seemed like genuine girls but I

couldn't help thinking that they weren't all that nice to her
when she was alive. One of the girls, Amanda I think her
name was, said she filmed the incident where the nurse hit
Vic. She forwarded the video to Vic but the police took her
mobile so I haven't seen it. Has anyone seen it?

Also, the head spoke to me. Commiserations and
all that. And then, get this, he said, Could we tone it down
on the Facebook page – and I'm like, Who are you to tell
me how to grieve? There are some good people on that
site and maybe you don't like some of the things that are
being said but home truths hurt.

And then this morning I went to the police station.
It's with much sadness that I tell you the post-mortem
is inconclusive. Bottom line – there was no alcohol and
drugs in her system. She might have fallen or she might
have been pushed down the stairs. My only consolation
is that she died instantly. I meant to ask the police about
the video footage but I couldn't speak. My fiancée drove
me home and we've just been sitting looking at photos of
Vic.

Thank you for helping me get through this, friends. I
need you all.

There are more than thirty replies to this, most of them
supportive.

Jesus.

That's horrific.

I feel for you, man.

And then someone calling themselves Admiral Nelson
has posted:

Hate to break up your party, but Victoria's mum is no saint. I know someone who worked with her and she has a history of violence. Is that true, Dave?

Dave doesn't reply but several other people land on the comment in seconds:

Piss right off, you wanker.

Have the guts to at least put your real name.

Get off this page! We're here to support Tori's mum and dad not throw mud.

Holly Standing has posted two dozen photos of Tori and her enjoying themselves over the summer holidays but Anna barely looks at them.

There's a long discussion about evidence, DNA and CCTV before someone says they saw Anna go into the police station and waited around outside but never saw her come back out.

We should have been at the back door

Won't happen next time.

And then the comments take another turn.

Where does the nurse live?

On the school grounds.

There are loads of houses on the grounds.

Anna's heart flips over. It wouldn't be that hard to find out which house is hers. At once her ears strain to listen and she straightens her back, her eyes wide. The only sound is the hum of the fridge-freezer and the rasp of her own breathing. She creeps to the window and pulls the curtain aside an inch or two. It's pitch-black outside. If anyone comes within range of the house the outside lights will be triggered.

She calls John; his mobile goes straight to voicemail. 'It's me, John. I'm sorry about earlier. I'm going a bit crazy, I know. We need to talk. Will you be home soon? The Internet trolls are discussing where we live. I'm going to check all the windows, double-lock the doors. Give me a call if you don't have your key. I'll wait up.'

She moves quickly round the house checking all the entry points, tightening window latches and double-locking the front and back doors. Then she calls DC Murray – it's almost eleven, she's not expecting him to answer, and he doesn't. She leaves him a message telling him about the Facebook page and asking whether it can be made clear that she is not in the frame for Tori's murder.

She sits down on the sofa and switches on the TV, channel hops for a minute or more and then switches it off again because she won't be able to hear if someone tries to break in. Would they break in? Or would they smash a window? Paint KILLER NURSE on the front door? Put dog mess through the letterbox?

'What do you think, Monty?' she asks. He has curled himself into a ball on her lap, a warm, heavy weight that grounds her and reminds her that she is loved and needed. 'We make a good team, you and me.' She loses her fingers in his fur and rests her head against the back of the sofa.

It's not long before her eyes close.

Chapter Twenty-Seven

With the first bang on the door, her eyes spring open and Monty leaps off her knee. As the second bang sounds, she's on her feet and Monty has scarpered under the couch. She grabs hold of the poker before the third bang shakes her insides so violently that the tremor travels down both her legs into her feet. She stumbles to one side and grabs hold of the mantelpiece. The police! Call the police! She feels her back pockets but her mobile isn't there; she must have left it on the kitchen table.

She runs from the living room through the hallway to the kitchen, the fourth bang sounding even louder so that she screams again and quickens her pace, sliding on the kitchen floor and jarring her knee against the chair leg. Her mobile isn't on the table and the landline phone isn't in the cradle. It never is because they barely use it. The back door! She'll go out the back door and knock on Geraldine's door.

Her shaking fingers fumble with the double locks until, by some miracle, the door swings open. She listens, hears another bang from the front and stifles a scream. She's only wearing socks and immediately the wet ground soaks through to the soles of her feet. She tiptoes over the grass and triggers the light, feels exposed in the open space and runs back to the house wall, where she stands stock still. She can hear voices at the front.

'I think she's' – a bout of coughing – 'locked me out.'

It's John! John is talking to Geraldine. Anna lets out her held breath, her eyes filling with tears of relief.

'Sorry for the noise. I'll go round the back.'

When John brushes past her she follows him to the back door. 'John?'

He swivels round, surprised. 'What are you doing here?' His body is rocking from side to side. 'Why are you outside? I've been banging on the front door.'

'I thought that …' She shakes her head. 'Never mind. Let's go indoors.'

John pushes in ahead of her, unsteady on his feet, bumping into the sides of the work surfaces as he moves through the kitchen. Anna pulls off her socks and throws them onto the floor. She finds another pair in the laundry basket and joins John, who is standing by the woodburner in the living room.

'Okay, so I'm pissed,' he says, hands out from his sides to help steady himself. 'But I want to say something before I pass out.' He sways on his feet. 'I don't blame you if you did sleep with Owen. In fact' – he lifts the side of his right hand to his forehead – 'I salute you for finding a way out for our family.' He gives a loud belch. 'We needed you to get the job because otherwise we'd have been homeless.' His lip drops. 'All the money I lost with buying that house.'

'John …' She goes to hug him.

'No. No, Anna. No, no, no.' He shakes his head at her and it topples him over so that he falls back onto the armchair. 'I take full responsibility for that prize fuck-up. You wanted to play it safe. It was me who pushed for us to buy it.'

'But I agreed.'

'Doesn't matter.' His head lolls on his neck. 'I'm rat-arsed.'

His eyes close and within seconds he starts to snore. Anna smiles down at him. 'Daft bugger.' She kisses his cheek. 'You're the man for me,' she whispers. 'You always have been.' She hugs his shoulders, then takes off his shoes and lifts his feet up onto a footstool. She fetches a blanket from the cupboard and covers him with it, tucking around the edges so that he is snug. She places an extra pillow behind his head to support his neck and sits down opposite him. She watches him with a mixture of love and envy. Perhaps she should do the same, she thinks, get blind drunk and slide into oblivion, except that the relief will be temporary and she'd rather avoid the morning hangover.

Monty makes no sound as he pads from the kitchen to the living room. He rolls on the rug between Anna and John, and when he's finished stretching himself, he jumps up onto John's knee. John doesn't stir; he is snoring loudly now. Anna gives him one last kiss, then climbs the stairs to bed.

The next morning, John spends fifteen minutes in the shower and when he comes into the kitchen he is dressed for work but walking slowly as if every step hurts. Anna places a mug of coffee and some toast on the table in front of him. 'Painkillers?'

'I've already taken some.' He looks up into her eyes. 'What did I say to you last night?'

'You don't remember?' Coffee in her hand, she sits down opposite him. 'You were very amiable.'

'Was I?' His expression tells her he finds that hard to believe. 'I'm worried, Anna.'

'So am I,' she says.

'I doubt we're worried about the same things.'

'Oh?'

I don't think you've been telling me the truth. And the problem with that is that it's got me thinking about other lies you might have told.'

'Now, John?' She thinks she knows where this is going. 'You really want to talk about this *now*?'

'It's been a long time coming. And frankly' – he gives a short laugh – 'before I end up perjuring myself for my wife of twenty-five years, I'd like you to do me the courtesy of telling the truth about your promotion.'

'Say that again?' She means the perjury.

'I think something happened between you and Owen that got you the job.'

Anna stares down into her mug of coffee. 'Sure, there were a couple of nurses on the short list who had more A and E experience than me,' she admits slowly. 'But I'd been working at Bishopglen for fifteen years. I'd proven my worth. It's not just about how many courses you've been on. A large part of my job involves building a rapport with parents and children.'

'What happened between you and Owen?'

'Because in your opinion, I'm not good enough for the lead role?'

'You wouldn't have been the bookies' favourite.'

'So you think I slept my way into it?' Her laughter is bitter. 'I mean, I know you have no respect for *him* but I didn't think that stretched to me as well.'

'You're oversimplifying it.'

'Am I?' She shakes her head, tears springing into her eyes. 'You've just accused me of having sex with Owen to get promoted.'

'Well, did you?'

'Fuck you, John,' she says so quietly that he doesn't hear her. She wipes the tears away with the backs of her fingers while her thoughts fumble around for an anchor.

'I am facing the worst situation of my professional and personal life and all you care about is old news.' She pauses before saying, 'There's plenty I could throw at you, by the way. Not least the fact that if it wasn't for you playing Good Samaritan, Tori would never have come to Bishopglen in the first place.'

'So I'm to blame?'

'I'm not blaming you,' Anna says. 'Simply reminding you that you had a part to play in this story.'

'And that hurts me.'

'Not as much as it's hurting me.' Her tone is sad. 'I am caught up in a murder inquiry and every day that I'm linked to the death of a child is twenty-four hours' worth of damage to my credibility as a nurse. The career I've spent years pouring my heart and soul into is being rapidly dismantled. And even if I'm exonerated tomorrow, a lot of people will believe there's no smoke without fire.'

'And is there smoke, Anna? Is there fire?'

She ignores this and pushes on with her train of thought. 'We'll lose our home, John. In case you've forgotten, this property is tied to my job.'

'I know that.'

'Isobel will lose her place in the school because even if she does want to remain here after her mother's disgrace, there's no way we'll be able to pay her school fees.'

'I know that too.'

'So what's your problem? You don't like that I get on with my boss? You're jealous of his achievements? You don't trust me? What, exactly?'

'I'm not jealous.' He makes a face at her. 'I would never want to be headmaster of a school like Bishopglen.'

'Well, do you want to be a headmaster anywhere? Because some people would say you lacked ambition.'

'I'm not a schmoozer and a paper pusher. You know that. I believe in the classroom and I believe in state education.' He points an accusing finger at her. 'You know perfectly well that I would have had Noah and Isobel in state schools if it wasn't for your insecurities.'

'Wanting the best for my children is an insecurity?'

'It's about principles, Anna.'

'You're a Labour voter through and through. I've heard it all before. But John, you know what?' she says lightly. 'Most of us adapt when we have families. We put them first.'

He gives her what Noah and Isobel call his sad-dad look. 'You're not the woman I married.'

'The woman you married was barely a woman.'

He's had three bites of toast and his face has gradually paled. He stands up. 'I'm not finished talking,' he says, before speeding off to the downstairs toilet.

Within seconds she hears sounds of coughing and retching. She clears his toast and coffee away, puts a glass of water in its place. She drinks her coffee and waits for him to come back. Every so often over the years, they've debated – sometimes argued about – the merits of private education. Usually Matt and Lynn have been with them – Matt is the only one of the four of them who, as a child, attended Bishopglen. Not only did Anna, John and Lynn not go to Bishopglen but they were all state school educated, something John and Lynn see as a badge of honour.

'I'd be happy to have my girls in local schools,' Lynn has often said. 'This is all Matt's doing.'

'Snap,' John said. 'Anna's always had her heart set on a private education for the kids. I don't know why.'

They've had variations on this conversation since they met – socialist principles versus putting yourself and your family first. Lynn lives in a six-bed, four-bathroom home with ten acres of land so as far as Anna is concerned she can hardly claim to be one of the people. She never says this to her, of course, because she loves her friend, and what is friendship if not being able to honour the contradictions?

John returns to the kitchen table, looking even more delicate than before. 'Do you want me to call you in sick?' Anna asks.

'No.' He pulls his chair in close to the table again. 'I think it's almost passed. I can work with a headache.'

She reaches across and takes his hand. 'Please, John. I don't want us to fight. We're on the same side, you know?'

His head is nodding rhythmically. 'So tell me exactly what happened with Owen?'

'Nothing happened with Owen,' she says, her tone sincere. 'I love you and I love our family, end of.'

She watches his expression tighten and then relax. 'Okay, Anna.' He's still nodding. 'I'm going to choose to believe you because I think we have bigger fish to fry.'

'Absolutely,' Anna affirms. Her smile is tense. 'Thank you.'

'Let me tell you what I did for our family yesterday, for our *children*.' His voice is tight. 'The police asked me if I could give you an alibi for the night Tori died. And I said yes, that you'd been with me all night, and that I'd know if you left the bed because I'm a light sleeper.'

He's not a light sleeper, Anna thinks, but she nods in acknowledgement of his support.

'It wasn't possible for you to have driven into town to confront Tori, I said, because we only have one car and the keys were in my trouser pocket on the bedroom floor. You'd have had to search for them. And that would have woken me up.' His eyes are probing 'But you weren't in bed all night, Anna, were you?'

'I got up early to go for a walk – you know that already – but otherwise I was there.'

'In the middle of the night I went to the loo. You weren't in bed, Anna.'

He leaves space for her to say something. She's frowning, thinking back. 'I was. I must have been.'

'I stood at the top of the stairs but I couldn't even hear a whisper of you.' His tone is low. 'And now I wish I'd looked out of the window to see whether the car was there.'

'Of course the car was there! John! You know what I'm like after too much wine. I must have been sitting in the living room with Monty on my knee.'

'Must have been or was?'

'Was. I *was* in the living room.'

'And early in the morning when you went out? Where did you walk to?'

'Just … through the woods. Down to the loch and—'

'You were coming from the direction of the school.'

'I must have walked in a loop. It was dark.' She should say, shouldn't she? That she went up to the girls' boarding house. She tries. 'Well, that's not entirely true. I was up by the girls' boarding house but I didn't go any further, I was—'

'There are twelve-year-olds in my tutor group who lie better than you,' John interrupts, his tone icy. He leans in towards her. 'The police showed me a video taken by Tori's friend Amanda. The night Tori was hit she was talking to another person at the entrance to the woods.' His eyes are pained. 'DC Murray asked me if I recognised my wife and I said no, I could tell it wasn't you because you don't stand in quite that way. Your head leans at a different angle.'

'John—'

'Let me finish!' he says loudly. 'As I was denying it was you, every fibre in my being was telling me otherwise.' He's inches from her face. 'It was you. I know in my gut that it was you. You were arguing with Tori and then you hit her. And you've lied about it. To the police, to your children, to me. For days now, you've kept the lie going.' He pulls back in his seat. 'And now I wonder if you're lying about having gone to her house too.'

'John!'

'Like I said, Anna. I did this for our children. They don't need a mother in prison. But Anna.' His voice trembles. 'If you killed a child then God help you.'

Chapter Twenty-Eight

It's getting harder and harder for Anna to be in the house by herself. Thinking. Thinking. Thinking. She has so much time to think and she has to be careful not to slide into panic and negativity. John's accusations have unnerved her. Now that he has lost faith in her, she is expecting the world to follow suit, the Internet trollers to assassinate her with words, the police to slap her in handcuffs and take her to a cell, the women in prison to attack her with knives.

The hashtag schoolnurserotinjail has been used two hundred and fifty times on Twitter. She is being tried without evidence, without the presence of a judge or jury, a braying virtual mob ready to lynch her. The parent body who aren't against her, led by Mungo Todd, is trying to add counterweight by praising Anna and by reminding the universe at large that she hasn't been arrested, let alone charged, but it doesn't help. It feeds them. More noise. More publicity. Because the more they defend her, the more venom bleeds from the naysayers.

She hides her laptop at the back of the wardrobe and promises herself that she won't read any of it again today. She won't read it ever, not ever, because it's making her ill. Her hands are constantly trembling, her head hurts, her eyeballs ache with pent-up tears. Her resting pulse is normally around seventy beats per minute but now, when she holds two fingers to her wrist and counts the beats, she finds that her heart's rhythm is permanently raised, ninety or more beats per minute. Even when she sleeps, she doesn't rest. Every hour she wakes with a start and she's out of bed, fists pumped by her sides, ready to punch her way out of trouble.

She's more exhausted than she's ever been in her whole life.

The minutes pass interminably slowly. She calls Lynn at break time. 'Do you have time for a coffee today?'

'I'm sorry, I don't.' Her tone is regretful. 'The seniors are giving statements to the police today and I promised to stay with them.'

'Of course. I read the email.' An email had come that morning from Owen, addressed to all the senior pupils' parents. 'It's good you're going to be there for the girls.'

'I could come round about seven if that suits you?'

'Could you bring Matt? It's just that John isn't really talking to me. He accused me of killing Tori.'

'*What?*'

'If you killed a child then God help you. That's what he said.'

'I don't understand. Why would he even think that?'

She tells her about the video recorded by Amanda. 'The police showed it to him and now he thinks it was me.'

'Why? Did it look like you?'

'I don't think so but I expect he was won over by the part when Tori speaks directly to the camera and says it's me. She's very convincing.'

'And this from a man who works in a school! Has he forgotten that children lie?'

'Crazy, I know.' Anna sighs. 'If Matt is able to come too then ...' She trails off. 'I dunno. It might help.'

'Of course he'll come. He should be home by seven. We'll drop Lois round at my mum's and come over.'

They say their goodbyes and Anna loads the washing machine. It's good to keep busy, no matter how mundane the tasks. As she separates whites and darks she thinks about Isobel. Children do lie and it's a shock for parents to realise that they don't necessarily know their own offspring, the tiny baby that grows into the curious toddler, the keen child, the reticent, moody teenager. Parents don't know what their children think. They don't imagine that they lie to them. They don't know that they have secret lives, that they are both more and less resilient than they give them credit for.

Anna believes she's under no such illusions about her own children. They're both teenagers, and teenagers are meant to lie to their parents. It's a necessary signpost to adulthood. They have to break the parent–child bond so that they can live independently, make their own decisions and learn from their own experiences.

And that reminds her: Isobel has yet to reply to her text asking her to come to the family dinner tomorrow evening. Anna will have to elicit John's help. And after this morning's outburst she not sure he'll support her.

She hopes he's willing to help.

Life without John by her side is just too sad and lonely to contemplate. She sits in the living room and closes her eyes, tries to visualise a beach, gently rolling waves, sunshine warming her skin. She breathes deeply, feels her lungs expand, holds the breath and then releases slowly. She manages this for several breaths, feels her extremities tingle, fingers and toes suffused with oxygen. *John said she wasn't the woman he married.*

She opens her eyes to mull that over. She thinks back to their first few years as newlyweds, setting up home together. She learned how to cook and clean so that the house was always spotless, the air sweet with home-baked bread and biscuits. She washed the football club kit, helped organise fundraisers, was welcoming when his teammates came round afterwards to share curry and a beer. She ground her own spices back then and always had at least two curries to choose from – one meat and one vegetarian. She made her own naan bread. It was important for her to be seen as someone who made an effort, gave much more than she received.

And how she wanted his family to like her. She wasn't without insight – she knew this was a reaction to her own upbringing – but big families were unknown to her, their fluctuating dynamics a mystery. She was an only child, to a mother who didn't socialise. Apart from her grandmother, not many people ever visited the house. John, on the other hand, was one of four siblings. He had over twenty cousins and extended family gatherings were frequent. By the time she met John her mother was dead, her father living in Spain with Angela. They rang each other on birthdays and Christmas Day, the conver- sations brief and stilted. He never invited her to visit and she never asked him to stay with her. They didn't even come to her wedding because he had a golf tour- nament that was too important to miss. When John's parents asked her why he was unable to make it she told them his wife was ill, the lie out of her mouth before she could stop it.

Over time she realised that John's family dynamics were underpinned by a generosity that meant intermit- tent bad behaviour from one member or another was tolerated and forgiven. They were a cheerful, spontan- eous group – John had chosen her and that was enough for them. Her striving was unnecessary and in some part of her brain she knew this – they had open arms and hearts – but still she couldn't help herself.

Being so deeply in love didn't suit her. She worried that John would leave her. She imagined he would intuit that her heart wasn't as pure and shiny as his, that her moral code was greyer, that she had been forced to nurture in herself a ruthlessness and a singularity that he would never possess. At times those first few years were an agony of anxiety. If he was even ten minutes late, her mind would begin to prod and poke at her, throw up the same two options to torment her: he was growing interested in another woman – a better version of her, a woman who was prettier, kinder, more honest; he had found out the exact circumstances of her mother's death and he was shocked to the core, too shocked to look her in the eye again, because if she could do that, live with that, what else was she capable of?

And then she fell pregnant.

Quickly, within two months of deciding they wanted to start a family, she was pregnant with Noah. She was congratulated and cosseted by his parents, sisters and brother. It's biology, she was tempted to say. I'm not clever or talented. I haven't consciously done anything except have sex. But she didn't say any of that. She allowed herself to bask in the attention, pleased to be adding to the family.

It was when Noah was born that she began to grow into herself, to find her calling as a mother and wife. It turned out that the creation of a family was what she was good at. Being a mother broke her open, and when the pieces fused back together again, her insecurities fell away. She had a reason for living that was much deeper and wider than herself. Her sense of purpose was focused on this new person – a warm, breathing, miniature human being. Every second her love for him grew and she couldn't stop it. She didn't want to stop it. This relationship had transformed her into a new version of herself and she was happier than she had ever been.

When she was pregnant with Isobel, she was concerned that there wouldn't be enough space in her heart for a second baby, but she needn't have worried. An everyday miracle occurred and her heart expanded, doubled in size, to make room for both her babies. She was broken and re-formed and this time there were two little people to put before herself. They were a family of four. She and John had willingly brought two souls into the world and now it was their duty, and their pleasure, to raise them. 'Our mission should we choose to accept it,' John joked before playing the *Mission Impossible* theme tune on his electric guitar.

He's right, Anna thinks, she's not the woman he married – she's more focused, more confident and much more determined than her.

And he doesn't play electric guitar any more.

She's lost in the ebb and flow of her memories when the doorbell rings. She stands up and automatically goes to open it, and then she remembers to be cautious. She climbs the stairs and looks out of her bedroom window. Flora Manson is back on her doorstep, holding a newspaper in her hand. She rings the doorbell several times but Anna doesn't go back downstairs until Flora posts the newspaper through the letterbox and walks back to her car.

Anna lifts the newspaper off the doormat and is shocked to see her own face on the front page. The photograph has been taken from the school's website – Anna in her uniform, smiling at the camera. Further down the page is a photograph of Tori in her school uniform, looking apprehensive.

Anna reads the article, her heart sinking.

Bishopglen Independent School is a place of privilege that occasionally opens its doors to those children and young adults whose parents can't afford the luxury of a private education. One of these girls was Victoria Jane Carmichael, a girl of exceptional talent who would have gone on to achieve great things were her life not so violently cut short. It's human nature to want to lay the blame for Victoria's death at someone's door and that someone is Sister Anna Pierce.

There is a paragraph about Anna's role in the school, all of it taken from the website, and then:

Anna Pierce has her house in order. She has photographs of her children on the walls in her hallway. Her kitchen is clean, home-made cakes fill the dome-shaped cake-stand, walking boots line up by the back door, a ginger tom is asleep next to the Aga. So far, so normal for a woman like her. And what sort of a woman is that?

She is controlled. She is icy when questioned. I asked her whether she would talk to me about the investigation, and having invited me into her home, she then refused to talk to me, marched me to the door. Why? Because she thought I would be a mouthpiece for her. She thought that I would favour her.

She thought wrong. This is a woman who is cosy with the establishment, protected by the professionals who surround her, closing ranks against what they would see as prying eyes and the rest of us would call the truth.

Anna's jaw tightens. She stops reading every word and skims the rest. It's more of the same, Flora Manson running her and the school down when she is woefully short on facts. Anna is astonished that someone can say so much while saying almost nothing at all. She has taken a few simple truths and exaggerated and distorted them to suit her own agenda.

Anna pushes the newspaper deep into the recycling bin and goes out for a brisk walk, anxiety and dread her twin companions.

Chapter Twenty-Nine

In the afternoon she makes two dozen mini sausage rolls – Matt's favourite – and smoked salmon blinis – John's favourite. They have enough lager and wine in the garage for four people on a work night. She texts John to say sorry, that she hopes he's feeling better and that the Sykeses will be popping in at seven – is that okay?

He texts back: I won't be drinking. Is company really a good idea?

They won't stay long, is her reply.

She waits for more from him but nothing comes and so she carries on preparing the house, cleaning the downstairs loo, vacuuming, laying out snacks and drinks as if everything is as it should be and this is four friends meeting for a catch-up. In this alternate universe, John won't be hung over, Anna won't be accused of a crime she didn't commit and the friends will all be easy with each other.

He's normally home by six on a Thursday but it's gone six thirty when the front door opens. He's bending down to untie his shoelaces when she goes into the porch. 'Hi.'

He grunts a reply.

'Do you feel like eating? I made some snacks and there's lentil soup left over from yesterday.'

'I'll get my own, thanks.'

'I can— okay.' She bites her lip. 'Lynn and Matt will be here soon.'

'I get it.' He gives her a weary stare. 'I'll be my usual friendly self.'

'I don't—' She takes his arm. 'I'm sorry, John. I know that I've upset everyone.'

'I don't want to hear it, Anna.' He sighs. 'Let's just get through this evening.'

She stands aside to make way for him to go upstairs, knows better than to try to force him to talk. Occasionally, he can be huffy and he always comes out of it himself, given time. But they don't have time, so she hopes that Matt and Lynn will fast-track him through the moodiness and out the other side.

When the Sykeses arrive Anna is shocked to see that Matt's right eye is framed with purple and yellow bruising. 'What happened to you?' Anna moves close to him, frowning as she assesses the damage.

Matt's hand automatically rises up towards his eye, his fingers feeling gingerly around the orbit. 'It's nothing, really.'

'Julia Raeburn took a pop at him,' Lynn says.

'*What?*' Anna is appalled.

'We felt we had to do something about the Facebook page,' Lynn says. 'And I thought she might listen to Matt because he's a thousand times more reasonable than me.' She widens her eyes. 'Goes without saying.'

'I have no history with her, so …' He shrugs. 'I asked her to stop mouthing off on Facebook, maybe even agree to speak to Victoria's dad for us but she became very angry, very quickly.' His face slumps. 'Tactical error on my part.'

'Have you been checked over at the hospital?'

'Yes, they did an X-ray but there's no fracture.'

'She must have some right hook.'

'She used the end of a golf club,' Lynn says, wincing. She takes Matt's hand and he turns to face her.

'I should have seen it coming,' he says. 'She was loading golf clubs into the back of her car.' He rubs his eye. 'Lesson learned.'

Lynn kisses his cheek. 'She's a nutter. You couldn't have stopped her.'

'You have to report her to the police,' Anna says. 'She can't be allowed to get away with it! It's—'

'Bang out of order.' John has come down the stairs to join them. 'She should be prosecuted for assault.'

'I know.' Matt shrugs again. 'But honestly? I think our priority at the moment is seeing you through this bad patch.' He raises a smile for Anna, then looks at John. 'You got a cold beer?'

'Sure.' John claps him on the shoulder. 'Come on through.'

Anna is about to follow them when Lynn grabs her hand. 'Is John okay with you again?'

'I don't think so. He's only just home so we haven't had a chance to talk.'

'I told Matt and he agreed that we would work on him.' She hugs Anna. 'You know, one day we'll look back on this and think – what a week that was! An absolute nightmare!' She pauses. 'And I know it sounds callous, but we'll reflect on Tori's death for about a minute and then we'll move on to the weather or where we're going on holiday.'

'You're probably right,' Anna says, not believing her, not believing her at all.

The snacks go down well. John has found his appetite and twice he even catches Anna's eye and she feels her anxiety shrink. They talk about his day at school – the chemistry experiment that went wrong – a client of Matt's who has more money than sense, and then Lynn mentions the senior girls, and how well they did when they were questioned. 'It wasn't the DC Murray you've talked about, Anna. It was a young officer called Emma Pritchard. She was very relaxed with the girls. Although none of them knew anything so there really wasn't much they could say.'

'Even Amanda?' John asks.

'Amanda was questioned separately,' Lynn replies. 'She's another one who has a habit of telling lies,' she adds, her eyes flicking towards Anna.

'Is Isobel okay?' Anna asks. 'I'm not expecting you to tell me anything she said,' she adds hastily. 'I just wondered how she was looking. I texted her last night to ask her to come home to dinner tomorrow.' She reaches across to touch John's arm and is relieved when he doesn't pull away. 'Noah is coming home.'

'Again?'

'It's Pippa's party on Saturday.'

'Not quite the party we expected,' Lynn says. 'We did consider cancelling it altogether but the senior girls have prepared a lovely tribute to Tori so hopefully it won't come across as poor taste.'

'I asked Noah to come home one day early so that we could have a family meal,' Anna continues. 'I'm just not sure whether Isobel will come.'

'She will,' John says. 'She hates missing out.'

'Would you mind texting her?' Anna asks. 'She's more likely to come if you ask her.'

'She's a daddy's girl,' Lynn affirms, popping a blini into her mouth.

John takes his mobile from his pocket. 'I'll do it now.'

Anna fetches some wine and a couple more beers from the fridge and as she puts them on the table a reply arrives on John's phone.

'Is this you doing Mum's dirty work?' John says, reading from the screen. 'No. I would also like you home for a family meal,' he says, keying the letters in as he speaks. 'See you at seven tomorrow.'

Once again the reply is almost instant. 'She's coming,' John says, putting his mobile back in his pocket.

'I thought I'd make Mexican,' Anna says. 'She loves chicken fajitas.'

'And your sweetcorn relish is not to be sniffed at,' he says, his smile slight but warm. Her heart lifts.

'So.' Matt glances at Lynn, who gives a barely perceptible nod. 'If I may, I'd like to talk to you both about what I mentioned before – the solicitor's fees.' John goes to speak and Matt holds up his hand. 'I don't want to embarrass you but we're friends and, to my mind, friends help each other out.'

'We're in agreement,' Lynn says.

'Nurses and teachers – the smooth running of society depends on people like you,' Matt says.

'The company's made a healthy profit this year,' Lynn adds.

'So please just email me your bank account details so that we can deposit enough cash to cover the costs.'

Matt sits back in his seat as if it's a fait accompli. Anna says nothing. John's antipathy towards her is lifting and she doesn't want to spoil that. Her fingers are crossed under the table.

'Thank you.' John tilts his beer bottle at Lynn and then Matt. 'I …' He hesitates, glances at Anna. '*We* really appreciate the offer but—'

'Before you turn us down,' Lynn interrupts, 'I want

to say something.' She sits up straighter. 'When I had postnatal depression after Pippa was born, who helped me the most? My mother? My mother-in-law? The health visitor? Matt?' She touches Matt's knee by way of apology for including him in the list. 'No. None of the above. You helped me, Anna. *You*. You sat with me while I cried. You drove me to the doctor. You minded my beautiful baby girl and you ran a bath for me when I was too exhausted to do it for myself.' She presses a hand to her chest. 'And now this is my chance to give something back.'

Anna mouths, 'Thank you,' while John presses a finger and thumb over his eyelids.

'It's a thank you, but it's a selfish thank you,' Lynn continues. 'I don't want you drowning in debt. I want things to continue as they are. I want Isobel to be able to stay at Bishopglen. Our two families are connected, aren't they?'

John nods. 'Yes, but I'm wary of crossing a line. I don't like the idea of mixing money with friendship.'

'Why?' Matt asks. 'We won't be going short. We have enough put aside for the kids. We have everything we need.'

'You don't know what's around the corner,' John says, throwing out his arms. 'You might suddenly need extra cash for an operation that can only be done privately in America or a pissed-off employee who's threatening the business. If this situation has proved anything, it's that you can never be sure what's heading your way.'

'I have enough money invested for the first eventuality, and the second would be covered by company insurance.'

'You know what I mean,' John says.

'No, I don't. Listen, John.' Matt leans forward, his tone earnest. 'It just so happens that in our society what

I do for a living attaches a higher monetary value than what you do.'

'You and I share socialist principles,' Lynn adds. 'Cut us some slack here, John.'

'Well …' He's weakening. 'Anna?' He looks at her, his eyebrows raised.

'I think accepting the money relieves us of a lot of pressure,' Anna says quietly. 'We could see it as a loan.'

'That we never pay back?' John asks with a sigh.

Anna shrugs. 'Our fortunes could change.'

There's a prolonged silence while John wrestles with his pride and then, finally, he stares across at Matt and Lynn. 'Thank you. Sincerely.' He holds up a finger. 'We'll accept your generous offer on one condition. If, at any point, you change your mind you must be honest and tell us. Somehow we'll find the money to pay you back.'

'Great! That's sorted then.' Matt rubs his hands together. 'Anyone want the last sausage roll?'

It's gone nine when Matt and Lynn leave. Anna stands on the front step and waves them off. High up in the trees, the crows are gathering for their evening debrief, cawing and screeching their news. She watches them fly from branch to branch, one bird taking flight as another lands, the branches dipping and swaying as if choreographed by an expert. She's smiling up at the birds, enchanted by their seemingly effortless skill, when out of the corner of her eye she senses movement in the rhododendron bushes ahead of her. She narrows her eyes in concentration and makes out a person-shaped shadow lurking in the space between the bushes.

Her breath catches. 'Hello?' she calls out. The shape stays still. He – or she? – is about twenty yards ahead of her. 'Hello?' she calls out again and the shape moves.

It's a man, and he's wearing a ski mask. *It isn't cold enough*. That's her first thought. *It isn't cold enough for a hat, never mind a ski mask.*

He steps onto the path and raises a finger, which he drags across his throat, then points at Anna. Her feet don't move. Her eyes are watching him but she isn't processing his actions. Her thoughts are turning on an empty loop, her mind completely blank, as if all her thoughts have been sucked out of her head.

And then the fear hits. Visceral and intense, it jump-starts her voice so that she screams loud enough to be heard a hundred metres away. The man turns and starts to run, and she sees another person behind him, smaller and thinner, perhaps a woman or a teenager, also dressed in black and wearing a ski mask. John is down the stairs in seconds and Anna points wordlessly towards the fleeing pair. John chases them and Anna follows. They've had more than a head start and she doesn't expect John to catch them but she follows to make sure he's okay. The wood isn't dense but branches grab hold of their clothes and tree stumps bite at their ankles, slowing them down. The two figures are about twenty metres in front, heading towards the driveway that lies east of the school and north of the loch. John moves faster than Anna so that by the time she reaches the edge of the wood, the two figures are nowhere to be seen.

'Remember YNZ,' John shouts to her, and she sees the car in the distance, speeding down the driveway. 'I've memorised the first part.' He pulls her in for a hug and holds her tight enough to squeeze the breath from her lungs. 'We'll call Murray. He'll be able to trace the number plate.'

He takes her hand and they walk back through the trees. Geraldine and Miranda are outside the row of cottages and when they see John and Anna coming, Miranda steps forward. 'Is everything okay? We heard a scream.'

'We're okay, thanks,' John says.

'There were two people in the bushes,' Anna adds. 'One of them threatened me.'

'How?' Miranda's eyes are wide. 'What did he say?'

Anna tells them about the ski mask and demonstrates the gesture; Miranda's hand jerks up to her own throat. 'That's awful!' she says.

'Very frightening,' Geraldine agrees. Anna gives her a grateful smile before saying goodbye to both women and following John inside.

'We need a stiff drink,' John shouts from the living room. 'Do you want to open the whisky we've had since Christmas?'

'Will do.'

'Remind me what the last three letters were,' he says.

'YNZ,' she calls back, and while he phones Murray, she opens the whisky, her hands shaking as she lifts two crystal glass tumblers down from the top shelf in the cabinet. They don't have many wedding presents left intact but two of the tumblers have made it through the years. She piles ice into each glass and pours the amber liquid over the top, watches as it fills the spaces between the cubes then gulps back a mouthful of whisky greedily, the burn in her throat a welcome distraction from the adrenalin surging through her bloodstream.

'I couldn't get through to Murray but another officer took the message,' John says when he joins her in the kitchen. 'He'll call us as soon as he has some news.'

'Thank you for coming to my rescue.'

'Always.' He takes the tumbler of whisky and nudges his glass against hers. 'Cheers.'

They both take a drink. It's Anna who shudders and John smiles. 'I can get you some wine if you'd rather?'

'No, this hits the spot.' She notices that John is energised by the whole incident, seems to be enjoying the thrill of it. 'I forgot to tell you – Flora Manson came to the door again, and when I didn't answer she put the latest edition of the *Courier* through the letterbox.'

'Uh-oh,' John says.

'Yeah.' Anna widens her eyes. 'Her article is as you would expect. A hatchet job.'

'Where is it?'

'In the recycling bin.' She shrugs. 'I was going to call Everett but then I thought – what's the point?'

'I'm sorry, love. I really am.'

'Thank heavens for good friends, though, eh?' she says, blinking away tears. 'What would we do without Matt and Lynn?'

'We're lucky,' he admits. He pours more whisky into his glass. 'And I've been thinking about what I said to you this morning.' His expression is reflective. 'It wasn't you in that video, was it?' He shakes his head at his own lack of conviction. 'I was nervous and Murray was pushing for me to say it was you. And …' He trails off, takes another mouthful of whisky before saying, 'I should have trusted you. I'm sorry.'

'And I should have trusted you,' Anna says, relieved that they're talking again. 'I was the one who started with the accusations.'

'Tough times,' he says. 'We need to stick together.'

'Like glue.'

'Like lovers.'

They share a moment of eye contact before Anna takes his free hand and kisses his fingers, one by one. The alcohol is skipping through her bloodstream and she feels happy, spontaneous, tactile. They take the whisky with them and go upstairs, place the glasses and the bottle on the chest of drawers and fall back onto the bed. They have the sort of sex that makes everything better – both deep and superficial, profound and frothy with laughter.

Afterwards, John falls asleep and Anna lies with her head on his chest, hearing every beat of his heart, her cheek rising and falling with the swell of his ribcage. Her head is empty, her muscles tension-free. For now she's warm and safe, and that is enough.

Chapter Thirty

When Isobel was eleven and she was excluded from school, the psychologist recommended they all attend family counselling. It wasn't as daunting as it first sounded. Noah and Isobel mostly expressed their thoughts and feelings through art. Anna had thought they would be too old for that approach but they didn't take much persuading; it was less confrontational than sitting still with all eyes upon them. They each chose a project: Noah's was space science and Isobel's was bridge engineering. Over the six sessions they made papier mâché models, drawings, collages and scrapbooks. And while they worked they talked about what they felt. John and Anna listened while the therapist led the session.

It turned out that there wasn't much wrong with their family that some quality time together and Anna's promotion couldn't fix. After the final session Anna stayed behind to ask the therapist her opinion on her parenting.

'I don't give opinions,' the therapist told her.

'Ever?' Anna asked. 'I know you're a skilled observer, and if you could share your insights I'd be really grateful.'

The therapist thought for a moment before saying, 'Do you think you need to be liked?'

'Doesn't everyone?' Anna asked. Her tone wasn't defensive, more interested.

'Perhaps,' the therapist replied. 'To a greater or lesser

degree. But I sense that it is particularly important to you.'

It was on the tip of Anna's tongue to say that she wasn't sure how that affected her parenting. But she merely smiled, thanked the therapist and left the room because she realised two things simultaneously. First, she wanted her children to like her and so often, especially with Noah, she was more of a friend than a parent. And second, she realised that sometimes it's better not to explore the reasons behind things, because for her to look at her own behaviour and her motivations, to *really* look, to delve deep into the hidden corners of herself, would involve a degree of courage that she simply didn't possess.

Before Anna sets the table, she asks John if he will sit with her. 'We need to talk,' she says.

'Sounds ominous.' His smile is soft. 'If this is when you tell me you're leaving me for Owen then let me have a shot of whisky first.'

'Will you stop with the Owen thing!' She pushes his shoulder, laughing. 'I've loved you from the moment we met. I don't know how I can keep proving that to you.'

'I do.' He pulls her close, his hands travelling up and down her spine with the sort of gentle pressure that makes her want to melt.

She laughs again and then almost immediately she's frowning. 'John, we really do have to talk before the kids arrive.'

'Okay.' He pulls out a chair. 'Opposite or side by side?'

'Opposite. I'm hoping to hold your hands throughout.'

'I can do that.'

They sit down at either side of the kitchen table and meet their hands in the middle. 'Okay. So.' Anna takes a deep breath. She begins by reminding him what Isobel said when she pushed her over and that the words continued to play on her mind. 'I had to find out whether she knew something she shouldn't or had done something she regretted.' She feels a tightening in his fingers when she confesses to sneaking into school and printing off Isobel's medical and pastoral care records. 'I used Geraldine's log-in and the next morning, she noticed. Owen asked me whether I'd done it and I said no.'

'You lied to him?'

'Yes.'

John looks surprised at this. 'Do you still have the printouts?'

'I threw them on the fire.' She summarises what she read, watches him frown when she tells him that Isobel is worried about someone close to her having done something that could get them into serious trouble. And whatever that something is, Tori knew about it.

'Who?' John asks. 'Who could she be talking about?'

'The obvious people are you, me, Noah and then maybe Hester. I don't think it's Pippa because she said she couldn't tell Pippa or her boyfriend Andrew. It was too big a secret to share and she was worried they wouldn't keep it to themselves.'

John's head is slowly shaking. 'I don't think it's me. Not that I can think of, but then ...' He shrugs. 'Are you sure this isn't just Isobel being melodramatic? I mean, this is the girl whose world is ending if chicken and pineapple are on the same plate.'

'I know,' Anna acknowledges with a smile. 'But I don't think so.'

'Noah's barely been around this year.'

'And he never met Tori so I don't see any connection there.'

'And you?' John says. 'Can you think of anything you might have done?'

Anna has one preoccupation, one major secret, one colossal lie. But it happened years ago and no one ever knew about it. 'I can't think of anything,' she says.

'So Tori knew about this secret something, and Isobel was worried that at any point she might drop the bomb.'

'Yes.' Anna bites her lip. 'And I'm sorry I didn't tell you before I broke into the medical centre but I didn't want you to be complicit.' She interlaces their fingers. 'And then when I realised it was important you knew about what Isobel had been saying to Geraldine, you had just come back from the police station and you were angry with me.'

'Bad timing,' John says.

'Bad timing,' she affirms. 'I've apologised to Geraldine and I'll tell Owen next time I see him.' She smiles. 'I feel so much lighter now that I've told you everything.'

John squeezes her hand. 'So how do we play this today?'

'How about if you keep things rolling along until about halfway through the food? And then I'll bring up Tori and see what happens.'

'Are you going to ask Isobel outright?'

'I am. I'm going to tell her that I've read her pastoral care record. I know she'll be angry with me but I think the time for worrying about that is long gone. We have to be straight with each other.'

'I'll support you with whatever you say,' John tells her. His forehead creases in a frown. 'Here's hoping it doesn't backfire.'

Tori felt bad about showing Isobel the video. She'd felt an hour of triumph but when Isobel didn't show up for her prefect's duty at break time, unease crept in. She'd expected Isobel to be freaked out – that was the whole point, wasn't it? – but when a message filtered through to the chemistry lab that Isobel was unwell, Tori counted the minutes until the end of the lesson then ran to the boarding house. She found Isobel in her bed, curled up under the duvet.

'Isobel?' She touched her shoulder. 'Do you need to go to the medical centre?' Isobel stared at her as if she had two heads. 'Of course … you can't really go there because your mum's on duty.' She bit her lip. 'I'm not going to do anything with the video! I'm really not. I was just proving a point and now I've proven it and …' She trailed off. Isobel was staring at the wall. She looked beaten, the way her mum had when her dad left them. 'I'm s—' She couldn't get the word out, wasn't able to say sorry – because girls like Isobel? They were privileged. They got everything their own way. If this was enough to break her then she needed a reality check. Far worse was happening to children all over the country, every minute of every day.

As Tori turned to go, Isobel sat up and said, 'How can I trust you not to show the video to anyone else?'

'Because I'm telling you you can.' Tori's expression was blank. 'I'll delete it. Look!' She showed Isobel the video on her mobile and pressed delete. 'There. Evidence destroyed.'

'How do I know you don't have it backed up somewhere?'

'Because I've made my point.'

'What you did was sick,' Isobel said, her voice cracking. 'Messing with someone's life like that. What's wrong with you? You don't even know him.'

Tori shrugged. 'Think of it this way, Isobel.' She opened the door and stared back at her. 'You'll be more careful about what you say now you know it can come back to bite you. A valuable life lesson, don't you think?'

* * *

Anna stands in front of the table checking that everything is ready. She has prepared a Mexican feast: nachos, fajitas, tortillas, salsa, guacamole, corn relish and corn on the cob, sour cream and cheddar laced with chilli. In the fridge, she has half a dozen Mexican beers and several margarita mocktails made with strawberries, sparkling water and lime juice, sugar crystals clinging to the rim of the glass. John is standing behind her, his arms wrapped around her waist, and Anna leans back against him. They are completely as one and it makes her feel peaceful as if nothing else matters, not Tori's accusation, nor Isobel's secret. Even Tori's death seems less of a tragedy through the prism of her closeness with John. The top of her head is just beneath his chin and she swivels round to place her lips against his neck, share a kiss before the front door opens – Isobel and Noah are home. They take off their shoes and dump bags in the hallway before coming into the kitchen. Anna is hanging back but Noah sees her at once and gives her a hug. 'You doing okay?'

She nods, swallows down her nerves. Now that Isobel is in the room she's afraid she's setting her daughter up. Perhaps it would have been better to meet somewhere quietly, just the two of them. But would Isobel have agreed to that? Anna doubts it. And that's why she's had to rope in John and Noah – not that Noah has any idea how uncomfortable this dinner could become.

Anna stands close to the Aga, refolding the dishtowels that hang over the rail. Mothers should be approachable, dependable, someone to halve troubles and share problems. Her daughter's been struggling and she hasn't been able to confide in her own mother. What sort of parent does that make Anna?

When Isobel sees the table her eyes linger on each of

the serving dishes. She reaches for a handful of nachos to dip into the salsa and then the sour cream, leaving a ripple of red running through the white sauce.

'Beer, Noah?' John asks.

'Love one.' Noah touches Anna's arm. 'What are you having, Mum?'

'Just some fizzy water,' she replies. 'I'll have a drink later.'

'Mum has made your favourite mocktail, Isobel,' John says. He holds one out to her and she takes it in her hand but doesn't bother to say thank you. They all sit down in their usual places: John next to Anna, Isobel opposite John, Noah opposite Anna. Noah starts telling them about a visiting professor from NASA who came to speak to them about the space programme. 'He was involved in designing the Falcon 9 rocket that made the uncrewed flight test in March.'

He goes on to talk about the engine and Anna tunes out as she carries the spicy chicken from stove to table. She slices lime wedges for the beer and replenishes the dips, then sits back down again.

'Fascinating stuff,' John says to Noah. And then to Isobel, 'It can't be long until you're off to York University for the science fair.'

'I know. You don't have to remind me,' Isobel says, with a bored tone. 'You could have been an astronaut and Mum could have been a doctor.' Her tongue flicks out to lick some of the sugar off the rim of the glass. 'Noah and I will make sure to live your lives for you.'

'That's not what I meant,' John says. He is wearing his sad-dad look. 'And as it happens' – he reaches for Anna's hand – 'I love my life. I don't need anyone to live it for me.'

Isobel has the grace to look sheepish. 'I stand

corrected.' She stuffs some nachos into her mouth and mumbles, 'Sorry.'

John's mobile starts to ring, the theme tune from *Match of the Day* sounding through the kitchen. He glances at the screen and stands up. 'It's the police calling me back.' He walks off to take the call in the living room.

'What's that about, Mum?' Noah asks.

She tells them about the incident with the figures in ski masks. 'I've been taking some flack on the Internet.' Isobel has yet to look directly at Anna but now she does, her interest piqued. 'They know where we live. I don't think they'd target either of you but you need to be careful just in case.'

'Well, that's just weird,' Isobel says. 'We were all questioned by the police yesterday and they were definitely looking for information against Tori's mother. Stuff like – Did you ever meet her mum? Did she talk about her mum? Was she happy at home? Andr—' She corrects herself quickly. 'One of my friends says Tori's mum attacked Tori's dad twice when they were getting divorced. So it's ridiculous that they're targeting you when her mother is prime suspect.' There's a note of flippancy in her tone. 'Like mother like daughter, I guess.'

'Tori was violent?' Anna asks.

'Not exactly,' Isobel replies.

'They traced the number plate.' John is back. He kisses Anna on her forehead and sits down. 'They wouldn't tell me the man's name but they've been round to his house. He admitted to going on the Facebook page, said he felt you deserved to be scared.' He raises his eyebrows. 'Murray says they took him into the station and gave him a warning. He won't be bothering us again.'

'I'll drink to that.' Noah raises his beer and they all clink glasses in the centre of the table.

It's now or never, Anna thinks. 'I have something to say,' she announces. 'And you'll have to bear with me because it might not make easy listening.'

Noah looks interested and John takes her hand. Isobel is busy piling salsa onto her refried beans and doesn't look up.

'Before I start, I want to admit that I know I'm not perfect. I make mistakes and I hope to learn from them.' Her voice is strong. 'But what I can say with absolute certainty is that I love all three of you more than I could ever express.' Her lip trembles. 'My aim is to protect us as a family.'

Isobel glances up at this point. Anna can see she's struck a chord.

'That said, I did something I promised I would never do.' She takes a breath. 'Isobel, I read your medical and pastoral care files.'

Isobel has a mouthful of nachos. She continues chewing, her cheeks growing increasingly red.

'It was wrong of me but I did it for what I thought was a pressing reason.'

Isobel swallows the final mouthful of her strawberry mocktail and takes the empty glass over to the sink. She opens the fridge door and helps herself to a second one. Everyone else at the table has stopped eating and is waiting for her reaction.

'And I've gathered us all here because I know, Isobel, that you're worried about someone very close to you and I'd like you to tell us who that person is and what they have done.'

Chapter Thirty-One

She expects Isobel to shout and scream but she doesn't. She sits down again and stares at the mocktail. 'You promised you'd never read my files,' she says quietly. 'You promised me privacy.'

'I did.'

'It was you who broke into the surgery, wasn't it?'

'Well … yes. But I used my keys.'

'Mr Wiseman had me in his office today, questioning me like *I* was the criminal.'

'I'm sorry.'

'Why didn't you just ask me directly? Why all this staging – I'll make a Mexican! That's Isobel's favourite then she'll tell me what she's up to.' She's mimicking Anna's voice. 'John, you'll need to help me! You text her. She'll listen to you.'

'You were ignoring my texts.'

'So you break into the school to get my personal files and it's my fault for ignoring you?'

'I'm not saying it's your fault.'

'I'm sure it's against the law.'

'I don't think it is,' Anna replies. 'I was asked not to go up to school but I still had my keys and I'm still head of the department.'

'I could tell on you.'

'You could. But I don't think you will because you care about this family too much.'

'Caring about this family should be about being honest.'

'Which is exactly what I'm trying to do.'

'You're too late,' Isobel bites back, her veneer beginning to crack. 'Too fucking late.'

'Isobel,' John warns.

'Were you in on this too?' She glares at her dad. 'Did
she convince you to help her? Sneak around the school
in the middle of the night? Break my trust?'

'No, but I do understand why your mum is worried,'
John tries to explain.

'It's fucking out of order!' Isobel pushes her chair
back and stands up. Everyone else stands up with her.
'You should be ashamed of yourself! Imagine if I did
something like that.'

'Isobel, please.' Anna's tone is conciliatory. 'I know
I've gone behind your back and I'm truly sorry for that
but I need you to tell me what happened so that we can
fix it.'

'It *is* fixed.'

'How?'

'It's fixed because Tori's dead,' she says.

No one speaks. Anna feels as if the air is now energised with a stark significance. She holds Isobel's eyes
and says quietly, 'Do you know anything about how Tori
died?'

Isobel frowns and then gasps. 'Oh my God! You think
I pushed her down the stairs?' She is incredulous. She
falls back against the wall, staring at the faces around
her. 'What do you take me for? A fucking murderer?'
Her eyes are smarting. 'Ever since I scratched that boy
when I was eleven. *Eleven*,' she repeats. 'You've been
suspicious of me. Watching me. Gauging my temper.'

'That's not true,' John says.

'Maybe *you* don't think it but *she* does.' She throws a

hand in Anna's direction. 'I tried with Tori. I really tried with her. I was friendly. I included her in whatever we were doing, even when Pippa and Hester didn't want her there.'

'She kept a diary, Isobel,' Anna says quietly.

'And it's missing.' She widens scathing eyes. 'No, I didn't take it. Did you?'

'Of course not.'

'I've never even seen it. I only know about it because the police told us it was missing.'

'Whatever it is that you're worried about, could have been recorded in the diary.'

Isobel leans in towards Anna. 'It's not your business. Get your own life.'

'Iso.' Noah's tone is gentle. 'Why not just tell us what happened?'

'Don't you start.' She gives him a dark look. 'You should be on my side.'

'And if the diary is found?' Anna says. 'And this incident is in the diary. What then?'

'I know you two' – her glance takes in both her parents – 'always want to see the good in people, even when it's not there, but the fact is that Victoria Carmichael was a liar and a manipulator. Her diary is probably full of lies! I don't give a fuck if it turns up. I'm done worrying about the whole thing.'

'I agree, she was a tricky girl,' Anna says. She pauses to re-order her thoughts. All the talk about the diary has thrown her off balance but she soon finds her way back to her point. 'A few hours before she died, she sent me a text saying she had something to tell me. I don't think she intended—'

'She had you figured out! You've always got to be the favourite, Mum. You've always got to be the person people turn to. She was playing you! For fuck's sake.' Isobel turns to her brother. 'I'm going to the pub. You coming?'

'Sure.' Noah briefly locks eyes with Anna. 'I'll get my wallet.'

'So what?' Isobel dares her parents. 'I have fake ID and sometimes I go to the pub. I don't smoke weed and I don't take pills.' She walks towards the front door. 'And I've never smoked crack!' she shouts back over her shoulder. 'You should be thankful!'

When the door closes behind them John says quietly, 'That went well.'

Anna stares at the half-eaten food on the table. 'I think it's time for some wine.'

John is in bed and Anna is emptying the dishwasher when Noah and Isobel return from the pub. They are quiet when they come in, no whispering, no drunken laughter. She hears one set of footsteps climb the stairs and then Noah comes into the kitchen. As soon as he sees Anna, he turns to leave again. 'You okay, love?'

'Yeah.' He hovers on the threshold.

'Did you want something?' He continues to hover. 'Don't mind me. I'm just finishing up here.'

She senses his reluctance as he approaches the sink, his steps uneven. 'I need some water.'

Anna hands him a glass and he runs the tap. She can't help but notice that there's a slight tremor in his hands. 'Did you drink too much?'

'No.' He gulps back the water. 'I just don't want to go to bed dehydrated.'

He is swaying on his feet but she doesn't think it's from alcohol. He is pale, shocked. 'Noah?' She touches his upper arm, feels goose-bumps through the short sleeves of his T-shirt. 'Are you okay?'

'I'm just …' His jaw tenses.

Anna feels a chill wind run through her. 'Did Isobel tell you what she was worried about?' she says quietly. 'Is it to do with you?'

'I'm really tired, Mum. I'm going to bed.'

'Noah.' She grabs for his arm. 'Are you the person that Tori knew something about? I mean …' She trails off, unable to fully articulate her suspicion.

'Isobel's right, Mum.' Noah's eyes meet hers. 'You need to drop this. Now. I mean it.' His tone is uncharacteristically harsh and she flinches. He walks away from her, takes the stairs at a run, his bedroom door closing with a definitive click.

The conversation is over, for him.

Anna lies awake.

Her eyes are wide open; sleep is nowhere close. John has been conked out for at least two hours. 'I think we have to back off now, Anna,' he said as she climbed into bed. 'Tori's dead so whatever was wrong is no longer an issue.'

One half of Anna agrees with him while the other half can't let it drop. What is wrong with you? she asks herself. Her own voice comes back in reply: You worry that one of your children will make a mistake that will haunt them for ever.

Admitting that to herself makes her feel better. She's not mad or suspicious, she's programmed to be wary where her children are concerned – and it's more a reflection of her than them. She has to exclude their involvement in Tori's death, not because she really believes them to be guilty, but simply for her own peace of mind.

She climbs out of bed and creeps along the corridor to Noah's bedroom. He's not an especially deep sleeper so she moves as quickly as she dares, leaving no time for the voice inside her head to switch from – you have to find out what's going on! To – you're overreacting; leave him alone!

Noah has pushed the duvet down to his waist, his arms resting on top. He's snoring quietly, his brow slightly furrowed, the way it always was when he was a baby. John used to say that Noah worked all his problems out overnight and that was why he was always so happy-go-lucky in the daytime. Never a moment's worry, that's what she always says about Noah when people ask. And it's absolutely true. He's good-natured, his default is a smile, he makes friends easily, he works as hard as he needs to and plays just as hard. That's why it's ridiculous to suspect him of anything.

But she's here now. In his bedroom, in the dark, because she needs to be sure that she's right to trust him.

Noah's mobile sits on the bedside cabinet and is plugged into the charger. The first thing she does is unplug it and then she positions his phone under his thumb and presses the button. The mobile lights up and Anna moves back into the hallway. His background photo is of the four of them when they climbed the Cuillin Mountains on the Isle of Skye. She scrolls through his texts. She doesn't really think Noah is the sort of boy who takes part in sexting or anything even remotely exploitative but this way she can be sure. She scans his emails and his photos. She feels a deep, liquid relief when she finds nothing except stuff from his friends: a girl called Lizzy who clearly likes him, uni friends discussing lecture rooms and study groups, rugby fixtures and trips to the pub.

She returns his phone and goes back to bed.

So that's that, then.

Chapter Thirty-Two

She wakes to the sound of the world ending. It's a crash so loud that the air in the bedroom fractures as if the very atoms themselves have been split. Anna screams automatically, no time to think or censor herself, and then there is another crash. This time glass scatters over the bed like jagged confetti and a brick lands a hair's-breadth from her upper arm.

'Fuck!' John shouts. Then he makes a sound she's never heard him make before. It's a visceral, animal moan. His left hand clutches the duvet and his right is raised to his face. A shard of glass has pierced his cheek and blood is running down his neck and onto his chest in a thick, red line. 'Anna! There's something in my face!'

'Don't pull it out!' Anna yells at him. She runs to the bathroom and seconds later is back with a towel. 'Let me hold this to your cheek,' she says. 'Help me put pressure on the wound.' She arranges his fingers on the towel, making sure they are either side of the broken glass. 'Press as hard as you can but be careful not to push the glass in any deeper.'

'You should make sure the kids are okay,' John tells her, wincing as he speaks so that more blood leaks from the wound, soaking into the material, turning white to pink and then pillar-box red.

'I will in a minute.' She positions herself between him

and the window so that if another brick comes through it will catch her, not him.

'What if they've been hurt?'

More blood; the towel is almost completely red.

'We'd hear the glass shatter.' Anna presses harder. 'Try not to talk, love. Rest your head against the headboard,' she says gently.

'What's going on?' Isobel appears at their bedroom door. Her eyes are wide with shock. 'Dad, are you okay?'

She begins to walk forward and John shouts, 'Stay away from the window!' His voice is so loud, so serious that Isobel bursts into tears.

Anna repositions John's fingers, then slithers off the bed and catches hold of Isobel's shoulders, pulling her into the corridor with her. 'It's okay, darling.' She strokes her hair. 'Dad's face is cut but he will be okay.'

'I don't understand. What's going on?'

'Do you think it's the same people as before?' Noah has joined them, his eyes panicked. 'Shall I go after them?'

'Absolutely not!' She glances back into the bedroom. 'John, if you start to feel dizzy, tell me. Noah, call the police and an ambulance for your dad.' Isobel is sobbing on Anna's shoulder. 'Your dad will be fine.' She hears her own voice, calm and even, while her heart is racing like a train. 'He'll be okay. He'll need stitches, but he'll be okay.'

Two bricks. Anna can see one on the bed and another on the floor. Will there be a third? She wants to return to the bedroom to be with John. She hears Noah on the phone: 'Please, come quickly, my dad is injured. Yes, he's conscious. My mum's a nurse. She knows what to do.'

There were about five seconds between the first and the second brick and now at least two minutes have gone by. 'Come into the bedroom, Isobel,' Anna says. 'You sit on the bed and hold Dad's towel. His arm will be tired.'

'There might be another brick, Anna,' John warns.

'I think it's unlikely. Too much time has passed. They'll have run off.'

'That's so much blood,' Isobel whispers, hanging back.

'Liquid spreads. And because it's red, it always looks more dramatic than it is,' Anna says, but really she's concerned. Any injury to the face causes significant blood loss because the head has such a rich blood supply. She fetches another towel and quickly swaps them round. 'Hold here, Isobel. Look.'

Isobel does as she's asked, wedging herself on the outside edge of the bed as she puts pressure on her dad's wound.

'Don't be afraid to press hard,' Anna tells her.

Both sets of neighbours also come to help. Miranda puts the kettle on. 'I'll make tea!' she shouts upstairs.

Geraldine assesses the situation and quietly makes everything better. First of all she gets shoes for everyone. 'You don't want to be stepping on glass.' Then she takes the bloody towel into the bathroom to soak, comes back into the bedroom and carefully removes pieces of broken glass from on top of the duvet.

John's face has grown paler and Anna begins to pile pillows under his feet and legs. 'Face is pale, raise the tail,' Noah says, his expression pinched. 'I remember that from your first-aid lessons, Mum.'

It feels like an hour but it's actually only about ten minutes before the police and the paramedics arrive. Professionals from both emergency services surge into the bedroom and take charge. Anna is grateful to be able to hand John's care over to the experts. 'You have a nasty cut on your arm, there,' one of them says to her. 'You'll be coming in the ambulance as well?'

'John's the priority,' Anna says. She has a tremor in

her legs that is spreading up to her torso. 'He's the important one.'

'For sure,' the paramedic replies. 'But you mustn't forget yourself, Anna. We'll prioritise your husband and see to your injury when we're in the rig.'

'I'll hold the fort here,' Geraldine says, her arm on Anna's waist to steady her. 'When the police are finished, I'll set things straight.'

'Thank you, Geraldine.' Anna blinks tears from her eyes and allows herself to be led into the hallway and lowered onto a chair. 'I really can't thank you enough.'

'We'll come too, Mum,' Noah says. He's dressed in jeans and a hoodie and is carrying a tray of mugs. Geraldine takes the tray from him.

'Has anyone seen Monty?' Isobel is also dressed now. She has a tissue scrunched in her hand and she lifts it up to rub at her eyes.

'He'll be up a tree or under a bush somewhere,' Anna says.

'He'll come back when everything's calmed down,' Geraldine says. 'And if he's doesn't, then I'll take a pocketful of treats and go on a search for him. Don't you worry.'

Geraldine's words have the desired effect and Isobel immediately looks calmer. Geraldine goes to give the tea to the crew in the bedroom and Anna is left with her children. 'I think the best thing would be for you both to pack an overnight bag and go to the Sykeses' house. You can help get things ready for Pippa's party.'

'But what about Dad?' Isobel asks.

'Dad will be well looked after. I'll stay with him.'

'But Mum, I can't enjoy myself at a party when Dad's injured!' Isobel's eyes are wild again. 'It feels wrong.'

'I understand that, darling, but we might need to hang

around for a while. I promise I'll call you regularly with updates.'

'Mum's right, Iso,' Noah says. 'We'd just be spare parts in the hospital. We're better going to the Sykeses'.'

'We'll join you later when your dad's all patched up.' Anna hands her mobile to Noah. 'Call Lynn while I get myself dressed.'

Her bedroom is busy with police officers and para-medics, so Anna takes her clothes into the bathroom. Before she gets dressed she sits down on the lid of the toilet seat and breathes. Her insides are jangling like sleigh bells, her senses heightened and her eyes popping as if she's drunk three cups of strong coffee on an empty stomach. She could do with a good cry but there's no time for that. She needs to support John.

There's blood on her nightdress. Seeing this prompts her to examine her arm. The paramedic was right – she has a significant cut that is oozing blood down into the crease of her elbow. She finds a bandage in the first-aid kit under the sink. She wraps it around the cut and tucks the edges in. Her face feels sticky and she checks herself in the mirror; she looks tired but, surprisingly, not panicked, not scared, not worried, despite the fact that the world has taken a crazy turn and she has her husband's blood smeared across her chin. She washes her hands and face and then dries them.

The bricks were meant for her, she thinks as she cleans her teeth. If the brick had travelled a couple of feet further, it could have hit her on the head and knocked her out. She pulls on underwear and trousers. If it had been a foot to the left, her face would be cut and that would be fairer considering she has brought all this trouble into the house. Not deliberately, not willingly. But it's her fault. Were they foolish to have stayed here after the ski mask man's threat? Or is this someone else?

Every which way she turns she finds herself wondering at her own mistakes. What if the glass had landed three inches lower and sliced through John's carotid artery? What if the bricks had gone through Noah's window? There is a shorter distance from window to bed. He could have been killed. What if whoever did this had climbed up onto the flat roof and got into Isobel's bedroom?

Her body convulses with a penetrating shudder at it dawns on her how serious this might have been. A whimper escapes from her mouth and she claps her hand over it to prevent another sound. *This is the time to be strong, to step up. Do not fall apart.*

There's a knock on the bathroom door. 'Mum.' It's Noah's voice. 'They're taking Dad downstairs to the ambulance.'

'Just coming.' She pulls on a T-shirt and jumper and opens the door. Noah looks worried. She touches his upper arm. It's meant to be reassuring but he goes to catch her as if she is clutching at him and might fall. 'I'm okay, love. Really.' She gives him a half smile. 'Did you get through to Lynn?'

'Yeah. She's coming to collect us.'

The police are taking photographs of the smashed window and have bagged both bricks. 'We might be lucky and find some prints on these,' a young PC tells Anna.

'That's great. Thank you.' Anna steps to one side as the paramedics help John to his feet. His face is now heavily bandaged. She hadn't noticed before but his left arm is a mass of tiny lacerations and one large, jagged lightning-shaped cut close to his elbow. The paramedics lead him slowly to the bottom of the stairs, all the while talking to him: 'How are you feeling now, John?'

'Bit woozy, but … not too bad.'

Anna grabs her handbag and kisses Isobel and Noah goodbye before following John into the ambulance. John is given pain relief and Anna's arm is re-dressed by the time they arrive at the hospital. It's not yet nine in the morning so the Accident and Emergency department is quiet. The paramedics take them straight to the treatment area where they're greeted by a nurse and a doctor. The nurse listens to the handover from the paramedics while the doctor examines John's wound.

'This is a nasty cut,' the doctor says, frowning.

'Just as well I'm not a model,' John says. 'My career would be over.'

'And what is your career?' the doctor asks, as he gently moves the glass stuck in the wound.

'I'm a chemistry teacher.'

'Really? Ever watched *Breaking Bad*?'

'I have,' John replies. 'And before you ask, the chemistry's pretty accurate.'

The doctor takes off his gloves and drops them into the pedal bin. 'I'm not going to remove that glass yet. I'm going to bleep our max-fax registrar.' He whips open the curtains and lets them fall together again behind him.

'Maxillo-facial,' Anna tells John. She's standing beside the trolley, taking everything in. 'They might want to give you an anaesthetic before they stitch you up.'

'Did worse playing football.'

'I have some IV fluids here, John,' the nurse says. 'And a bag of O negative blood.' She brings a drip stand and several packets over to the bed. 'We're lucky the paramedics put this line in for us.' She opens the small portal on the back of his hand. 'Saves a bit of time.'

'Do your worst, Sarah,' John says, reading her name

badge. 'I promise I won't flinch.' He's managing to stay
upbeat but Anna can tell that he's flagging.

'I'll get the blood started first,' Sarah says. 'And then
we'll give you the bag of fluid.'

'I could do with a drink of water,' John says.

'We're going to hold off on oral liquids and food for
now. Just in case you need an op.'

'Whatever you think is best,' he says, his eyes closing.
'I met my wife in an A and E department. She's a nurse.'

John is taken into theatre just after midday. Anna calls
Noah and Isobel to let them know, then she finds a
vending machine and buys a cup of coffee and a cheese
sandwich. She finds the ward John will return to and
sits next to the bed they have allocated for him. She
goes through her handbag, wishing she'd brought a book
with her; but then she probably wouldn't be able to
concentrate on it anyway. She could go downstairs to
the shop at the hospital entrance and buy a magazine
but she's comfy in the chair. She plays a dozen games
of solitaire on her phone and then finds herself back on
Facebook, just to see whether anyone has mentioned the
bricks through her window. Anna skims through the first
dozen or so posts and then comes to one about the
newspaper article:

Suzy Meeks
Just read the *Courier*. Great piece by Flora Manson.

*

Reply Steve Mulberry
What does it say? #schoolnurserotinjail

*

Reply Suzy Meeks
Basically that she's one of those controlling people.
#RIPVictoriaCarmichael

*

Reply Steve Mulberry
Psychopath springs to mind. #schoolnurserotinjail

*

And then, an hour later:

Steve Mulberry
Wait for it, folks! I've just heard that someone threw a brick
through her window this morning. She was taken off in an
ambulance. #schoolnurserotinjail

*

Reply Suzy Meeks
Hope they don't work too hard to save her.

*

Reply Steve Mulberry
Bitch is getting what she deserves.

*

Reply Julia Raeburn
While I don't condone violence of any sort, I can't deny
that I gave a cheer when I read this!!!

*

So says the woman who punched Matt in the face, Anna
thinks. She's about to log off when a post by Holly
Standing catches her eye.

Me and Tori having fun in the summer. #loveyouTori

*

Anna scrolls through the photos: dozens of selfies and posed shots in Glasgow city centre, in bars and restaurants, and by the seaside. She zooms in on Tori's face, sees the light in her eyes, the fun in her smile. No matter what Isobel says, she finds it hard to believe that Tori was all bad. Maybe she did play Anna for a fool some of the time but surely not all of it?

When she gets to the last photograph, she's about to close the app when she spots someone. She zooms in on the face. Her mouth drops open.

Since Anna married John, her life has been a smooth run. There have been ups and downs, of course, but her life's roller-coaster has generally been a gentle affair – a roller-coaster for toddlers, not the adult version that dips and lunges and leaves your stomach in one place, your dizzy, screaming head in another.

But seeing the face of a person she loves standing close to Tori in a Glasgow club takes Anna into a nightmare theme park, where she is tied to a big dipper, her life nose-diving into the ground.

'Could we remind ourselves what makes for a successful group dynamic?' Anna asked the class. Although it was almost the end of term, she did this periodically when she sensed that the boundaries were blurring.

'Listening,' Hester called out and Anna wrote it on the whiteboard.

'Respect,' another voice called out.

'Respecting each other's viewpoint is key,' Anna agreed as she wrote it up.

'Every team member engaged in what's taking place.'

'What happens in this room stays in this room.'

She added both of these to the list. 'It's important to have each other's backs, don't you think?' There was a muted murmur of agreement. 'Okay.' She put the board marker down on the desk. 'So the topic for today is consent. In the broadest sense, consent means giving permission for something to happen.' She paused, stared round at each of the faces upturned in her direction. 'But what does that actually mean? Legally and personally.' She glanced at the clock on the wall. 'You have twenty minutes to discuss this in your groups and then you'll share your thoughts with the class.'

They immediately congregated in their separate huddles, desks moved to one side, chairs scraped across the floor. Anna walked from group to group, catching snippets of sentences:

'... but in the context of a healthy relationship ...'

'... nothing to do with gender inequality ...'

'... but wait! Teenagers make impulsive decisions because they are motivated by short-term gains.' It was Tori who was speaking. 'I watched a TED talk on it. It's to do with the connections in the brain.'

'Sex without consent is rape. End of,' Isobel said. 'And fifteen-year-olds can't consent to sex with someone aged sixteen and over. It's the law.'

'But criminalising young adults for something that's natural,' Tori said. 'How can that be right?'

'What has this got to do with consent?' Isobel said. She was growing impatient, Anna noticed. This often happened during the group work as Tori tended to provoke debate in a way that the others couldn't handle.

'Suppose you're a nineteen-year-old boy and you meet a girl in a club,' Tori said, her expression animated. 'It's fair to make the assumption that she's eighteen, isn't it? You hook up and have sex with her and then you find out she's fifteen.'

'So you're saying that if a man has sex with a fifteen-year-old girl, he shouldn't face prosecution?' Isobel asked her.

'Maybe but maybe not. It depends on the context. Because a fifteen-year-old can pretend to be sixteen. What's the guy supposed to do? Ask to see her passport?'

'I don't believe that happens to decent men,' Isobel said.

'What?' Tori's eyes were wide. 'You don't believe that decent men can be caught out? Their names added to the sex offenders register? Their whole lives ruined?'

'No, I don't,' Isobel said, irritated now. 'I think that, as usual, Tori, you're stirring for the sake of it.'

Tori's expression darkened. 'So much for respecting other people's opinions, Isobel.'

Chapter Thirty-Three

The party is already in full swing when Anna arrives at the Sykeses'. Their house is lit up, inside and out. Oversized fairy lights are strung from tree to tree and across the top of the wooden lintels above the windows. Gold-coloured balloons are clumped together at intervals along the path, blowing in the breeze like gigantic flowers. Anna pushes open the front door and is immediately greeted by a meld of music and loud voices. The downstairs is mostly open plan, stretching for over thirty metres to bifold doors that lead out onto the decking.

The first person she bumps into is Matt. He grabs her in a hug. 'How's John? What's the latest?'

'The surgery went well,' she tells him. 'They picked all the glass out and his cheek has been very neatly stitched up. He came out of theatre mid-afternoon and is asleep now. They're going to keep him in overnight.'

'Good news.' Matt smiles and hands her a drink. 'Low-alcohol punch. Lynn has been round the garden checking the bushes for hidden bottles of vodka.'

'Thank you.' She sips the drink. 'Your eye looks better.'

'The bruising is still there but Pippa has put some of her foundation over it. I think it's a case of ensuring I look as normal as possible.' He points his glass over Anna's shoulder. 'She's making sure she's the centre of attention this evening.'

Anna turns to glance over her shoulder and spots Pippa on the decking. 'She looks gorgeous.'

'Aye. She's growing up.'

Pippa is wearing a short, backless silver dress that shimmers in the light. ('It's close to a thousand pounds but she's only seventeen once,' Lynn had told Anna.) Pippa has one arm round Isobel and the other round Ed Wiseman. Several of their classmates are taking photographs on their phones while they pull silly faces. Anna's pleased to see that Isobel looks relaxed and happy.

'Lynn has got the guest house ready for you all,' Matt tells her.

'Thank you for coming to our rescue – again.' She widens tired eyes. 'The nightmare continues. It should have been me who got hit by the brick, not John.'

'Don't be daft. John would do anything for you. You know that.' He clears his throat and his face twists with discomfort. 'Anna, I don't know whether you've seen the local rag …' He trails off.

'I have,' Anna says quickly, her hand resting on his arm. 'I'm front page news.' She rolls her eyes. 'Lucky me.'

'It was no sooner through the door than it went straight into the bin,' Matt says. His eyes flick towards the clock on the wall – eight fifteen. 'Tori's parents are arriving at nine. Lynn's organised a' – he stares down at his feet – 'ceremony, I suppose you would call it.'

'She told me. I'm really pleased it's happening. I'll be sure to keep out of the way.'

Matt's forehead creases. 'I don't want to …'

'I understand, Matt.' She kisses his cheek. 'The last thing any of us want is to spoil Pippa's party.' She smiles. 'Have you seen Noah?' Her voice is surprisingly even.

'I expect he's in the barn. We hired some games tables so most of the lads are hanging out down there.'

Anna excuses herself to go to speak to him. Isobel doesn't notice her as she zigzags through the throng of teenagers on the decking and onto the gravel path. The garden slopes for over one hundred metres towards the loch at the bottom but she doesn't need to go that far. Almost immediately to the right of the house is the converted barn. Several pupils say hello to Anna as she passes by, oblivious, it seems, to what's been playing out online and in the local press. Then someone grabs for her arm and she jumps before she realises it's Lynn. 'Anna! How's John?'

'He's okay.' She tells Lynn about his operation and thanks her for preparing for their stay. 'I just need to have a word with Noah and then I'll come to join you for a proper drink.'

'We've got Tori's parents arriving shortly but don't feel you have to leave.'

'Matt told me. I'll hide so they don't see me.' She carries on walking and calls back, 'You look great by the way!'

Lynn does a twirl, her red silk skirt floating outward, before she continues walking up to the house.

Matt's right – the barn is full of young men and half a dozen girls who are joining in with the games: table football, darts, table tennis and a computer game in the corner on a screen larger than Anna's kitchen table.

Noah is playing table tennis and Anna doesn't interrupt him. She waits for him to finish because there's really no rush. She stares again at the photo Holly posted on the Facebook page. Noah, her son, with his arm around Tori. He told Anna he didn't know her. But only a month ago he was with her in a Glasgow nightclub.

After the lesson, Tori's resentment towards Isobel burned in her chest. She tried to ignore it. She tried to douse it in water

*by thinking of all the reasons Isobel would fail in her life.
She wasn't very bright, very pretty, very anything at all.
She was a big fish in this little Bishopglen pond, and univer-
sity would strip her of all her arrogance.*

*But Tori couldn't ignore the fact that Isobel's parents were
the ones she would have chosen for herself. And for that
reason, she was jealous of Isobel. She wanted, needed, to even
the score somehow, to rock her perfect family boat. She'd
heard a great deal about Noah because Isobel often spoke of
him. Tori would have given at least twenty IQ points – the
gift that set her apart from her peers – to have had an older
brother she could look up to, confide in, share the agonies of
their parents' divorce.*

*She had looked online to see whether she could find Noah's
profile. She couldn't. But there were photographs of him on
Ed Wiseman's Facebook page, multiple shots of them on
beaches, washing baby elephants, on mountain peaks. And
there was talk of what they were doing next. There was an
early event for those studying engineering at Glasgow
University. It was happening at the end of August.*

*That was all it took. At first it was simply a fantastical
notion – she could have sex with Noah to get back at Isobel,
to prove her point that decent men could be fooled. She'd
been put up a school year when she joined Bishopglen, so
she was still fifteen. Her birthday wasn't until the end of
October and that made her the youngest in her year by a
long way.*

*She suggested to Holly that they go to Glasgow for the
evening. Holly's cousin lived there and often let them bunk
overnight on his sofa. She made it seem like an accident
when they joined a group of fresher engineering students at
a venue in the West End. The evening played out with the
ease of something that was meant to be. She had done her
homework and so she knew he was interested in space science.*

It didn't take much manoeuvring to get chatting to him. She pretended she'd also been to the Far East on a gap year. At one point she saw Holly's WTF? expression as she told him all about the fisherman's boat she sailed on in Laos. She pretended she was about to study engineering too.

He was staying the night in the halls of residence and she told a wide-eyed Holly that she was going back with him. While neither of them were virgins, their sex lives thus far had involved boys they'd known since nursery school. Tori convinced her she would be safe and left with Noah. Even up to that very last second, she thought, This will never work! He'll realise I'm fifteen. Something I say or do will give me away.

They got into his room and started kissing. She brought a condom out of her back pocket and he said, 'Are you sure?' She smiled and kissed him some more.

The sex was better than she'd had with any of the boys at the skate park – for starters it was on a bed, there was foreplay and he took his time. Afterwards, she knew she should have felt something resembling remorse but she didn't because she was now imagining the look on Isobel's face when she told her.

She filmed him when he was asleep. She zoomed in on the used condom on the floor and their clothes scattered like debris around the room. She propped the phone up against the glass on the bedside table and woke him up. Then she filmed them having sex again.

Noah finishes his game of table tennis and moves off to the side to let someone else play. He doesn't notice his mum at first but when he does, he comes straight across. 'How's Dad?'

'He's doing really well. Your uncles and aunts were there when I left so he's got plenty company.'

'Thank God.' He gives a relieved smile. 'That could have been serious.'

'I need to talk to you, Noah.'

'What? Now?'

'Yes, now.' She takes his arm and walks them both round the corner of the barn, glancing up towards the house to make sure that Isobel hasn't spotted them. She finds the photograph on her phone and holds the screen out towards him. His face pales and he looks away, shifting on his feet. 'You told me you didn't know her,' she says quietly.

'I didn't know her.' He shakes his head several times, his breath quickening, before he says, 'I didn't know her, Mum, and I *swear* I didn't know she was fifteen.' He presses his fingers into the corners of his eyes. 'She told me her name was Daisy and that she was also going to be studying engineering. She had this whole story about a gap year in Laos and she knew about space science and – Fuck! I was such a fool! I had no idea she was the Victoria Carmichael Dad had spoken about. And even when you told me she had accused you of hitting her, I still had no idea! I swear to God.'

Anna is frowning as she focuses on the fact that he mentioned Tori's age. 'Please tell me you didn't have sex with her?'

He doesn't speak; the expression on his face gives him away.

'Jesus, Noah! That's against the law!'

'I know! I know that! Of course I fucking know that! She targeted me, Mum, because of something that happened during a lesson. One of your lessons.' He points an accusing finger, then immediately rolls his head back on his neck. 'Sorry. Of course it's not your fault. I'm not trying to shift the blame.'

There is a gear change in Anna's brain and the pieces of the puzzle drop into place: she remembers a Sex and Relationships lesson back in June, she remembers hearing her daughter say something to Tori, her words almost a challenge.

Anna hugs Noah, feels the bones of him shivering under her arms. 'I'm sure you would never have had sex with her if you'd known she was under age.'

'She did it to get back at Isobel.' He blows out his breath. 'She filmed us together and showed it to her.' His face contorts. 'There had to be something wrong with her, Mum. Who does that? Who films themselves having sex?'

Anna's concern deepens. 'I didn't know there was a video.'

'She deleted it in front of Isobel. I think she regretted what she'd done but who knows?' He starts pacing, almost tripping up as his foot catches on the uneven ground. 'If the police had found it on her mobile I think they would have questioned me by now.' He shakes his head, his face lined with worry. 'I'm sorry she's dead but poor Isobel. She's been bricking it for weeks now.'

Anna reaches for his sleeve to stop the agitated circling. 'And you weren't in town on the Friday night she died?'

'What do you mean?' He frowns, confused.

'Did you go and see her last Friday?'

'Jesus! No!' He backs away from his mum. 'Is that what you think?' She watches his eyes as he grapples with what she is suggesting. 'You think I could have killed her?' He bangs the flat of his hand on his forehead. 'Fuck, Mum! First Isobel and now me? I didn't even know I knew her until Isobel told me in the pub last night.' He holds up a hand. 'Wait! I can prove that I was nowhere near here on Friday.'

He moves past Anna and goes back into the barn, where Ed Wiseman is standing by the pool table chatting to Pippa and Isobel. Isobel glances across and catches her mum's eye, then she marches straight over to speak to her. She's wearing a T-shirt dress and her feet are bare. 'You've left Dad on his own?' she accuses Anna, no 'Hi Mum' or 'Good to see you.'

'Of course I haven't,' Anna replies, her tone calm. 'The Pierces have descended. When I left, they were reminiscing about a spaniel they had when they were growing up.'

'Oh. Okay.' She stares at Anna, thinking. Her hair is curled around her shoulders and her eye make-up accentuates the soft grey of her eyes. 'What's going on with you and Noah?'

'I … he told me about what happened with Tori.'

Isobel's expression grows wary. 'Don't tell anyone,' she grinds out. 'I mean it, Mum.'

'I'm not going to tell anyone! Do you honestly imagine I would?'

Noah is back by her side with Ed's phone. 'Here you go.' He scrolls through photos and then shows Anna the automatic record of date, time and place – Friday night, after midnight, in Glasgow Halls of Residence. 'Only electrons can be in two places at once,' he says.

'Thank you, love. I'm sorry.' Anna is flooded with relief. 'I'm sorry that Tori did this to you, and I'm sorry that you had to keep it a secret, Isobel.' She looks at her daughter. 'I can only imagine how stressful this has been for you.' It's on the tip of her tongue to say, *I wish you'd told me*, but she'll leave that for another time.

Ed calls to them from across the barn and Noah and Isobel are drawn back to their friends. She watches them as they walk away, Noah's arm round Isobel's shoulder.

She's sad that Tori did what she did, and Noah has learned a hard lesson, a lesson that could have got him into serious trouble, but maybe now the madness is over. She has good kids. She can breathe again. She can stop worrying that they or John were involved in Tori's death: John was at home, Noah was in Glasgow and Isobel was in the boarding house. Perhaps no one will ever know what happened to Tori, but that's for the police to work out, not her.

It's eight forty-five and she needs to stay out of the way of Tori's parents, so she walks further down the garden towards the loch. She dodges a couple of girls who are deep in conversation and another couple sitting on a fallen tree. Then she spots Owen. He's staring out at the still water, a bottle of lager in his hand. She hasn't spoken to him since she denied using Geraldine's log-in. Now would be a good time to put that right.

'I need to make a confession,' she says when she's in earshot and before her courage fails her.

He turns towards her. 'Oh?'

'It *was* me who logged in as Geraldine.'

'I thought as much.' He has another lager at his feet. He reaches down and passes it to her. 'I had to inform the governors. There may want to follow it up.'

Anna registers this with slight nod. 'I've apologised to Geraldine.' She takes a drink from the bottle and stands beside him. 'I'm sorry I lied to you.'

'But are you sorry you did it?'

She inclines her head. 'I'm sorry I felt the need to do it. I was being paranoid. I thought Isobel was up to something.'

'And was she?'

'No. Or at least not the way I thought.' She raises her eyebrows. 'It was more about me than her.'

'How come?'

'I worry about them.' She shrugs. 'I worry about my kids making a mistake. I can't help it.' She holds the bottle a little tighter. 'Did I ever tell you how my mum died?'

'A car crash, wasn't it?'

'There's a bit more to it than that.' She takes a deep breath. 'I was much the same age as Tori when it happened. And, like her, I told a lot of lies. My dad was marrying Angela. I was angry with them both, with my mother, with the world. There had been a story in the paper about a girl who'd been sexually abused by her father and I decided that was the best way to get back at him.'

'You can't lie about something like that,' Owen says and she hears the warning note in his voice.

'I wrote in my diary that he'd been forcing me to have sex with him,' Anna continues. 'That it had started when I was thirteen. And then I left the diary in his house, expecting Angela to read it. She was always going through my stuff.'

'Fuck, Anna.' She looks at him now and his expression leaves her in no doubt how he feels about this. 'That's heavy.'

'I know. I didn't think through the consequences.' She briefly closes her eyes, wonders at the fact that she's sober and is saying these words out loud. 'He dropped the diary back at the house. His fiancée hadn't read it and neither had he, which was a relief because I'd spent the whole day at school realising it was a horrible, cruel mistake.'

'Thank God for that,' Owen says.

'Not really, because when I came home my mum was in a state. *She* had read it. She was all set to go and rip my dad's balls off until I told her I'd made it up. She wouldn't believe me at first but when I pointed out the similarities between my story and the girl in the news she had to believe me. She was horrified that I could be so spiteful.' Anna pauses to let a five-second silence sharpen the edges of her guilt. 'She slapped my face a couple of times and then went out to drink with her friends. The last words she said to me were, "You're a wicked girl, Anna! And I am going to think up a serious punishment for you."' Her voice lowers. 'She wasn't a great driver at the best of times and when she was angry or upset she was careless. She went through a red light and a lorry coming the other way ploughed into her.'

Her words hang helpless in the air before Owen says, 'You can't blame yourself for her death. She was the adult. She was the one behind the wheel.'

'I do blame myself,' she says firmly. 'And because it was such a fatal mistake, I've always worried that one of my children – especially Isobel, because she can be impulsive like me and not think things through – might do something similar, a misstep that would change the direction of her life for ever.' She clutches the bottle tighter still; her knuckles are white. 'My mother's death is on me, Owen. And it always will be.'

'I don't know what to say.' He shakes his head, defeated. 'I understand why you feel the way you do but rationally you must know that you were a child.' He rummages in his pocket and pulls out the joint he got from his brother. 'Would this help?'

'There are teenagers everywhere,' she says.

'You're right.' He doesn't look disappointed; he looks relieved, as if an option has been taken away from him and lightened his load. He throws the joint on the ground and stamps it underfoot. 'More than either of our jobs are worth.'

Anna folds her arms. In truth, she could do with a fast track to relaxation. Although she now believes her children are not involved in Tori's death, John is in hospital and she is still on the police's radar. The burden is yet to be lifted from her shoulders. But tempting as it is to smoke the joint, she remembers what happened the last time.

It was a month after Anna had secured the head of department post and she was feeling buoyant. That morning all four of them had been to see the cottage they would move into. Noah and Isobel chose their bedrooms and John was pleased to find a tiny room at the top of the house, barely enough to turn around in, but with a skylight that was perfect for a telescope. That evening there was a barbecue in the Sykeses' garden for the parents in Pippa and Isobel's class. John's mum was ill so he had to leave early, the kids were busy playing in the barn and Anna ended up outside with Owen. He was leaning against the waist-high wall, a bottle of tequila and a shot glass beside him.

'We saw the house today,' she told him. 'It's going to be perfect for us.'

'I'm glad it's working out.' His tone was subdued.

'You okay?'

He told her his father had just died, and far from being indifferent that the man he cared little for was dead, he felt the ache of lost chances. 'He wasn't cut out to be a father or a husband but …' He shook his head. 'I wish, as adults, we'd managed to find common ground.'

They had a heart-to-heart over tequila shots, and discovered they shared a dysfunctional childhood that made them determined to parent in an active, thoughtful way. 'I want

Julie Corbin

282

my kids to know they're loved,' Owen said. 'And grow into kind and decent adults.'

When he pulled a joint from his pocket, she didn't say no. She inhaled deeply and leaned back against the wall; they were shoulder to shoulder. They passed the joint back and forth between them one more time, neither of them speaking, until Anna shook her head. 'No more for me.'

The seconds lengthened as the dope and the alcohol skipped through Anna's bloodstream. She was suffused with wellbeing. Peace, happiness, light – all the good stuff. She remembered a creeping paranoia from the few times she smoked dope when she was younger but not with this joint. This felt different, better. Laughter sat in her chest just waiting for the moment to bubble up and sing. But before she caught hold of those bubbles she remembered that Owen was bereaved and when she leaned in towards him, it was to give him a comforting kiss on the cheek – that's all – and she would never have even contemplated such a thing but for the fact that she was high, and dusk had bled into darkness so that the only light came from the galaxy of stars that spread like dropped diamonds across the sky.

Owen turned his head towards her just as her lips approached his cheek. She didn't think his turning towards her was deliberate; it was more reflex than a conscious act. And when their lips met Anna felt something she hadn't for a while: this was someone who understood her, knew the essence of her and didn't find fault.

Five seconds of leaning into each other, experiencing a kiss that lit fire, before the outside light was tripped and, at once, they drew apart so that when Lynn came round the corner, Anna was on her feet and Owen was finishing his drink.

Nothing else would have happened, Anna told herself as she lay in bed later that night, rigid with the reality of her betrayal. John had always sensed a connection between her and Owen and now she had proven his point. But while she would never deny, to herself at least, that there was something between them, an unexplored sexual tension that they both kept a lid on, it didn't mean they would ever act on it.

A kiss was just a kiss. And Anna knew with absolute certainty that life was about what you focused your attention on. You made up your mind what you wanted and then you focused on getting it. And if you were lucky enough to get it then you focused on keeping it. You didn't forget that this was a hard-won prize you were holding. She had planted a flag for her family and she protected that flag, ensured it kept flying no matter how attractive a face temptation wore.

They hadn't kissed − not since that first time − never since then. They didn't seek each other out. Their paths barely crossed. He had never told anyone and neither had she. If there could be integrity in a stolen kiss then they had managed it. Both of them knew that what they really wanted lay at home. That success was not about the individual; it was about family.

Should an otherwise loving and loyal marriage be ruined by a five-second lack of focus?

Anna didn't think so.

Chapter Thirty-Four

They talk about the shock of the bricks coming through the window – 'Don't these people realise that they could kill someone?' – and John's operation: 'He's expected to make a full recovery. He'll be left with a tiny scar. That's all.' And how much Lynn and Matt have helped them. 'They're so supportive. I don't know what we'd do without them.'

'I've always been impressed that you got past Lynn telling John.'

'Eh?' Anna is smiling. 'Telling him what?'

'That she saw us together, here, that night.'

Anna stares at him. 'I don't understand.'

'She came outside to speak to us. Remember?'

Anna does remember. 'But the light tripped seconds before we saw her. By the time she came into view we'd pulled apart.'

'They have security cameras on the edge of the roof.' He points up to the house, his hand moving from left to right. 'It wasn't so dark that the camera wouldn't have recorded a clear enough picture of us both.'

Anna's jaw drops open. 'I don't believe you!' She is shaking her head, completely flabbergasted. 'Lynn wouldn't do that! She's my best friend! She would talk to me. She wouldn't go to John behind my back!'

'She never told you? But I thought—' He stops. 'I'm sorry. I thought you must have known.'

'Are you sure she told John?' Anna asks, still disbelieving.

Owen nods. 'A week after it happened, he came to have it out with me. I was down by the loch. He swung at me, accused me of giving you the job because we were having an affair. I denied it, and he said that Lynn had caught us kissing. I denied that too and he said that he knew for a fact it had happened, which I took to mean he had seen evidence.'

Anna has fallen back against a tree, her mouth open. 'That can't be right! She's my friend, for fuck's sake!' She gasps. 'John has known about this for five years?'

'I'm sorry, I would have mentioned something sooner if I thought there was a chance you didn't know.'

'And did Lynn tell Katia?'

'No.'

'So she tells John, but your wife remains oblivious?' Anger ignites. 'This is fucking unbelievable!'

She starts up towards the house but Owen grabs her arm. 'Don't, Anna. Don't go up there. Tori's parents have arrived.'

The mood is changing up at the house. Everyone has gathered on the decking and a hush has descended over the group. She hears Lynn's voice addressing Tori's parents. 'Welcome to our home,' Lynn is saying. 'We want to lend our support to you both.'

Anna begins to retch and the two mouthfuls of lager she swallowed come back up. She allows Owen to lead her into the shadow of the trees where she can no longer hear Lynn's voice. 'No wonder John has always been suspicious of us.' She wipes the back of her hand across her mouth. This whole time he's known that she was lying. But then, the accusation he's frequently thrown at her was that she was having an affair and that's why she got the promotion, not that she shared a five-second kiss with Owen a month later.

Splitting hairs.

Smoke and fire.

Deceit is deceit.

John mustn't have believed Owen. He must have thought – must still think – that the kiss was evidence of the affair.

And Lynn is two-faced. The woman she considers her best friend. The woman Anna would have sworn blind would stick by her no matter what has been speaking behind her back. She thought they had solidarity, as women, as friends, as mothers and colleagues. 'I don't get it,' she says. 'I would never do that to her. I wouldn't do it to anyone! Not even Julia bloody Raeburn.'

'Could she have thought John deserved to know?'

'Maybe.' Anna throws up her arms. 'But then talk to me about it!'

'She's a woman who likes to be in control. Did you ever tell her there was an attraction between us?'

'No! Of course not.'

'Could she have been annoyed you didn't tell her?'

'Why? Because friends are supposed to share absolutely everything?' Anna puts a hand up to her forehead. 'We're grown-ups, for Christ's sake! Messing in my marriage? That can never be okay.'

'I'm sorry, Anna. I—'

'My husband is in hospital. I'm worried about my children being in danger. I'm being destroyed online and also in the press.' She points an accusing finger at him. 'And you tell me this now? Your timing is off, Owen. Really fucking off.'

'I saw the newspaper article. The school's lawyers have spoken to the editor and owner, who are scrambling to prevent a libel case. There will be an apology in the next edition.'

'After the damage is done,' Anna says. She rests her head against a tree, the bark rough against her cheek. 'I need to think about this.' She takes a breath. 'I'm not going to say anything to Lynn. Not yet. Not until I've spoken to John.'

'That sounds wise.'

'If information is power then I'm best not to let her know that I know.' She shakes her head. 'Fuck. I can't play those sorts of games.' She stares up at the sky, comforted by its vastness. In the grand scheme of galaxies she is less than a speck on a minuscule planet that is profoundly insignificant. How can any of these betrayals and deceits really matter?

Except that they do. 'I'm supposed to be staying here with the kids but I can't do that now.'

'You're welcome to stay with us,' Owen says.

'It's not the best idea,' she says shortly. 'The kids can stay here and I'll stay with John's mum.'

She walks out into the clearing just as a loud rendition of 'Happy Birthday' begins on the decking. Lynn is carrying a cake, bright with candles, towards an excited Pippa. Anna begins to walk up the hill, hugging the treeline. She doesn't say goodbye to Owen. She's far too angry with him. How could he sit on that information for five years?

She follows the path round the side of the garage and makes it to the front without being seen. A car is leaving the driveway – Tori's parents, she thinks. She's dodged that bullet, at least. But she's wrong. She's about to climb into her car when a voice says, 'She liked you, you know.'

Anna freezes.

'My daughter. She really liked you. Sister Pierce this and Sister Pierce that.'

The central part of the driveway is lit up but the edges are in shadow and Anna's eyes focus on a gloomy corner where a shape is hunched on the ground.

'She looked up to you. You were kind.' She makes an attempt to stand but her foot slides and she immediately gives up. 'Kind.'

Anna runs across and sits down on the ground beside her. 'Saskia.'

'Not like me. I wasn't kind. I was a bitch of a mother.' Her head flops down towards her chest. 'And now it's too late.'

Anna reaches out, feels the woman's hands grip hers tightly. 'I am so, so sorry for your loss, Saskia. Truly I am.'

'She hated me drinking.'

'This is an impossibly difficult time for you.'

'I know you would never have hit her. That's all just stupid.' She makes a gurgling sound and then she gasps and begins to sob. Anna hugs her, feels her grief pass through her in a shuddering wave as she helps her to her feet. Her arm around her waist, she leads her towards her car. 'Let me give you a lift home,' she says. 'You shouldn't be alone at a time like this.'

On the drive back, Saskia stops sobbing and is then completely quiet. This worries Anna and she frequently glances across at her. There is hopelessness in the stoop of her shoulders and the glassy expression in her eyes.

'I won't remember any of this,' Saskia tells Anna when she helps her upstairs and into bed. 'I drink and then I black out.' Her eyes glaze and then clear. 'It couldn't have been me who pushed her, could it?' She's digging her nails into the soft skin of Anna's forearm as she speaks. 'Do you think it was me?'

'No! You didn't push her. Of course you didn't. Why would you have done that?' She strokes Saskia's hair until she settles her head back against the pillow. 'You loved Tori. You were her mother.'

Saskia nods. 'She knew I loved her, didn't she?'

'She did,' Anna tells her. 'She really did.'

Anna's mood is sombre when she leaves Saskia to sleep off the booze. The whole situation is desperate. There but for the grace of God, Anna thinks as she drives to the hospital. It's eleven thirty, well past visiting hours, but she goes anyway and spends five minutes persuading the lead nurse on night duty to buzz her onto the ward. As she reaches the nurses' station, she sees that the nurse has a copy of the *Courier* in front of her. 'Yes, that's me,' Anna says, expecting judgement to follow – a dismissive stare or a tut of disapproval.

'In a job like ours, sometimes you can't do right for doing wrong,' the nurse says.

'You're right,' Anna replies. 'And what's even worse is that most people believe what they read in the papers.'

'Not me.' The nurse stands up and indicates for Anna to follow her along the corridor. 'Fake news is everywhere now, isn't it?' She opens the door to the single room where John is lying on his side, eyes closed. 'Looks like your husband is already asleep but by all means go in and say goodnight.'

Anna pulls up a chair and takes John's hand. She speaks quietly, leaning in close as she talks. She tells him about Tori's mum: 'She's in a terrible state. It's heart-breaking, and I know it's selfish, but I feel so relieved that she doesn't blame me.' She mentions the party, not referring to her conversation with Noah because what she needs to talk about is that kiss. 'I found out this evening that Lynn told you she caught Owen and me kissing.' She pauses but his eyes remain closed, his breathing steady. 'It was a one-off mistake, John. As God is my witness I've never done anything like that before or since. I should have told you about it but I couldn't bring myself to say the words. And so I buried it, the way I bury most things that I don't like about myself.' She kisses the back of his hand. 'I should go now but I'll be back first thing in the morning.' She kisses his forehead. 'I love you.'

It's when she's at the door that he calls after her, 'I've waited five years to hear that.' He opens one eye. 'I love you too, Anna.'

Chapter Thirty-Five

It's three days later, and John's first day back at school. A semicircle of tiny, neat stitches marks his cheek. 'The kids are bound to ask me what happened and I'm going to tell them the truth. Let them see what encouraging online hatred can lead to.'

The police have caught the two men who did it. Fired up by the vitriol on Facebook, they each threw a brick at the window. They'll be charged with grievous bodily harm and could even face time in prison. It's stopped all the online chatter dead in its tracks and many previously posted messages have been deleted. Julia Raeburn's posts have all been taken down and Anna wonders whether it's because of guilt or fear. Has she reflected on the things she said? Or is she just afraid that the police might widen their net?

Noah has returned to university and Isobel is boarding as usual. Everyone is back to normal apart from Anna – but it won't be long, because Everett has been in touch. 'Good news!' He's spoken to DC Murray and she is no longer a person of interest. 'You can draw a line under this and move on,' Everett tells her. 'Not only are the fingerprints on the back of Victoria's T-shirt not yours but your prints are nowhere to be found in the house.'

'What about Tori's accusation that I hit her?'

'No evidence there either. The video is unclear and has been discounted.'

'The prints on the T-shirt – they're not her mother's, are they?'

'No, they're not. They're checking the database to see whether they can come up with a match.'

Anna is relieved that Saskia is in the clear. She has spoken to her each morning since she drove her home. Not surprisingly, her mood is low and she is quick to tears, but one of her work colleagues has moved in and is helping ensure she is both nourished and limiting her alcohol intake.

Just one more thing to fix. Anna has arranged to meet Lynn at her house for breakfast. She doesn't want to jettison their friendship but she has to understand her motives for going behind her back and telling John about the kiss. When she arrives at the house, Lynn's car isn't in the drive but a text has arrived telling her that she's been delayed and to go inside.

When Anna opens the front door, Toast comes bounding out, running past her to turn happy circles on the flowerbeds at the edge of the driveway. 'Your mum's not going to be happy with you,' she tells him when she catches him. 'Look at the state of your paws!'

She takes him into the utility room to clean him up. He licks her face as she suspends him over the sink and uses a disposable wipe to remove the dirt. 'There you go, Toasty.' She puts him on the floor and he immediately rushes off to get a toy. The utility room is furnished in pristine white units, the recycling divided into clearly labelled bins. Anna drops the used wipe into the correct bin and nudges the drawer closed with her hip. As she's leaving the room, her eye catches a flash of red on one of the shelves. When she looks more closely she sees that it's the red edge of a book that's been placed on the top shelf but is sticking out a couple of centimetres. A red book, A5 in size. Inside her mind, connections cleave together like magnets. She stands on her tiptoes and reaches for the book. On the front cover it says: This diary belongs to Victoria Jane Carmichael. KEEP OUT.

Anna's scalp tingles. She blinks several times in quick succession. Questions gallop through her brain: *What? Why? How come? How did Tori's diary come to be in the Sykeses' home?*

She opens the book, flicking from page to page as she gets a feel for its contents. Many of the pages are beautifully illustrated with colourful flowers, mathematical equations, cartoon drawings of people, dogs and cats. Some of the pages are bordered with symmetrical patterns, others with hearts, especially when she's writing about her dad. Often the hearts are broken in two, framing the page with sadness.

The first entry is dated 12 September 2018:

Brand-new diary. Brand-new school. I've been at Bishopglen for a whole week. And it's okay, I suppose. I was hoping it would be better. I thought I'd feel like I belonged here, that I'd meet girls I'd really get on with.

I don't think that's going to happen. The girls can be divided into three types: the popular ones who shine at everything, the click-bait divas who only want to be celebrities, and the studious, non-make-up-wearing girls – mostly Chinese or South Korean.

I'm sharing a room with a girl called Amanda. She's from Shanghai. Her real name is Ping Ho but she chose Amanda as her English name. Her English language is almost as good as mine and she's gifted at maths and physics – she should be the scholarship girl, not me.

Anna skips a couple of pages …

Boarding school is nothing like the old Enid Blyton stories or Harry Potter's Hogwarts. And it's not like a long-lasting sleepover either. It's just school with beds and no break from classmates.

~~I don't miss Mum.~~ I do miss Mum. A bit. The nice side of her.

I don't miss her drinking. She's an alcoholic. She says she isn't. She admits that she's 'alcohol-dependent' but insists that doesn't make her an alcoholic. (??) She won't get help because she doesn't need help. I need to 'shut my face and fuck off'.

Cheers, Mum.

(And if you're reading this, Mum – you shouldn't be. Nothing good comes from reading other people's diaries.)

I met Sister Pierce when I went to the surgery for a painkiller. Before I even said my name she guessed who I was; she told me she'd been looking forward to meeting me – ME? Who looks forward to meeting ME? – and that she'd heard so much about me.

As I was leaving, I said something like, 'I hope I don't let Mr P down.'

And she said, 'You deserve your scholarship, Victoria. Be proud of yourself.' She laid her hand on my shoulder. 'You have so much to offer.'

Her kindness made my heart double in size. It sounds pathetic but it's true. She's the most genuine person here.

Anna groans as she reads this. Then she turns the pages faster, pausing to read when certain words catch her eye …

I thought Dad would have called by now. Six whole weeks!! I know he's on holiday with what's-her-face but it's only Sicily or maybe Sardinia. I did get a text – Good luck with starting your new school, Vic. Speak soon, Dad xx

BTW I know I promised myself I wouldn't lie, that this would be a fresh start. We have a kitchen where we're allowed to make snacks. Hester (Head Wiseman's daughter – full of herself, pretty, moody) had left some buttered toast on a plate then gone to answer the phone. When she came back, it was gone. I was sitting pretending to read a magazine but I could see her from the corner of my eye looking on the floor, in the sink, in the fridge.

'Did you see my toast?' she asked me.

'No.' I glanced up at her. 'Maybe you ate it already?'

She shook her head at me and left the room, no doubt to tell Pippa and Isobel that I'd eaten it.

I threw it out the window. 😱

I was stupid. I wish I hadn't done it. 😟

I'll try again tomorrow.

Dad says he'll take me to the cinema the weekend after next. #hopinghopinghoping.

So Dad cancelled on me which made Mum happy because it proves her point that 'he left us both, Tori. Not just me.'

I felt sick inside. I wanted to cry but the feeling was beyond tears.

I still feel sick inside.

I know his girlfriend has a daughter. I try not to care.

I feel really low. All the world is dark. Darkness has seeped into the very bones of me. I swear to God, I wish I didn't have to wake up. Every day it's the same depressing shit.

I defaced a library book, wrote fuck and cunt in bubble writing, and I stole a mobile phone, threw it into the loch over lunch hour.

At my mentoring session I sounded off to Sister Pierce. 'I have almost no control over my life,' I told her. 'Go here. Go there. Do this. Do that. Adults are constantly telling me what to do, how to behave. Adults whose lives are way more fucked up than mine will ever be. It's a case of do what I say not what I do. And at the end of it all we die.'

'Is this about your dad?' she said.

I cried. I cried so much she ended up excusing me from PE so that I could sleep in sick bay. She even tucked me in, like I was a baby.

Like I was her baby.

Anna stops reading and covers her face, sadness enveloping her for a minute or more before she continues.

I've had an idea!! A way to prove a point to Isobel. I've got the summer holidays to work on it. I like a project. It will take research and planning and I'll probably have to rope Holly in on it.

Anna checks the date for this entry – 27 June 2019; just after the lesson about consent. This was the beginning of her plan to trap Noah but first there are several entries about the Sykeses.

I was stacking shelves today when Mrs Sykes spoke to me. 'I didn't know you worked here, Tori,' she said.

'Holiday job,' I told her. 'I'm saving up to go and visit Amanda in Shanghai.'

Lois was with her and she reached out to take my hand, staring up at me with the sort of adoration that I seem to inspire in seven-year-olds. 'Pippa's in Paris,' she told me. 'But she never plays with me so I don't miss her.'

Some more chit-chat and then Mrs Sykes asked me whether I'd like to babysit – £10 an hour. 'Seeing as Lois likes you so much.'

'Yeah,' I said casually, my heart hammering. (£10 an hour?? When the going rate is £6!!)

Their home reminds me of one of those lakeside houses that you see in American films – all wood and windows, spectacular views of the metallic blue water and the moody sky, a sunshine smile one minute and a storm of cloudy temper the next. (I'm a poet but I don't know it.)

A view like that makes you feel as if you own the whole world. You can even see the tip of Bishopglen's church spire poking up above the trees on the far horizon. There's underfloor heating so you can wander about in bare feet in December (the cleaner told me this – she's called Magda. She comes every day to clean the kitchen and bathrooms. 'Not

Mr Sykes's study,' she says in her half-Glaswegian half-Polish accent. 'He need his privacy.')

Lois is fun to be with – she's quirky and not too demanding. I've been three times this week and we're in a routine now: first, we walk Toast down by the loch, hang about in the boathouse skimming stones off the pier, play skipping games in the barn and then we go back up to the house to make ourselves a snack. In the afternoon we lie on the long couches and read – Lois with her book and me with mine. Five hours a day – 150 quid! Easy money. (Mrs Sykes goes out to eat lunch, or have her nails done or maybe she's shagging some buff guy at the country club – fuck knows.)

Lois said something to me today – a bit weird – 'Mummy loses her temper sometimes but she doesn't mean it.'

'All mums lose their temper,' I told her.

'When Mummy hit Daddy he was crying,' she told me, bug-eyed with sincerity. 'I saw them. I'm not supposed to go into Daddy's study but my blanket was in there and I sat down behind the big chair.' She paused as she remembered. 'It was to do with the white powder.'

'Right,' I said. 'Shall we make pancakes?'
???

Anna is surprised at this. Lynn hitting Matt? She's never seen any signs of this. Could Lois have got it wrong? She doesn't know what to make of it so she continues reading, drawn into the diary as she waits for the next revelation.

Smooth as clockwork.

I did it!!!

I shagged Noah.

And I filmed it.

When I left him lying there, innocent as a newborn, I felt elated like I'd just got away with robbing a bank.

Now I just feel flat.

But wait till Isobel sees the video.

Anna's lips tighten as she reads this. She feels her sympathy for Tori momentarily fade. It's one thing thinking about taking revenge but to actually carry it through? The deceit, the damage she could have caused. 'Pot, kettle, Anna,' she whispers to herself.

I've made over £700, add that to my money from shelf stacking and I'm up to £1,272!! Shanghai here I come!! I'm thinking of going at Christmas but that would leave Mum on her own so I might have to wait till Easter.

It feels amazing to have all that money. I keep checking the balance online. It makes me so fucking happy, like I've actually done something. Like I've changed my life. #happyhappyhappy

Today was my last babysitting day before school begins again. They were going out for the evening so Lois was ready for bed. She was wearing a nightie with embroidered flowers. She literally looked like an angel. She sang me 'Somewhere Over the Rainbow' which she's practising for a school concert and then – we're sitting with mugs of hot chocolate watching *Incredibles 2* for the nth time – she said,

'I hate it when Mummy gets angry. It was because Daddy didn't put the white powder in the safe.'

Second mention of white powder. I'm not surprised that they use cocaine on the weekend but they'd get a shock if they knew their daughter was talking about it. 'Were you hiding in Daddy's study again?' I asked her.

'I'm not allowed to say.' She held her fingers up to her lips and whispered, 'Ssh.'

'I won't tell anyone.'

'That's why Pippa had to go to France because she was asking and Mummy said, you'll understand when you're older, and Pippa said you're such a hippogriff.'

'Hypocrite,' I corrected her.

'Hypo-cryth.' (She was really trying but her tongue just couldn't do the gymnastics.) 'And Mummy said, Pippa this is about family! And she was really shouting.'

She fell asleep on my knee and I carried her up to bed. The carpets upstairs are so thick and soft that my feet sank into the wool – luxury squared. The whole house is an ode to perfection. Comfort like this is so seductive. Money is power. (I can see why people steal. I mean, really steal, not the fucked-up self-sabotage stealing I do) – although I have saved all that money so go me!

When they arrived home Mr Sykes pushed past me and went upstairs. 'Matt has to make a quick phone call and then he'll drive you home,' Mrs Sykes said. She was unsmiling, more tense than I'd ever seen her. It made me anxious and I tried to make it better by starting a conversation. When has that ever worked?

This was the convo verbatim:

Me: 'How was your dinner?'

Her: 'Very tasty. We went to the Pierces'.'

Me: 'I really like Sister Pierce. She's been SO good to me. She's my favourite person at Bishopglen.'

(Granted, it was a bit lovey – but wait for it.)

Her: 'She's not as nice as she seems.'

Me: 'Funny!'

Her: 'I'm not joking, Victoria.' Her expression was set hard. 'You think she's so perfect?'

Me: 'Well ... she's your friend, isn't she?'

Her: 'She was responsible for her mother's death. In effect, she killed her.'

Me: I'm about 90 per cent sure she's joking. 'We'd all kill our mothers given half the chance!' Nervous laugh.

Her: 'You think murder is funny?' She was really in my face. 'Do you?'

And then I saw it – her fists were clenched. Her eyes were sparking, firing, flaming – like a boiler about to blow. It was SCARY.

I took a step backward, my hands up in surrender. 'I'm sorry. I don't think murder is funny. I really don't.'

She slammed her hand against the wall and walked off.

Fuck.

I'm guessing she has problems with impulse control when she's been drinking. The therapist needs therapy. Go lock yourself in a room, bitch.

I stood there for about ten minutes waiting for Mr Sykes. He's one of those men who doesn't hold eye contact. He's borderline weird but I'm used to him not speaking whenever he drives me home so I

spent the journey on my phone pretending to send
texts.

Anna has to stop reading. Her hands are shaking and
the words jump in front of her eyes. Anna never told
Lynn about her mother's death. Never, ever. The only
people she's ever told were Geraldine and recently Owen.

And Lynn is violent. *Since when? How could Anna
have missed this?*

She shakes her head against this news, believing and
yet not believing. Was Matt's injury caused by Lynn, not
Julia Raeburn? When Isobel holidayed with them a couple
of years ago she mentioned to Anna that Lynn had a
temper. Anna hadn't asked her for details because she
thought Isobel was just being critical.

She continues reading.

I told Isobel today that I shagged her saintly brother
Noah – I showed her the video – she almost shat
herself. I proved my point about consent and criminalising young people. I told her I won't do anything
with the video, and I won't.

(I feel a bit ashamed, if I'm honest. He seemed
nice, Noah. Gullible but nice.)

Also, I'm a bit worried she might tell her parents.
I don't want them to be disappointed in me. I don't
want that.

I really don't want that.

Dad is getting married.

Dad is getting married.

Dad is getting married.

Why can't he love me? What's so wrong with me?

Three lines were scored out and scrubbed so hard with the pen that the page was torn through.

> News flash – Sister Pierce hit me. Can you believe it?? Mrs Sykes is right – she's not perfect after all. I was trying to get her attention because of Dad and what was the best thing for me to do and she –

Anna closes her eyes tight. She can't read this. It hurts too much. She lets several seconds tick by and then she opens her eyes again. She's barely breathing as she turns the page to the last entry, written on the night Tori died.

> People lie. People wear masks, have secrets. I know that – but the more I think about it, the more I think that the Sykeses' behaviour is weird, especially Mrs Sykes.
>
> It's dark.
>
> It's scary dark.
>
> Instead of fighting with Sister Pierce – no wonder she hit me – I should have told her about her friend. She should know that her friend is not to be trusted. This will be a peace offering because I've made enough trouble for her. I didn't think she'd be suspended. I thought Mr Wiseman would throw me out of his office. Everyone knows I'm a liar, for fuck's sake. Why believe me now?
>
> I've ruined things for her.
>
> I've ruined it for myself too.
>
> I'm going to do better.
>
> It's almost eleven but I'll text her. Hopefully, she's still up and she'll agree to come and see me.
>
> Fingers crossed x

Chapter Thirty-Six

Anna closes the book. Her heart has slowed right down. She feels strangely calm. She goes into the kitchen and sits down on the sofa by the window, Toast lying beside her. The seat is a perfect combination of soft and supportive. It's upholstered in a subtle blue-grey tartan, an expensive wool blend. Everything in this house is placed with a designer's eye. The sun streams in through the patio doors and falls upon the marble work surfaces. They gleam. Dazzle. The whole room dazzles. The house dazzles. As a couple, Matt and Lynn dazzle with their friendship and their generosity. Their openness. Their honesty. Their perfection.

Anna has valued Lynn's friendship above all else except the love of her family. She has seen Lynn almost every day for twenty years. They are close friends who have shared everything.

That's what she's always believed.

Anna waits, her back straight, her expression blank. Five minutes later Lynn comes through the front door. 'Sorry I've taken a while. I stopped off to get us some croissants.' She pauses to kick off her Italian loafers. 'And Lois was a bit reluctant to go into school. She's still upset over Tori. Pippa and Isobel have promised to look out for her.' She dumps the shopping on the work surface and walks across to Anna. 'You okay? You look like you've been crying.' She reaches out and touches her cheek. 'You have been crying.' She pushes Toast off the sofa and sits down beside her, concern puckering her forehead. 'John is okay, isn't he?' Anna nods and Lynn takes her hand. 'I expect it's relief. I always cry after the event. I'm strong while it's happening but afterwards? I'm a basket case.' She smiles and stands up again. 'I'll make us a coffee. Warm the croissants.'

'What event?' Anna asks.

Lynn gives a slight shake of her head. 'Eh?'

'You said you always cry after the event. I'm wondering what event – or events – that might be?'

Lynn stares at her, perplexed. Anna's seen this expression before. She does it in staff meetings where she's pretending not to follow because she doesn't want to be pinned down. It forces the other person to keep pushing, and many staff shy away from this because confrontation in the workplace is to be avoided unless absolutely necessary. It's not only the English who are polite – the Scots can play that game too.

But Anna's not playing that game. She's not playing any game. Not today. She intends to ask Lynn why she spoke to John behind her back but when she opens her mouth to speak she cuts to what's more important. 'The night we had the curry, the night Tori died, did you go to see her?' she asks.

'What?' Lynn's spine lengthens. 'Anna! What on earth?'

'You were with me when I got her text.'

Lynn shrugs. 'I was.'

'So when you and Matt left you could easily have gone there.'

'Why on earth would we?'

Anna walks into the utility room and is back seconds

later with Tori's diary. 'I found this on a shelf.' She places it on the marble surface.

Lynn steps back in shock. 'Where has this come from?' Her arms are folded as she stares down at the diary. 'Did you bring this here?' She is wide-eyed. 'Did you?'

'No.' Her tone is patient. 'I think you brought it home after you took it.'

'Me? Anna!' She runs a hand through her perfectly cut hair, light catching on the warm-blonde strands. 'This is insane! You know me! Think about what you're accusing me of!'

'I'm not sure I do know you.'

'What?' Her mouth twists.

'Tori had found out some things about you. I …' She hesitates. It feels too outlandish to voice. And yet. 'I think you might have guessed what Tori meant in the text. She wanted to tell me about you.' She swallows hard. 'So you went to speak to her.'

'I know you've been through a lot, Anna.' She tries to take Anna's arm but she shakes her off.

'Tori's mother said she was writing in her diary that evening, so whoever took the diary must have gone there around the time of the text message.'

'Well, a) I hardly think her mother is reliable and b) perhaps it was Isobel?' Lynn poses, her expression dark. 'She comes here a lot. She could easily have taken the diary from Tori and hidden it here. And she had reason to dislike Tori.'

'Why? Why did she have reason to dislike her?'

'All the girls did!'

'Why Isobel?'

'Look.' Lynn sighs as if this is more than she wants to reveal but now she's being forced. 'I heard rumours about Tori trying to trap Noah.'

'No, you didn't,' Anna bites back. 'You could only know that if Tori told you, and she wouldn't. Or Isobel told you, and she wouldn't either. So you must have read the diary.'

'You weren't the only person Tori confided in, Anna.' She stares towards the front door and when she looks back, Anna draws a quick breath. 'We both put our families first, don't we?' Lynn says softly. 'That's something we have in common. Why else would you have hit her if not because you were thinking of your family?'

Anna feels as if this is the first time she has ever truly met Lynn's eye, and she is both fascinated and repulsed by what she sees there. No warmth. No sparkle. Just a flat, hard determination.

'Nothing in this world is free,' Lynn says.

Anna lifts the book and starts walking towards the front door.

'Wait!' Lynn catches hold of her sleeve. 'Give me a chance to explain.'

'You pay my solicitor's fees and I turn a blind eye? Is that it?'

'Not a blind eye.' She searches the air for the right persuasion. 'Anna, I did it for you too.'

'Did what?' *Surely she's not talking about murder?* 'You went to her home and you took her diary but—' Anna has never felt more bleak. 'Tell me you didn't push her? Tell me it's not your fingerprints on the back of her T-shirt?'

'She talks about Noah in there.' Lynn points to the diary. 'He could be prosecuted for having sex with a fifteen-year-old and spend his life on the sex offenders register. Noah! Your kind and generous son trapped by a spiteful, manipulative girl! How could that ever be fair?'

'She regretted trapping him.' Anna is trying to process the idea of murder. Of Tori being deliberately pushed by Lynn – a therapist, head of pastoral care, her best friend.

'But could she be trusted?' Lynn says. 'She was jealous of all the girls. She's made Isobel's life hell these past few weeks. Don't you have any sympathy for what your daughter's been going through?'

Anna wants to leave now. She has to leave. She has to take the diary to DC Murray. She has to let Murray draw his conclusions and continue with the investigation. But before she does that she says, 'How did you know about my mother?'

'You told me!'

'I didn't.'

'Oh, for God's sake! You're so petty!'

'Tell me!' Anna shouts.

'I came round the night you were confessing to Geraldine, of all people! You were completely out of it. You didn't notice me coming in. Neither did she, for that matter.'

Anna takes a second to think, accepts that it could be true because she has no recollection of how that evening ended. 'So why tell Tori?'

'Why not? She had a crush on you! She thought you were perfect! She needed to see that you were flawed just like the rest of us.' She narrows her eyes. 'Sometimes, Anna, I get tired of your holier-than-thou, all-the-children-deserve-a-chance bullshit.'

'It's not bullshit.' She walks to the door but Lynn gets there first, her back against it so that Anna can't open it. 'Move aside, please,' she says.

'Don't throw yourself under a bus,' Lynn whispers. It's a clear warning and for the first time Anna feels a flicker of fear. It passes quickly because Lynn is small, slight. Anna could match her. She's sure of that.

Anna pulls on the door handle.

'Leave the diary here and I'll let you go.'

'Are you threatening me?'

'Yes.'

'You're in no position to threaten me, Lynn.' She leans in to her. 'Did you kill her?' Lynn doesn't reply but then she doesn't need to because Anna sees the truth written across her face. 'Why? Why would you do that? Because she knew you hit your husband? Because she thought you might be using drugs?'

'You had your chance,' Lynn answers quietly. She steps away from the door, and as Anna pulls at the handle, a shadow falls across her hand.

Anna turns. It's Matt. Matt is behind her. She thought he was at work. *Don't panic.* This is Matt. Gentle, generous Matt. The man who was bullied at school for being soft and kind. 'Matt.' He's watching her, hands in pockets, a sad expression on his face. 'I need to go.'

'I'm sorry, Anna. I can't let you …' He shrugs. 'We have too much to lose.'

'She hits you.' Anna points towards Lynn. 'Domestic violence wears you down. You could be free of that.'

'Matt understands that I can be impulsive,' Lynn says lightly. 'He knows I'm working on improving myself.'

Matt's eyes are like lamps, unblinking, as he stares at Anna.

'I know that you love Lynn,' Anna says. 'But what she's done is wrong.'

He walks towards her, his hands coming out of his pockets. Anna manages to get the door open and she's running down the driveway towards her car, sliding, slipping, but not falling. Running faster than she's ever run before. More scared than she's ever been before. So scared that she can barely breathe. She's at the car door when she feels his hands on her shoulders. He pushes into her and she falls heavily, the weight of him landing across her back. She cries out, just once, and then darkness floods in from the edges and yanks her under.

It was the middle of the night but Tori was still awake because she hoped that Sister Pierce would answer her text. There was a quiet knocking at the door and Tori jumped up, ran downstairs. 'Sister P—' The name died on her lips. 'Mrs Sykes, what …?' Words failed her.

'Sister Pierce sent me. She wasn't able to come. She thought that I could help you instead.'

It was just about plausible. Except that what she wanted to tell Sister Pierce – your friend is a nut job – she can hardly say to Mrs Sykes's face.

She came inside and walked towards the living room. 'I wouldn't go in there if I were you.' Tori held her arm. 'My mum's decided to decorate again so the furniture is covered in dust sheets.' It wasn't true. She said this because she wasn't sure whether her mum was crashed out on the sofa with several empty wine bottles on the floor next to her – as she so often was – or whether she'd made it as far as her bedroom.

Mrs Sykes followed her upstairs to her room, her eyes immediately homing in on her diary, a beacon red colour that screamed SECRETS. 'What did you want to tell Sister Pierce?' she asked.

'I'd rather not say.' She shouldn't have let her come inside. It was a stupid mistake. She was distracted by the shame she felt at her mother's drinking. 'I'm actually really tired.'

'Were you going to tell her about me?'

'What about you?'

She sighed. 'You know we have cameras in our house?'

'*I know you have some outside.*'

'*We have one in the living room, too. I saw you talking to Lois.*'

'*What?*' *Fuck! They spy on anyone who's in their living room? She would dwell on that later.* '*I haven't hurt Lois!*'

'*She told you something.*'

'*Oh!*' *Tori thought back.* '*About the white powder? I don't care how much coke you do.*'

Mrs Sykes's expression changed — relief. Tori saw relief. Why? Why would she be relieved? And then, '*It's not as if you're dealers, or anything.*' *The words were out of her mouth before she could stop herself, a throwaway comment, a preposterous idea, but then Mrs Sykes wasn't laughing and nor was she angry. She was staring at her blankly, all emotion wiped from her face.* '*I'm joking!*' *Tori laughed but it was already too late because reality hung between them like a carcass on a hook — the stench, the nakedness, the ugly truth.* '*Hidden in plain sight,*' *Tori whispered.* '*Perfect family. Perfect cover.*'

By the time she felt the hand on her back it was too late. She seemed to fly, so long was she in the air before she hit the floor at the bottom of the stairs. She screamed, loudly and instinctively, and surely it would wake her mum, surely it would, except that when she'd been drinking she could sleep through the high-pitched wail of the smoke alarm.

There was a dizzying blink of pain, followed almost at once by profound, weighty numbness. Her cheek was on the floor and she wasn't sure why. She tried to breathe in but her ribcage wouldn't lift and her lungs were empty. She tried to speak but she couldn't feel her tongue. She was used to being able to think straight — thinking straight was what she did best — but suddenly there were no words.

Just silence.

Chapter Thirty-Seven

It's Further Education Day and Bishopglen have invited Davison High to share the experience. All the Scottish colleges and universities, and many of the English ones, have set up stalls in the main hall. Isobel and Andrew volunteered for car park duty so that they could be together and are manning a post where the car park ends and the school buildings begin. Parents are dropping their children off as they normally would; visitors, less sure of where they're going, are coming up to ask for directions.

'That's Julia Raeburn.' Isobel points out a slim woman with a blonde bob who is urging her children out of the car. 'She's a right cow.' She takes a deep breath. 'I'm going to confront her.'

She strides off full of purpose and Andrew follows her. 'Iso! Think about it! Your mum and dad wouldn't want you doing this!'

'I don't care. I'm doing it,' Isobel says. And when she's a few metres away from Julia, she calls out, 'My dad could have died!'

Julia starts back, shocked. Her two boys glance up at their mother and then at Isobel and Andrew, interested.

'You two need to go up to school,' Isobel tells them. 'You don't want to be late! You'll lose house points.'

They run off without saying goodbye to their mum, and Isobel stands in front of Julia, arms folded. 'The stuff you wrote on that Facebook page incited violence.'

'It will be to my eternal shame,' Julia replies, hand on heart, a tad dramatically in Isobel's opinion. 'I'm so sorry. I went too far and I'm … embarrassed.' She tells them that she got carried away, that she does this sometimes because she feels at a loose end. 'I had a career, you know? When we lived in London.'

'Well, Internet trolling isn't a career,' Isobel says.

'I know—'

'And hitting Mr Sykes with a golf club isn't a great move either.'

'Pardon?'

'I've seen his black eye.'

'What?' She doesn't laugh or get angry. She looks genuinely confused. 'I'm not sure why you're saying this.'

'Because you hit him.'

'I didn't.' Her expression remains confused. It's blindingly obvious that she hasn't a clue what Isobel's talking about. 'I know that online I've said some very hurtful things but I've never *physically* lashed out at anyone.'

'Did he ask you to stop posting on the Facebook page?' Isobel says, her arms unfolding, her tone losing its ferocity.

'No. Owen Wiseman spoke to Victoria's dad but—'

'Okay.' Isobel gives Andrew a significant look then takes his hand, pulling him back towards their post.

'Isobel!' Julia grabs for her arm. 'Your mum will be returning to work soon, won't she?'

'Yes,' Isobel replies. She holds eye contact, sees a scared little girl behind the successful woman with the big house. 'You're not that powerful.'

She takes a huge breath of relief and Isobel almost feels sorry for her – almost.

As they're walking away, she says to Andrew, 'I should have guessed Lynn was lying.' She's always found Lynn a bit too *Stepford Wives* – all perfectly groomed and smiley – but now she knows that under the surface there lurks an uglier creature.

It was one o'clock in the morning. Isobel was on holiday with the Sykeses. They were staying in a chalet in the Alps and Isobel was out of bed going to the toilet when she heard raised voices in the living room. She crept along the hallway and peeped around the corner. Matt and Lynn were standing in the middle of the room and Lynn was shouting, a barely coherent mix of venom and spite spewing from her mouth like vomit. It was an argument way beyond anything Isobel had ever witnessed between her own parents, and when Lynn started kicking Matt, Isobel scuttled back to bed, her eyes wide with alarm.

'What's going on?' Pippa asked her when she came back into the room.

'Your parents are fighting,' Isobel said quietly. She pulled the covers tight around her, shivering with shock. 'I mean, really fighting.'

Pippa snapped on the light. 'They do that. It's normal for them.' She rubbed at her eyes. 'Please don't tell anyone, Iso.'

'I won't.'

Isobel lay back down and tried to fall asleep but in her mind's eye all she could see was Lynn's small frame landing a kick that would make a premiership footballer proud. She tried to tell her mum when she got home but her mum didn't get how serious it was and she didn't want to push it because she knew how much she liked Lynn. Every now and then she remembered the fight and thought how scary it must be for Pippa and Lois, living with a mother who cracks like that. And when she had the chance to change her mentor she did it, chose Geraldine Whitlock who was a no-bullshit, trustworthy adult. And not her mum's best friend.

'Matt and Lynn are both a bit weird,' she tells Andrew. 'I went on holiday with them once.' She tells him about the incident.

'What the fuck!' Andrew is shocked. 'Rage like that' – he whistles through his teeth – 'it's not normal.'

'I'm going to tell my mum what we've found out.' She makes the call. It rings a couple of times then goes to voicemail. 'Pippa told me she was having breakfast at theirs this morning.' She glances at her watch. 'It's gone ten o'clock. She should have arrived ages ago.'

'Maybe she has her phone on silent.'

Isobel tries every five minutes until almost an hour has gone by. 'This isn't like her,' she says. 'I feel quite worried.' She frowns. 'Should I be worried?'

'Maybe she left her phone in the car or they've got music on and she can't hear it ringing.'

'Would your mum ignore you for an hour?'

He laughs. 'Never.'

'Exactly. My mum always answers her phone. Especially if it's me or Noah or my dad, and because I've been a bitch to her lately she'll want to make amends.' She flinches. 'Fuck. I really have been awful.' Her cheeks redden as she looks at Andrew. 'I pushed her over.'

'What?' His head jerks forward on his neck. 'Why?'

'Just because.' She shrugs. 'My dad went nuts at me.' She calls again, and this time she leaves a message. 'Mum, it's me. I don't know why you're not answering and I'm getting really worried now. Love you.' She stares at Andrew, tears in her eyes. 'There's no point trying my dad because he doesn't answer during school hours.'

'We could try the school secretary?'

'Or we could just go to Lynn's?' Andrew's recently passed his driving test and has a ten-year-old Fiesta. 'Most of the visitors have arrived by now and anyway, if they can't read the signs' – she points to the school map behind them – 'they shouldn't be going to university.'

Andrew grins. 'YOLO. Let's do it.'

'This is why I like you.' She kisses him, puts her arm through his and they run to his car. 'You need to go up the back road to the other side of the loch. Their house is on the hill. Wait till you see it.'

She'd wanted Andrew to come to Pippa's party but Pippa had said, 'No, I'm really sorry, Iso. My parents want to keep the guest list small, with Tori dying and everything.' In the end there were almost eighty people there and Isobel was hurt that Andrew wasn't one of them. Sometimes Pippa was like that – controlling, exclusive, mean. Hester told Isobel she was jealous because she didn't have a steady boyfriend. It was her party and she was the one who was going to get all the attention. She didn't want anyone there who might be happier than her.

The back road is twisty and potholed, hedgerows rising up on either side. They bump over the uneven ground, Andrew taking the opportunity to drive faster than the speed limit. Isobel holds onto the side of the car as he swerves to avoid a stray sheep that's escaped from one of the fields.

'Next driveway on the right,' Isobel says. They follow the road down and pull up in front of the house. 'I don't see my mum's car.'

'This is where they live?' Andrew's eyes widen as he takes in the remarkable build, a perfect harmony of wood and glass. 'What does Pippa's dad do?'

'He's got his own computer company or something,

I think. And there's family money.' Andrew follows her to the front door. She rings the bell, then steps back so that she is level with him.

Seconds pass, and Isobel moves from one foot to the other, impatience driving her legs. She rings the bell again and again and finally Lynn opens the door. 'Isobel! Shouldn't you be in school?' She looks Andrew up and down. 'And you are?'

'Andrew.' He holds out his hand. 'Pleased to meet you, Mrs Sykes.' Lynn doesn't take his hand and he lets it drop back down by his side.

'I'm looking for my mum,' Isobel says loudly. 'She was coming here for breakfast, wasn't she?'

'That's what I thought, but she never turned up.' Lynn glances behind her distractedly. 'Have you tried your house?'

'She didn't call you?'

'I'm a bit busy at the moment.' Lynn's hair is a mess. It looks as if she hasn't brushed it this morning. That never happens. 'We have a water leak. I'm about to call the plumber.'

'Do you need any help?' Andrew says.

'You two should go back to school.' She abruptly closes the door.

'Friendly.' Andrew takes Isobel's hand and leads her back to the car. She lets herself be led, is deep in thought as she climbs back into her seat. When Andrew turns the key in the ignition, she puts a hand on his arm.

'Don't go yet.' She's been thinking about Tori a lot since she died and she's thinking about her now. What would Tori do in this situation? She was the sort of girl who observed everything and everyone. She could think outside the box. She was sharp. Isobel couldn't deny that; it had often been annoying. She was super-quick at understanding mathematical theories and problem-solving. And her gut instinct was usually spot on.

So what would she make of this situation?

She would be methodical. She had a scientific brain and she was good with process. She would approach it with her mind not her heart and she would find the answer.

'What are you thinking?' Andrew asks her.

'Nothing's binary is it? Not human beings, anyway. No one's all bad and no one's all good. Tori was really attached to my mum and a few hours before she died she sent her a text saying she had something to tell her. And I told my mum she was just winding her up but what if she really did have something to tell her?'

'Like what?'

She sighs. 'I don't know.'

He reaches over and attaches her seatbelt. 'How about we drive to your house and see whether your mum's there?'

'Okay.' She nods slowly. 'But I feel like there's something I'm missing.'

Andrew leaves the tree-lined driveway and they head back the way they came. They're about half a mile along the road when Isobel calls out, 'That's Matt!' He doesn't see them. His head is down and he's walking, almost running back in the direction of his house. 'Turn around, Andrew. Let's offer him a lift.'

Andrew does as she asks. 'Hi, Matt!' Isobel winds down her window. 'Do you want a lift?'

He shakes his head and keeps half walking, half running along the road. The end of a keyring is hanging out of his trouser pocket – it's a clunky two-inch model of the Brandenburg Gate that Isobel bought for her mum after the S3 trip to Berlin.

She leans into Andrew's ear and whispers, 'That's my mum's keyring.'

'Are you sure?'

'Yes.' A door opens inside her mind. She glimpses what's beyond that door and when it tries to slam shut, she wedges it open, holds fast against the tide of questions that frighten her because what she sees is impossible, isn't it?

'Matt never takes any exercise. Their garden is massive. They never even walk their dog.' She's staring straight ahead. 'He must have driven my mum's car somewhere close. There's a parking spot back there, isn't there?'

Andrew doesn't answer. He's already turning the car around again and with a squeal of brakes they take two bends at speed before turning into the car park. 'There it is!' Isobel shouts. A lone car is parked in the furthest bay, beyond which the loch stretches out for almost a mile, the water tranquil, mirror-smooth. Andrew pulls up next to the car and Isobel jumps out, looks in the windows, pulls at the handle – locked – and shakes her head at her boyfriend before climbing back into the Fiesta.

'What now?' he asks.

'We go back to the Sykeses',' Isobel says. She clenches her teeth. She's scared – not of the Sykeses; she reckons she could deal with Lynn while Andrew dealt with Matt. *But where is her mum? Has Lynn hurt her? Could she have done that?* Isobel shudders and covers her mouth with her hand to stop herself from screaming.

'We'll fix this, Iso.' Andrew reaches across and strokes her hair. 'It's okay.'

They arrive back in the drive just as the front door closes. 'We're not ringing the bell this time,' she tells him.

They go inside. Matt's shoes have been kicked off just

320 *Julie Corbin*

inside the door. They both stand still, listening. At first the house seems pin-drop quiet. And then they hear the sound of distant voices. Isobel puts a finger to her lips and points towards the utility room. They creep across the hardwood floor, their steps silent as night.

'How could you be such a halfwit!' Lynn is shouting. 'I told you to get rid of the diary!'

'I was going to do it this morning. I was waiting until Lois was in school. I—'

'Stop talking!' she shouts.

'Tori's diary,' Isobel whispers to Andrew. They are standing more than ten steps away from the arguing couple. 'My mum must have found it here.'

'We have to call the police,' he whispers back.

Isobel nods. She still doesn't know what any of this means, has no time to speculate because each moment feels urgent, dangerous even. *She has to find her mum.*

They're turning to tiptoe back the way they came when Isobel sees him – Toast. He is halfway down the garden, scratching at the barn door.

'Toast loves my mum,' Isobel whispers.

She heard Matt and Lynn's voices, harsh and unforgiving, could make out only a couple of words 'too late', 'barn' and 'fault'. She was dragged by hands that were rough and cold. Pain. There was pain in every part of her and she cried out, moaned, tried to resist the thump and drag of her body. A rag that smelled of petrol was tied around her mouth, rope dug into her ankles and wrists, and then there was the prick of a needle as it pierced the soft skin in the crook of her elbow.

She drifted.

She floated off into a world of memories that became dreams and dreams that became memories.

She was drawn into the same dream or memory; she

wasn't sure which it was. It lapped at the edges of her brain like a hungry sea. Sometimes the details changed – there were so many whispers inside her head – and she wondered whether the moon was full that night? Was Tori crying? Did anyone see them?

But what never changed was the memory of her raising her hand.

Ali was on duty overnight and Anna had given her the handover. There wasn't much to say with the sick bays empty, evening meds given out and no crisis calls from the boarding houses. When Anna came out of the medical centre she set off towards the path through the woods. It was completely dark apart from a weak, cloud-covered moon, and with the end of automatic school lights twenty-odd metres behind her, she was using the light on her mobile phone to lead the way. Just as she turned off the main path to enter the woods, a voice called out, 'Sister Pierce!'

Anna jumped. 'Tori! You gave me a fright!'

'Sorry, Sister, but I need to talk to you.'

'Have you been given permission to be outside?'

'No, I …'

'Well then.' Anna kept the torch light at waist height and rested her bag on the ground by her feet. 'It's after nine thirty. You should be in the boarding house.'

'It's about my dad.'

'Is he okay?'

'Yes, he's fine but—'

'Can we talk tomorrow, then?' Anna was exhausted. It was the end of a fourteen-hour shift, and she hadn't slept well the night before because Monty was outside having a barney with something in the woods. Now she wanted nothing more than a comfy seat, shoes off and a glass of wine to help her unwind.

'*I need you* now. *I need to speak to you* now.'

This wasn't the first time Tori had insisted on 'now' and usually Anna obliged her but not this time. 'I'll see you tomorrow, Tori. Please go back to the boarding house before they have to send out a search party.'

It was as Anna bent down to lift her bag off the ground that Tori moved closer and said, 'You have to listen!'

'Tori, please.'

'Why won't you listen?' Tears spilled onto her cheeks.

'I will listen. Tomorrow. Please, Tori. Let me go home now.'

'I know something about you.'

Anna hesitated, one hand gripping the handles of the bag. Perhaps she should give in to her. Half bent, she turned her head to look at Tori, lifting the torch from waist height so that she could see the girl's face.

'I know you killed your mother.' Tori's eyes were bright, her lips tight with malice. 'You always act so good, so perfect, like you're better than the rest of us but you're not.'

There was a pause. Tori's taunt polluted the air like a noxious gas. And she was standing too close, pushing right up against Anna's side. Anna felt a rush of fear, of memory, of police officers and guilt, of secrecy and lies, feelings immediately quashed by the voice of professional reason that she always employed when dealing with pupils. She lowered the torch light down towards the ground and swung the bag up and over her shoulder.

'Don't walk away from me!' Tori's voice was raised. 'I'll tell everyone. I'll tell everyone in school. I bet Isobel doesn't know about it. I bet Mr P—'

Anna's arm shot out and her fist made contact with Tori's face. Tori screamed and lurched away from her. 'You hit me!' she shouted.

Anna turned the light up towards Tori's face again and saw that she was cupping her cheek. 'Tori, I—'

'*You fucking hit me!*'

'*I did not!*' *Anna said, denying it. Because she couldn't have.* She did. *But she couldn't have because she wasn't that sort of person.* '*You must have fallen against the tree!*'

'*You hit me!*'

'*Let me see.*'

Anna took a step towards her but Tori pushed her away. '*Piss off! Bitch!*'

She turned and stumbled off through the trees and Anna shouted, '*Wait! Tori!*' *But Tori was already gone and when she triggered the automatic light, Anna pulled herself back into the shadows.*

Anna made her way home, too tired to think about what had just happened, and when she got there, John had already poured her a drink. '*Thought you might need it,*' *he said.*

Chapter Thirty-Eight

They know they'll be seen if they go out onto the decking to reach the barn, so they tiptoe back through the open plan kitchen and out the front door. Isobel leads the way round the side of the house and into the back garden. At the same time, Andrew is on the phone to the police. 'What's the address, Iso?' he calls out.

She takes his mobile, tells the call handler the address. 'Please come quickly. Please. We're in the back garden.'

Toast hears them and sprints up the hill, throwing himself at Isobel's legs and barking several times before running back to paw at the barn door. As soon as Isobel opens it, he runs to the corner where Anna is lying on the floor, her hands tied and twisted behind her back.

'Jesus! Mum! Mum!'

The voice is Isobel's, Anna thinks, but there is a fog and it's cold and she's having trouble breathing. She tries to open her eyes. She's tried this already but hasn't been able to. This time, though, she manages it and she sees Isobel leaning over her, watches her face light up and then her eyes fill.

'Let me untie you, Mum.'

Her fingers are shaking and she has help from someone – Andrew, Anna thinks. This must be Andrew. As soon as they remove the rag from around her mouth she tries to say his name but the only sound she can make is a dry rasp so she points instead.

'Andrew,' Isobel confirms. 'He helped me find you.'

His strong arms lift her to her feet but she can't feel her legs, is incapable of walking. 'I'll carry you, if that's okay,' he says. 'The police are on their way but we should get out of here.'

Anna is limp in Andrew's arms, feels the sun on her face and wants to cry. *I'm not going to die. Not today.*

Afterwards, when she thinks about it, she's not able to say much about what happened in those next few minutes. A muddle of feelings and words, sunlight and pain: Andrew laying her down in the shade of the trees, Toast licking her face, raised voices – Lynn's and then Isobel's. The green of a petrol can, the flash of a knife, heart-stopping fear, screams and then sirens.

And later, much later, a hospital bed, her family around her.

'They drugged you,' John tells her. He is holding both her hands, his face ragged with worry. 'They were going to set fire to the barn.'

'With you in it,' Isobel adds. 'They were drug dealers, Mum. Can you believe it? And Matt had a knife but Andrew got it off him, punched him in the face, really hard.' There's pride in her voice. 'He was amazing.'

'Lynn's been arrested for Tori's murder.' Noah passes her a cup of water and she drinks. 'Her fingerprints were on her T-shirt.'

Anna nods, tries to take it all in.

Tori. This was all about Victoria Jane Carmichael, a child who should never have died and must never be forgotten. Anna has the truth to tell and she will. As soon as she is strong enough, she'll tell John everything.

About how her mother died, and how she hit a child and lied about it.

What sort of person does that make her?

She wants the answer to be that it makes her human. She is flawed. She has her triggers, just like everyone else. But she's a lot harder on herself than that, and by her own judgement she's crossed a line and now she has to make amends. Every day and in every way she can she'll make amends.

And then maybe, just maybe, she'll be able to forgive herself.

Acknowledgements

Thank you to Lottie Britton and the senior school nurses who kindly answered my questions.

My editors at Hodder & Stoughton, Cicely Aspinall and Jo Dickinson, and my agent Euan Thorneycroft who never fail to guide me towards the final draft with patience and good humour.

Sorcha Rose and Jasmine Marsh who, behind the scenes, have worked hard on my behalf.

My writing friends, Mel, George and Neil for their advice and encouragement.

And a big thank you to my readers for emailing me, for writing reviews and for sticking by me through the years.

TELL ME NO SECRETS

You can bury the past but it never dies.

Grace lives in a quiet, Scottish fishing village – the perfect place for bringing up her twin girls with her loving husband Paul. Life is good.

Until a phone call from her old best friend, a woman Grace hasn't seen since her teens – and for good reason – threatens to destroy everything. Caught up in a manipulative and spiteful game that turns into an obsession, Grace is about to realise that some secrets can't stay buried forever.

For if Orla reveals what happened on that camping trip twenty-four years ago, she will take away all that Grace holds dear …

Out now in paperback and ebook.

HODDER